WHISPERS OF THE LAKE

Other Books by Shanora Williams

The Bitter Truth
The Other Mistress
The Perfect Ruin
The Wife Before

WHISPERS OF THE LAKE

SHANORA WILLIAMS

kensingtonbooks.com

Content Warning: child abuse, emotional abuse, physical abuse, mental illness, murder, violence

DAFINA BOOKS are published by

Kensington Publishing Corp.
900 Third Avenue
New York, NY 10022

Copyright © 2025 by Shanora Williams

To the extent that the image or images on the cover of this book depict a person or persons, such person or persons are merely models, and are not intended to portray any character or characters featured in the book.

This book is a work of fiction. Names, characters, businesses, organizations, places, events, and incidents either are the product of the author's imagination or are used fictitiously. Any resemblance to actual persons, living or dead, events, or locales is entirely coincidental.

All rights reserved. No part of this book may be reproduced in any form or by any means without the prior written consent of the Publisher, excepting brief quotes used in reviews.

All Kensington titles, imprints, and distributed lines are available at special quantity discounts for bulk purchases for sales promotion, premiums, fund-raising, and educational or institutional use.

Special book excerpts or customized printings can also be created to fit specific needs. For details, write or phone the office of the Kensington Sales Manager: Kensington Publishing Corp., 900 Third Avenue, New York, NY 10022. Attn. Sales Department. Phone: 1-800-221-2647.

DAFINA and the Dafina logo Reg US Pat. & TM Off.

ISBN: 978-1-4967-4584-2
First Trade Paperback Printing: July 2025

ISBN: 978-1-4967-4585-9 (e-book)

10 9 8 7 6 5 4 3 2 1

Printed in the United States of America

The authorized representative in the EU for product safety and compliance is eucomply OU, Parnu mnt 139b-14, Apt 123
Tallinn, Berlin 11317, hello@eucompliancepartner.com

To anyone learning how to love themselves again.
Keep healing. You've got this.

Gorgeous Two Bedroom Cottage on Lake Aquilla

Take a breather in this cozy cottage on Lake Aquilla! Located in the heart of Sage Hill and surrounded by so much nature, you'll be left with no choice but to unwind, enjoy the views, and relax.

With just a short walk to the shore, you'll love putting your feet in the cool waters and spotting the fish.

Wake up to wide-open windows that reveal rippling waters that go farther than the eye can see. Make a cup of coffee in our newly renovated kitchen and sit on the patio to watch the sun rise over splendid mountains.

Take a hike on our trails to open up your mind or use our speedboat for a quick ride across the lake.

Whatever the decision is, you can do no wrong in Twilight Oaks, where *everyone* is welcome.

CHAPTER ONE

*F*uck *Happiness.*

The fleeting thought crossed my mind as I stood in the bedroom closet I shared with Cole and stared at the racks of clothes. What would happen to me now? Where do I go next? How do I find that dreaded happiness again? When it arrives, will it come temporarily, like a visitor? Or will it stay this time? Will it hold me forever?

Only yesterday I was smiling. Hopeful even, ready to put one foot forward and focus on my future. But today, tears fill my eyes and the various colors of clothes become one irritating blur.

People speak of happiness like it's some tangible, obtainable object—like you can simply grab hold of it, kiss it, and cling to it. Make it promise to never leave you.

Perhaps it is like an object in the metaphorical sense. You can hold on to it all you want, but the thing I've learned about Happiness is that it hates clingy bitches. Happiness is disloyal. Unfaithful. Unyielding. It doesn't care what happens to you when it walks out of the door. It's like a bad guest, one who shows up when they feel like it. Lingers around. Takes up space. Eats all your favorite snacks. It's the kind of friend who is so charming and loving that you forget all about their flaws and the way they walked away from you the first time.

Like I said, *Fuck happiness. It can go to hell for all I care.* I sniffled as I stepped deeper into the closet, wiping my face with the back of my arm. The brakes of a car let off a light squeal.

Cole was home.

A sudden flash of anger wrapped around me, so white-hot that I swear my skin was sizzling. I snatched as many of his pieces of clothing as I could off the hangers. My arms were full of trousers, button-down shirts, silk ties, jeans, T-shirts—whatever I could manage. All of it had to be worth thousands of dollars. I even bent down to grab a pair of his favorite Jordans—a custom-made eggplant pair that I always hated the color of. I snatched down belts, a case of watches, a pair of Versace sunglasses.

The front door closed just as I left the bedroom and rounded the corner, hugging the items. I could smell burning wood from here. Cole's eyes expanded when he caught sight of me. "Rose," he said, but I was already walking in the opposite direction, toward the back door. "Rose. Hey, what are you doing?"

I ignored him and walked straight through the door I'd left wide-open. I hoped a million mosquitoes had flown inside just to bite his ass up all night long. The sun was setting, and the air was cool. The firepit was ablaze and the flames enticed me the closer I got. The heat swelled, strong enough to make a person sweat. I swear the crackling of the flames sounded like someone was laughing while chanting, *Do it, do it, do it!*

Cole shouted my name, chasing after me as I approached the roaring fire. I hurled all of his clothes into the firepit, pulled off my wedding ring, tossed it in too, and watched it all burn.

Eve Castillo journal entry

I found myself staring at my reflection again. I stared for so long it seemed I wasn't even real anymore. My features became invisible, and my eyes did that weird thing where they glaze over. It's like an out-of-body-experience—like I'm not myself at all.

Then I blink, snap out of it, and feel the breath coursing through my lungs, the prickle of my skin, the beating of my heart. I wish I could stay that way—living outside my body, watching this ridiculous girl stand for so long she rots.

I wish I was happier, or that I had a simpler life.
I wish I didn't have to fake smiles.
I wish I didn't hate myself so much.

CHAPTER TWO

Three Months Later

Corporate parties should be illegal. I didn't understand how people really looked forward to these things. Socializing outside of working hours with coworkers? Being in the same room as your boss and enjoying an alcoholic beverage with them?

There's this odd, invisible line that lingers. Sometimes it loops and threatens to wrap around your neck like a noose. You must remain professional, but also let your guard down just a bit—but not *too* much, or people will judge you. If you're too forward, they'll think you're doing too much. If you're too reserved, they'll think you're standoffish. I was certain the latter was what some of my coworkers thought of me now.

Reserved.

Quiet.

Weird.

I checked my phone, feeling annoyed that Herbert wasn't here. He was the only person I could tolerate during these gatherings, but he was at home tending to his sick dog, Dozer, after leaving the vet. Dozer had gotten ahold of a dropped grape, the poor thing. Perhaps I should've used that as my excuse too—to be there for my worried friend and his sick pet.

As I sipped red wine, my eyes traveled across the room to my boss and *Premier Daily*'s senior editor, Twyla. She was flashing all her teeth as she spoke to a cluster of other correspondents, waving her hand dismissively at the appropriate times (likely from a compliment) and giggling when necessary. She'd gotten veneers. They made her teeth look like Jim Carrey's when he starred in *The Mask*. No one had the balls to tell her how bad they looked, though—not even me.

Her eyes swung my way, and she threw up a hand, as if pausing the entire party, before scuttling across the room to me in her Italian leather heels. I didn't miss the way some of my coworkers glanced my way, then rolled their eyes.

"Rose! Girl, what are you doing over here all by yourself?" Twyla pressed a hand to my shoulder, scanning me with big hazel eyes.

Twyla was light-skinned with brown freckles and big, bushy curls that took up a lot of space. She was mixed and often talked about not being able to properly identify with either race—Black or white. Some days she was too Black. Others she was too white. I always suggested she be herself. It seemed she still didn't know how to do that. In a month, she'd be getting cheek fillers. I couldn't imagine how that was going to look with her teeth.

"I'm just enjoying the view," I said, bobbing my head to the right.

Twyla glanced out of one of the floor-to-ceiling windows, where the Charlotte skyline loomed above. "Isn't it a great view?" she marveled.

"It is."

She batted her long lashes as she pulled her hand away. She was giving me that look again. The same pitiful look she'd given me when I returned to work two days after I'd called and told her I wouldn't be able to come in because I was mentally unwell.

Somehow (probably because of Herbert), Twyla found out Cole had cheated. But I bet it was when she found out who he'd cheated *with* that she developed pity for me. Since then, she'd been giving me sad, sympathetic looks. I couldn't stand it. It made me feel weak and stupid, like I didn't have a handle on my life.

"Are you doing okay?" she asked, like she'd done this morning and for the past three months.

"I'm good, Twyla. You really don't have to keep asking me that." I laughed it off, but I was dead serious.

"Yes, yes. Of course. So, how is the article on Cowan coming along? You've done great investigating on that so far."

"It's getting there. I'm still digging but I'm sure it'll turn out great."

"Good, good."

My phone buzzed inside my clutch bag. I placed my wineglass on the nearest surface. I saw the name *Zoey* pop up on my screen, so I silenced the call.

"Sucks Herbert couldn't make it," said Twyla. "Oh—by the way, good job on that interview with the business owners of South End. Keep going at this rate and you'll be moving up the ranks in no time." She passed me a wink.

I couldn't help smiling. As of that very moment, I was an investigative reporter. I worked mostly in politics, but also dabbled in city and business conflicts that happened in or around the Charlotte area. I was relieved to hear she'd liked my last one. Granted, it was a piece any junior reporter could've conducted, but I'd put my own spin on it. I made talking about city codes for breweries, shops, and boutiques sound like the next hot thing.

Lots of traffic made its way to *Premier Daily* and I caught a comment here and there about how people loved the reports by Rose. The next step was to move up to senior reporter, have a more serious status in the company and, eventually, branch out and travel to other states for grander stories.

"Twyla!" a deep voice called.

I looked as she did at Benson Parks, the only person in the room that made me feel slightly inferior. Not even Twyla could make me feel that way. Benson was just too damn good at everything, even looking like a snack, with his warm honey-brown skin, pale green eyes, and clean-cut hair. His shirts were always fitted just right. He looked good... and it was clear Twyla wanted more from him than just a few stories to edit. He waved for her to come back with a smooth smile that I'm sure made my boss's panties twist.

"I should get back over there." Twyla placed a hand on my arm. "You know how the younger reporters get when they've had one too many."

Benson was one of those younger reporters. I'd been reporting for three years more than he had, yet he was on the same level and vying for the same position I was. And they say misogyny is fading. Bullshit!

Twyla took off and I watched for a moment as she stood before him, looking into his eyes with stars in her own, nodding, grinning. My phone buzzed again. It was another call from Zoey. I'd have to call her back when I left... which was most likely going to be in the next ten minutes.

First, I had to pee. I polished off my wine and ventured out of the room to find the restrooms. A man and a woman brushed past me, nearly knocking me a step backward as they made their way toward the elevator. I peered over my shoulder, scowling at their backs.

Once I got to the stall, I heard giggling women enter the bathroom.

"I wish Twyla would just let her go already," one of the women said. Through the thin slit of the stall, I saw them stop in front of the mirror.

One wore a blue dress, the other a gray one. Janna and

Bree. *Of course.* Girls who wrote columns on fashion trends, donuts, and the best bikes to ride in the city. Newsflash, no one should ride a bike in *this* fucking city unless they want to be flattened like a pancake.

"Right?" Bree said. "She's not even that good."

"Did you hear about her husband?" Janna said in a lower voice.

"No." Bree gasped. "What are you talking about? Details, bitch."

"So, I don't know how much of this is true, but apparently, she walked in on her husband *cheating* on her. Like, right in her house, Bree. Can you fucking imagine?"

My throat thickened with a mixture of emotions.

Frustration.

Rage.

Sadness.

"Stoooppp," Bree said, exaggerating the word. "She did not."

"I swear that's what I heard. Apparently, it happened months ago, but Hailey saw a note about it or something when she was clearing Twyla's desk. Now Rose is clocking all these hours and coming up with all these stories because she has so much time on her hands. She's kissing Twyla's ass so hard, but I keep hearing Benson is going to get the senior reporter position. Poor woman is going to get her heart broken *again.*"

"Well, he should get it." Bree chortled. "He doesn't come with all that baggage. Seriously. Rose is so fucking weird. She makes all of us look bad."

That's it. Time to shut that shit down.

I flushed the toilet, unlocked the stall door, and trotted out. Both girls peered over their shoulders at me before looking at each other and fighting smiles. I took the sink between them, giving my hands a wash before reaching around Janna for a paper towel. After drying my hands and tossing the damp paper in the trash bin, I made a show of running my fingers through my box braids, completely unbothered by their presence. I even applied a new coat of lipstick to add to the nonchalance.

They fingered at their mascara-heavy lashes, swiped their lips with gloss, pretending not to notice me. Done with my show, I started to leave the restroom, but a darker thought snuck its way in and made me stop in my tracks.

"Janna, didn't you bring your boyfriend with you tonight?" I asked.

Janna gave Bree a nervous glance. "Yeah. Why?"

"Because I'm pretty sure I just saw him sneaking to the elevator with Virginia," I answered. "And I'm pretty sure they're going to her office right now so she can suck his dick and then ride it. But I could be wrong."

Janna's jaw dropped. Bree's eyes widened. She was lucky I didn't have petty dirt on her. I'd seen her washing up in the restrooms one early morning before anyone else was in, and she had a duffel bag next to her feet. It was dirt, but I wasn't low enough to make fun of a homeless person.

With a smirk, I twisted on my heels and left the restroom. If there was one thing about me, it was this: Even if I felt weak, I'd be damned if I let anyone shit on my job and how hard I worked.

Having a cheating husband was one thing, but being stellar in my career was another. I was good at what I did.

Janna and Bree knew this and were simply jealous of it. Normally I ignored them and their snobby looks, but things were changing now. I was done being the nice girl—the sweet lady who takes the high road. Sometimes it felt good to unleash my pettiness and hit people exactly where it hurt.

CHAPTER THREE

"This is really starting to stress me out, Rose." Zoey's voice cut through my phone's speaker again as I sipped the last dregs of my coffee.

I'd stayed up way too late working on details for my investigation and fact-checking things with Herbert over the phone. I meant to call Zoey back after the party last night but was too frustrated to do so. Instead, I drank half a bottle of wine and dove straight into work. Work was the only thing keeping me sane, it seemed.

"It's been too long," Zoey went on. "Do you think she's okay?"

I refrained from rolling my eyes just as a I heard a knock on my office door. Herbert stepped in, waving a few sheets of paper in the air with a huge grin pasted on his face.

"*More info on Cowan,*" he mouthed.

I silently thanked him as he slid the paper across my desk. I picked it up with eager hands, perusing the papers, studying the violent domestic report from Cowan's wife, Melissa. One he desperately tried to hide by paying off a lead detective on the case.

Robert Cowan, CEO of a massive tech company with headquarters in Charlotte, was "allegedly" drugging and raping some of his female employees. Melissa Cowan *allegedly* found out about this and reported it to the police. News leaked and I'd been on it like Winnie the Pooh on honey. The next thing we know, Cowan's wife revokes her statement and they're traveling to Ibiza and wherever the fuck rich people travel to these days.

On one of the papers were photos of Robert's wife smiling from ear to ear but there was no spark in her eyes. It's almost like she was being *forced* to smile, forced to enjoy their escape to restore their marriage. In other words, forced to live a lie. It made me wonder what Robert had on her.

This carried on for a month before video footage came out showing Robert Cowan at a bar with a twenty-four-year-old girl named Anabel who worked for his company. *Allegedly* dropping something into her drink. The footage was released yesterday morning.

This story was the only thing I could focus on at the moment (or perhaps it's what I chose to focus on). If executed well, it could top me with that senior reporter hat, the one Twyla so happily liked to dangle above my head like a carrot. What I should've been doing was sending an email to Anabel to see if she'd be interested in meeting with me for an interview, but that couldn't happen because my ex–best friend's little sister was on the phone.

"Oh, this is beautiful," I said. A grin split my face in half as I read over Melissa Cowan's revoked statement. It had taken some digging to get it.

"Rose? Oh my God, are you even listening?" Zoey's voice crackled through the speaker again and I briefly averted my attention from the report to the phone screen.

Sighing, I reluctantly set the paper down to pick up my phone. "Zoey, I'm sorry. What . . . uh . . ." I rubbed my forehead with the pads of my fingers, trying to remember what she was talking about. "What did you ask me again?"

"I asked if you've heard from Eve," she said, and I could tell she was talking through her teeth.

"Oh. That's an easy one," I told her, snapping my fingers. "No."

"No? Like you haven't seen her?"

"Sure haven't."

"Well, when's the last time you talked to her?"

"Hmm, let me think." I pretended to ponder it as I scanned the statement again. "Oh, right. It was three months ago. Around that time, she got so drunk she went to a man's table while he was having dinner with his *wife*, grabbed his tie, and kissed him right on the cheek."

I'd never been so embarrassed by Eve's behavior. That said a lot because she did embarrassing stuff all the time—ever since we were sixteen and the best of friends, actually. Now that we were thirty-two, it still hadn't changed.

"I haven't heard from her in three days." Zoey ignored my statement. "It's not like her to *not* answer my text or calls. She always calls me back if she misses one."

"Does she have some new boy toy you aren't aware of?" I asked, inspecting my cuticles. An unnecessary distraction because I'd just gotten a gel manicure two mornings ago with my sister Diana. I told the nail tech to surprise me. They're velvety pink. They call the style a *cat eye* or something like that.

"I don't know," Zoey said. "All I know is the last time I talked to her she was driving and said she wanted to take a break from working and traveling so much."

"Well, there you go, Zoey. She's probably just holed up somewhere moping or sniffing cocaine."

"Rose." Zoe's voice grew serious, despite the tremble in it. Hearing it caused me to lose a bit of the coldness. "I know you guys aren't as close anymore but . . . I don't know who else to call or ask about this. It isn't like Eve to *not* respond to me. She knows how bad my anxiety gets when she takes too long to answer."

I sighed, closing my eyes and lowering my defenses. As

much as this conversation was annoying me, she was right. Even though Eve could be a reckless woman, she never missed out on her sister's calls or texts. Zoey was all she had—the only family left. It was because of their parents that Zoey suffered bouts of anxiety and depression. Their parents were awful to them, and it wasn't until *my* dad, a social worker, intervened that their lives changed. They were immediately moved in with their grandmother. She and Zoey had been inseparable up until Zoey started college.

"Look, I'm sorry, Zoey," I murmured. "I'll tell you what. I'll swing by Eve's place after work and see if she's around. Okay?"

Zoe sniffled. "Thank you, Rose."

"Yeah, don't mention it. I'll call you when I'm there."

"Okay." She sniffled again. "Thanks. I have to go before I miss my next class. But *please* don't forget to call me."

"I won't, baby girl."

"Ew. Rose, I told you I hate that name!" She laughed.

"I know." I smiled. "Just wanna hear you cheer up before letting you go."

She giggled. "Thanks. Talk later."

As soon as the call was over, I drew in a deep breath and released it. Then I picked up my phone and scrolled through it until I found the name I hadn't tapped in months—Eve. I called but it went straight to her voicemail. That in itself was unusual. Eve never turned her phone off, like, ever.

She freaked out whenever she had to put her phone on airplane mode during a flight, which I always thought was dramatic, seeing as she was a travel vlogger . . . and since most airlines had free Wi-Fi.

Airline Wi-Fi just doesn't hit the same, Rose, she'd said one time.

"So? What do you think?" Herbert's head popped in through a gap in the door, a big smile on his face. "It's crazy, right? I knew that motherfucker was guilty." He pushed the door open a bit and walked in, sitting in the chair on the other side of my desk. "By the way, you look official up in here! Sitting behind your big desk in your big comfy chair."

I couldn't help laughing.

"You're moving up in the world, lady," he said.

"Well, I won't be moving up quick enough with Eve always doing something ridiculous."

"Oh Lord." Herbert rolled his eyes. "I swear that girl is always getting into hot water."

He wasn't lying there.

I stood and collected the statement as well as my laptop and a few folders. "That was Zoey on the phone. I told her I'd check on Eve, see what's up with her. In the meantime, can you have Nico politely hack into Melissa Cowan's social media? I want to see if she might've DM'd some of her friends on there about her issues with Robert."

"*Politely hack*?" Herbert busted out laughing. "There is nothing polite about hacking a rich person's socials. And you know that's illegal, right? You probably shouldn't be saying that out loud."

"Well, it's a good thing Nico is good at covering his tracks, huh?" I walked around the desk and wrapped one arm around his neck to give him an awkward sideways embrace. "Call you when I'm home. And kiss Dozer for me!"

Eve Castillo journal entry

I woke up this morning feeling a little . . . off. Like there's been a change . . . or that a change will come soon. That's the only way I can describe it. It doesn't feel good at all.

There's this ache in my chest, like a thick knot is forming. When I swallow, it hurts. When I breathe, the pain intensifies.

Some days I feel like I'm losing touch with reality. I do things and don't know why I do them. Rose says I need to see someone, that maybe something mental is at play and I need a diagnosis.

I can't take meds like Zoey. I don't need them. If I take them, I'll be weak, then who will Zoey look up to?

God. It was so much easier when we lived with Abuela. I wish she was still here. I wish there was someone around who understood me the way she did.

CHAPTER FOUR

Eve's car wasn't parked in the designated spot in front of her townhouse. I was currently parked there, staring at her front door. It was painted pale yellow with a wide glass arch at the top. Orchids were on either side of her small porch, wind chimes hanging from above.

I sat for a moment, annoyed by the fact that I had to, once again, check on Eve to make sure she was okay. There was a reason I hadn't spoken to her in three months. Well, actually there were many. But the primary one being that Eve was horribly irresponsible.

She was also obnoxious.

Reckless.

Attention-seeking.

For the longest time, I wanted to chalk her behavior up to her terrible childhood. Abuse from a parent is not okay. She required love.

Attention.

Affection.

She never received that from her parents. Now she was out in this cruel world, seeking love in all the wrong ways and places. For years I tried being by her side, protecting her, loving her as a true friend should. But every single time, she pushed my buttons until I'd simply had enough.

There are friends you keep for life who feel similar to your heart—an organ you carry with you at all times. One you take care of and listen to. One who means so much to you. Then there are the friends who are like dead limbs. Sure, it'll hurt cutting the limb off and yes, amputation will suck, but you'll find so much relief when you realize you don't have to carry such a heavy burden anymore.

Eve was my dead limb.

I dug through my purse and plucked out my keys. On one of the rings was a key to Eve's front door. She'd never asked for it back, which I found surprising because I'd asked for mine back immediately. Granted, I was no longer living in the house she had a key to by the time I asked, but it was the principle of the matter.

As I killed the engine of my car, my phone buzzed in the cupholder. It was Cole calling.

"Mmm." I ignored it, grabbing the door handle and climbing out.

I knocked first, just in case Eve's car was in a shop getting repaired or something. I waited, noticing up close the dead plants on the porch, the empty hummingbird feeder.

Strange.

Eve always kept the feeder full. She loved the birds, the rapid flaps of their wings, their tiny chirps. She'd watch them from her living room window sometimes. When there was no answer, I stuck my key into the lock, twisted it, and walked in.

Nothing was out of the ordinary. Eve's townhouse had two floors. On the first floor were the living room, kitchen, a bathroom, and laundry room. Upstairs you'd find a landing and two bedrooms, one of which Zoey slept in when she was away from college.

I walked along the hardwood floors, checking the dining table. A few pieces of mail were there as well as a Victoria's Secret catalogue. The living room was spotless. The kitchen too. I checked upstairs in her bedroom. Her bed was neatly made, corners tucked, pillows fluffed. The desk in the corner had a laptop on top of it as well as an old camera and a tripod.

I stood next to the desk, searching for a planner of some sort. Eve was the type to buy planners, use them for two weeks max, then never use them again. There was one planner, but it was blank. Not even the dates were written in.

I shifted my gaze to the laptop and flipped it open. A picture of Eve and Zoey was on the screen. The sisters looked very much alike. Deep, naturally tanned skin, voluminous curly auburn hair, pink lips that carried big smiles. Their heart-shaped faces, cat-like brown eyes, and button noses. The only thing that truly set their faces apart was Zoey's splatter of freckles on the apples of her cheeks and the bridge of her nose.

I needed her fingerprint or password to log into the laptop. I had no clue what the password could be and didn't bother trying. Instead, I closed the laptop and left the room. I checked her back patio just in case. It was vacant.

I left the condo altogether, mildly annoyed that I went there at all. Zoey said Eve was in the car the last time she'd spoken to her. I must've been right then. She was away somewhere, probably snorting her life away.

Once I was in my car, I gave Eve's phone one more try. When it went to voicemail, I left one. "Hey, Eve. Um . . . Zoey called me earlier and said she's really worried about you. I just dropped by your place to see if you were around. I, uh . . . I told her I'd check. Anyway, if you get this, call me back."

I hesitated on the last part. "And if you need help or something, just . . . call me, okay? Don't keep ignoring Zoey. You know how she gets."

I hung up, dropping the phone in the cupholder again. The last thing I wanted was for Eve to call me, worming her way back into my life just because I gave her an in. She'd done it before, and I hadn't stood my ground. This time I swore I would. If she called and was okay, I'd let Zoey know and that would be the end of that.

No friendly text messages.

No calls.

No FaceTime chats.

Nothing.

Why? Because best friends don't sleep with their best friend's husband.

Eve Castillo journal entry

Rose never should've married Cole.

He had secrets. We both did. Rose didn't know that Cole and I had met before—that we'd hooked up on a dating app almost half a year before she'd met him. We linked up at a bar, had a couple of drinks, and slept together that same night.

She married him so fast. I mean, I just blinked and boom. She was asking me to be her maid of honor ten months after meeting him. She's so in love. I don't know how to break it to her that Cole and I have slept together.

And not just once, several times.

I got tired of Cole and sort of ghosted him, so meeting Rose's new boy toy for dinner for the first time was a shocker. He glanced at me all night with this hungry look in his eyes. I don't know how Rose didn't notice.

But like I said . . . something is changing.

The good side of me wants to tell her. But the other part of me . . . it whispers for me to never tell her a damn thing. The last thing I want is to ruin her happiness.

CHAPTER FIVE

"How are you feeling about that, Rose?"

I looked from the bowl of Jolly Ranchers on the coffee table to my therapist, Dr. Cristine Nether. Her umber skin was deep and rich, her thick hair pulled back in a classy ponytail. She was such a pretty woman who could've passed for a model, really. I started coming to her office a week after setting Cole's belongings on fire. After slapping him so hard I still felt the sting in my hand for nearly twenty minutes afterward.

It was Diana's idea. She knew Cristine personally and Cristine agreed to squeeze me in every other week so I could have a chat with her. It was odd calling it a chat. It was more like she asked me questions and I answered them to the best of my knowledge while feeling a little guilty each time. Honestly, Cristine's job was no different than mine. Interviewing. Nodding. Responding when necessary. Gathering information to study later. Only this was an ongoing interview, one that didn't make me feel all that comfortable.

I'd visited Cristine four times now. The first time I came, I ranted to her until I was parched. I don't know what it was that made me word-vomit. It could've been her sure eyes or maybe her soft smile. The scent of lavender and undertone of lemon in her office that relaxed me. The cozy chair and how my butt settled into it nicely, making me never want to leave. The bowl of Jolly Ranchers that were so inviting.

I'd chosen the watermelon Jolly Rancher the first time. I sucked on it as Cristine waited for me to speak. Then I remembered Cole buying me a pack of Jolly Ranchers when I was on a deadline, so I spit it out in the trash can, returned to the love seat, and spouted off.

But today was different. I wasn't that angry woman anymore. Today I simply felt . . . *frustrated*. But not about Cole.

"She always does this," I finally said. "She never answers her damn phone when people need her, and I feel like she's selfish. I'm sick of it."

"Have you considered that she might be tied up?" Cristine asked.

"Please," I scoffed. "She always has her phone on her."

Cristine paused. "If that's true, shouldn't that make you worried about her? Perhaps something has gone wrong."

"No. I don't care about her or what she's doing anymore."

Cristine didn't react, but she did stare at me like she was waiting for me to be honest with myself. I couldn't stand when she did that. The judging-me-without-judging-me thing. She was too good at her job.

"I don't care enough to figure it out," I said after a while.

"You know, Rose"—she sighed, folding one leg over the other—"it's hard to let friendships like the one you had with Eve go. It's okay to feel brokenhearted about that too. You didn't just split apart from your husband. You also split from a long-term friend. That was a relationship you cultivated over many years. You don't simply stop caring about that person because they wronged you."

"I don't want to care," I told her, eyes burning. *Great.* The tears were on the way. "I just . . . I don't get why I still bother checking on her, or calling her, or looking into anything she does, when she practically ruined my life and any chance of happiness that I had."

"I get that." She paused. "And you still haven't spoken to her since that night you caught her?"

"No. She tried getting in touch with me for about a month, but I think she gave up when she realized I was never going to answer."

"What if you'd run into her today?" she asked. "What if she'd been home when you checked on her for Zoey? What would you have done?"

"I don't know." I shrugged, swallowing thickly. "I guess I would've just told her to give her sister a call and then left."

"Okay. But what if Eve stopped you and asked for a word? What if she wanted to apologize?"

I shook my head. "I wouldn't let her."

"Why not? Don't you think she owes you an apology?"

"She does, but that doesn't mean she deserves my forgiveness."

The room fell silent, my words clinging to the walls like ice and turning the place frigid.

"Look, I know we all make mistakes," I said, attempting to warm the room again. "I know we're all human and we mess up . . . but this isn't something I can just forgive. I've forgiven her so many times for things she's done that have hurt me. But what she did with Cole was just . . . it was *ultimate* deception. She doesn't just get to apologize like before and expect me to accept it."

"I understand that." Cristine studied me. "Do you still have the urge to be violent?" To slap someone again, is what she meant.

"Well, last night I did let one of my coworkers know her boyfriend was cheating on her after hearing her shit-talk me in the bathroom, so . . ."

Cristine almost laughed. Her lip quirked up on one side, but she regained her composure. Much too professional to let my pettiness break her role. "But no one was physically harmed?" she inquired.

"No. I don't have the urge to physically harm anyone . . . unless they try to hurt me first, of course."

"Okay. Well, that's good. That's progress." She paused, tapping the end of her pen on her notepad. "Do you still think about the attack that happened to you?"

"Every day," I answered, averting my gaze.

"Do you feel like that may contribute to why you struck Cole? Perhaps you had some pent-up frustrations about that as well? You didn't react to the attack like you wanted but had the opportunity to do something about your anguish this time?"

"I don't know. But I took it easy on Cole by only slapping him, in my opinion." My leg began to bounce as I tried to ward off thoughts of the attack. I squeezed my eyes shut, drew in a shaky breath and released it.

"Okay, Rose. Here's what I want you to do."

I opened my eyes to see her place her notepad face down and set her pen on top of it.

"I want you to put yourself in Zoey's shoes. She relies on you and is a person who loves you very much."

I blinked to ward off tears. "Okay?"

"What would you do if Diana hadn't answered her phone in days, but you called Zoey to figure things out because she's closest to Diana at the moment? How would you feel if Zoey told you she didn't care to look into it, even though you were extremely concerned?"

"I would feel frustrated. And a little . . . lost, I guess."

"Right." She smiled empathetically. "You may be wanting to put Eve in your past, but Zoey will still be in your future. You have a good heart, Rose. So what I want you to do is hold on to the goodness that resides in you. Your heart may feel like it's frozen over a bit, but don't forget about the love you have for the people who've kept it warm over the years."

Damn. She's good.

CHAPTER SIX

I'd expected to leave my therapist's office feeling better, or relieved at least. Instead, I was muddled with conflicting emotions. On the one hand, I wanted to call Zoey and tell her Eve wasn't home and I didn't know where she was. That would be that, and so be it. However, on the other hand, I knew it wouldn't be enough for her and that I needed to dig a bit deeper to calm her mind.

Zoey knew I had ways of figuring things out. She'd be angry at me for not trying harder.

As soon as I pulled into my driveway, I collected my things from the passenger seat and headed to the front door. Before twisting the doorknob, I gave Zoey's phone a ring.

"Hey, Rose. Anything?" she asked as soon as she answered.

"No, sorry." I tucked the phone between my ear and shoulder as I entered and locked the door. "I checked her place and there's no sign of her. She left her laptop though. Does she usually do that?"

"She has two laptops," Zoey answered.

"Oh, okay. Well, one of them was in her bedroom. Other than that, it appears like what she told you. She's crashing somewhere else and taking some time for herself."

"Hmm. Maybe." She was quiet a beat. "It's just—it's not

like her, Rose. You know? I know you guys are having your differences right now or whatever, but aren't you concerned too?"

"Not really," I returned. "Eve does stuff like this all the time. It's not new, Zo."

She let out an exasperated sigh. "I feel like there's something going on between you and Eve that's much deeper than her kissing some stranger, and you aren't telling me."

I set my purse down on the table, fighting the guilt swirling in my stomach. Why was *I* feeling guilty? I wasn't the one who committed the betrayal. Zoey had no idea what her sister had done with Cole, and Eve should've been glad I never told her.

"I just . . . I don't know who else to turn to right now." Zoey's voice was thicker, on the verge of tears.

There it was. The reason my guilt continued to manifest. I *did* still care about Eve. As much as I didn't want to accept it, Cristine was right. Eve still felt important to me in some way. She'd been my best friend for sixteen years. We'd experienced so much. I couldn't just write her off like she was nothing. My heart wasn't cold enough to do that.

Not only that, but Zoey was like my little sister too. No matter what my status was with Eve, I would never neglect or abandon Zoey. She was one of the few people who kept my heart warm. She reminded me a lot of Diana, my baby sister, who often acted like the older sibling.

"Well, if I hear anything, I'll let you know, okay?" I said. "Try not to worry yourself too much. I'm sure she's fine."

Even I wasn't sure about that, but Zoey took the bait.

"I'll try not to," she murmured. "I guess I'll go study now. Can I call you tomorrow if I still don't hear from her?"

"Of course, Zo. Call me anytime."

"'Kay. Thanks, Rose. I love you. Goodnight."

"I love you too. Goodnight."

When she hung up, I went to the kitchen, perusing the

fridge for something to eat. I grabbed the leftover chicken salad and searched the pantry for crackers. As I did, there was a knock at my front door. I paused on opening the crackers, glancing at the sidelight windows. I could see the arm of someone's suit, the familiar shadow lingering behind them. With a burst of irritation, I walked to the door, unlocked it, and snatched it open to face Cole Howard, my cheating-ass husband.

CHAPTER SEVEN

Cole stood on the other side of my door, dressed in a blue button-down beneath a beige suit. I tried not to let my eyes travel over him. I hated that he looked so good all the time, even when I irrevocably despised him.

Those beautifully annoying brown eyes.

That flawless brown skin.

His perfectly lined-up hair.

That smooth damn goatee.

I ignored it all and folded my arms as I asked, "What are you doing here?"

"I've been calling you for days," he said.

"And?"

He gave me a dry laugh. "I thought you'd have been mature enough to answer me at least once."

I narrowed my eyes. "What do you want?"

"I'm worried about you," he said.

"Maybe you should be more worried about keeping your dick in your pants." I flashed him a faux smile.

"Rose." He threw his hands in the air. "Come on, I'm trying here. We can still give this another shot."

I pinched the bridge of my nose, one arm still folded over my chest. "Look, I'm seriously not in the mood for this tonight. Stop coming to my apartment and expecting me to be open to the idea of you being here. I never will be. Why do you think I moved out of the house in the first place?"

The whole point of getting this apartment was so I wouldn't have to see his face again. But he'd found out where I moved to when he saw the security deposit in my bank account. At the time, he still had access to my accounts. He wanted to know where I was, so he called my complex and figured out which apartment I was in. That was my fault. I should've changed all of my passwords and changed ownership of my accounts first thing. Instead, I spent days and nights crying in bed.

"It's just . . . well, I miss you, Rose."

"Goodbye, Cole." I stepped back and started to close the door.

He wedged a foot in the crack to stop it.

I lifted my gaze to his with a frown.

"Have you heard from Eve?"

My brows stitched together so fast I didn't have a chance to control my reaction. "*What?*" He couldn't be serious right now.

"Eve? I—I was just wondering if you'd heard from her. She agreed to meet me last night."

"Meet you last night for *what?*"

"There's something I wanted to talk to her about. Just wanted to, uh, apologize for . . . everything. But the main reason was so I could ask her if she knew any ways I could win you back. She knows you the best, so I just figured—"

"Get the fuck away from my door, Cole." I couldn't stand here and listen to anymore of his bullshit. He truly was an asshole.

"But Rose, I—"

"GET AWAY FROM MY DOOR, COLE!"

He flinched and had the nerve to look flabbergasted. Perhaps he was. I hardly ever raised my voice. I also didn't burn people's clothes and then slap the shit out of them before walking away, yet here we were. This man brought a lot of ugly out of me.

I swallowed my rage, closed my eyes to fight the burn, counted to ten in my head like Cristine suggested when I felt a violent urge coming, then sighed as I opened them again. "I don't need you trying to win me back," I told him in the calmest voice I could muster. "We are *done*. The divorce papers were sent to you weeks ago. I don't want this to get ugly so please just get off my doorstep, sign the damn papers, and leave me alone. I am *never* taking you back."

He opened his mouth like he was going to speak. Before he could, I shut the door in his face and locked it. I stepped back far enough to see his shadow near one of the side windows. He lingered for a while, then sighed. After a few seconds, his shadow moved, footsteps sounded, and he was gone.

Biting back tears, I returned to the kitchen and grabbed my leftover dinner. After pouring a glass of wine and taking a large gulp, I sat at the dining table and reached for my laptop.

I needed to focus on this article and turn it in to Twyla, but for the life of me, I couldn't concentrate. Not only because of Cole's random appearance, but also because of what he'd said about Eve.

Why were they still in touch with each other? What made him think she had any power to salvage our marriage? If anything, this made their situation appear worse. For all I knew, they were still sleeping together. They were both idiots. I wanted to say that to Eve's face. I wanted to say that and a hell of a lot more, but I would never be able to arrange that if she didn't answer her damn phone.

I ran my fingers over my forehead to smooth the frown lines before picking up my own phone. Once I found Nico's name, I gave him a call.

"Hey, Rosette."

"Nico." I fought a laugh. "I told you to stop calling me by my full name. Only my dad has that privilege."

"My bad. It's a nice name though. I don't get why more people don't call you by it."

"Rose is easier to say, I guess."

"Sure, Rosette. Look, if you're calling about the Melissa Cowan stuff, I'm still working on it."

"No, it's not that," I said, though that was important too. "This is about someone else."

"Okay. Who?"

"Eve Castillo. I need you to track her location for me."

Eve Castillo journal entry

I'm ashamed right now. Ashamed and so stupid. I bought a peach cobbler, vanilla ice cream, and a bottle of wine. It's Wednesday and Rose and I always meet for our movie nights and girl time on Wednesday.

Cole answered the door. He looked surprised to see me. "Rose is working late with Herbert," he'd said.

"She is?" For some reason my heart dropped. Did she text me this?

I checked my phone and sure enough, there was a text in there from Rose twenty-ish minutes ago. I must've missed it while I was shopping for the food and wine.

"Oh my Godfrey. I feel so stupid."

Cole flashed me a smile and I tried not to react to it. Even though I'd ghosted him, I couldn't deny that Cole was attractive.

"Godfrey will never get old." He chuckled. Then he invited me in.

I'm sitting here writing this because I shouldn't have accepted his invitation. I should've just gone home. We ate some of the peach cobbler and I hoped Rose would turn up soon so the awkwardness would pass.

Eventually Cole offered to pour some of the wine I'd brought and said I was welcome to watch a movie on the sofa if I wanted to wait for Rose. He said he was going to catch up on some work emails.

I hesitated.

"You wouldn't be a bother," Cole said, smiling.

I told him sure. He popped some popcorn while I sat on the sofa with a blanket. I sent a text to Rose and asked if she'd be home anytime soon. She responded after Cole had brought me the popcorn and another glass of wine and said she'd be off in another hour. She apologized for bailing at the last minute.

I told her it was okay, but if she wasn't going to be here soon, I figured I needed to leave. We could catch up another time.

I let Cole know as much as he worked at the dining table. He looked surprised to see that I was leaving. He said something about how he was wrapping up on the emails and knew the perfect movie we could watch until Rose came home. He was talking like we were a couple—like he didn't have a freaking wife who was my best friend.

"I should go," I kept saying as I slipped into my sneakers.

I grabbed my purse and keys, ready to leave. But before I could, Cole caught me by the elbow and spun me around. He kissed me. I snatched my mouth away and froze. And for some reason that I couldn't understand at the time, I let him kiss me again. This time, I didn't stop it.

"I miss you," he whispered on my mouth. "I wish it was you."

I swear it just happened. We started kissing. He cupped my face in his hands, and we made out against the door.

It felt wrong.

Dirty.

Deceitful.

But it also felt . . . good.

Rose would kill me. She'd never talk to me again if she knew. She was like a sister to me. It was so cruel of me. I didn't stop him until my phone chimed with another text from her.

He looked at me. I looked at him. Then I told Cole I had to go. I ran out of the house with tears in my eyes. I wouldn't let it happen again. It was a mistake. One I regret so, so much.

CHAPTER EIGHT

There's always this little voice in the back of my head judging me. I'd hear it ask things like: *Why do you still have Eve's number in your phone? She slept with your husband! Why do you even care about her?* I wish I had it in me to *not* care. I really wanted to be the kind of person who knew how to ghost others and not feel guilty about it later.

The truth is, Cole and I were reaching the finish line way before he'd had sex with Eve. Our marriage had only been going for two years and was already on the rocks. I was working too much; he was working too little. He'd gotten laid off from one of the top engineering companies in Charlotte and was trying to start up his own business. Soon it'd gotten to a point where he was working way more than I was.

We weren't making much time for each other. In the beginning, it was so romantic. He'd send me flowers and take me out on dates. We'd walk the boardwalk in University, and grab ice cream from Ninety's. We would hold hands and kiss until we were breathless. A lot of that changed within a year. I couldn't fully blame him for what he'd done with Eve.

Eve didn't know at the time that I was thinking about moving out of the house. She had no idea that I was refusing to go home because I didn't want to get into an argument with Cole over bills and money. She had no clue that he'd been drinking a lot more, that he was vulnerable, desperate, lonely.

But she'd made her choice. Instead of walking away, she let it happen. She let my drunk husband come on to her, probably kiss her, then eventually fuck her on the couch I used to share with him. The couch where he'd be watching some sports game and I'd have my head on his lap while reading a novel. The couch where we dealt with losses and celebrated our wins. The couch where we had the discussion that I needed some time to myself—that our marriage wasn't working. That we'd rushed into it and now I wasn't sure what to do.

This wasn't all on Eve. It was on Cole too. But for some reason, I was hurt by her the most.

Cole and I were drifting apart at the time of their affair, but I'd had it in the back of my mind that we'd be okay again. That once we both had time to breathe and Cole gained some footing with his new business, we could have a nice dinner and a deep discussion about our future and move things along. That all came crashing down when I came home one night for my laptop charger and saw them.

His pants around his ankles.

Her dress in a puddle on the floor.

Her lips red and raw.

His breaths ragged.

The flare of his nostrils.

Her apologetic, fear-filled eyes as she shoved him away and ran toward me, completely naked—and with the best fucking body ever, mind you. A body ten times better looking than mine. She exercised four times a week. I was lucky if I could squeeze in exercise four times a month.

I had nothing to say to either of them that night. I'd already been distancing myself from Eve because of her ridiculous actions, but this took the cake. We were done. *I* was done.

Instead of letting her plead her case, I backed out of the house and slammed the door. I got in my car and rushed to Best Buy before they closed so I could buy a new charger. While lying on a hotel bed that same night, I looked at apartment listings with puffy eyes.

I hadn't talked to Eve since.

CHAPTER NINE

Sage Hill, North Carolina. That was Eve's last known location.

According to what Nico sent this morning, he couldn't trace her phone and assumed it was off, but he found out when she'd last used her laptop by sifting through her emails. It was the night before Zoey called me to say she was worried.

In the emails, Nico also discovered that Eve had booked a two-bedroom cottage on Lake Aquilla. I ended up searching for the listing of the house to get a better visual of where she was.

According to the online booking calendar, the cottage was still reserved today, September 7th. I couldn't put in a booking until September 9th.

This meant one of two things: Eve was still there, or someone else had booked right after she'd checked out and was staying for, what, one night? I checked some of the reviews and saw several complaints about spotty cell service and Wi-Fi. That alone didn't make much sense because Eve needed reliable Wi-Fi like she needed water.

I remembered what Zoey told me the day before. Eve wanted a break from traveling and vlogging. Perhaps she'd purposely booked the cottage so she wouldn't wind up scrolling through social media or comparing her content to others.

She did that a lot. All that to say, it still didn't make sense that Eve wasn't answering her phone or any of her texts. I texted Zoey right after gathering the information about the cabin and asked if she'd heard from Eve yet.

Nothing.

Diana hadn't and neither had our dad.

If there was one thing I knew about Eve Castillo, her phone was *always* in her hand. She was always texting, scrolling, posting, chatting. She was always online, even when she pretended not to be.

Seated in my office, I took a sip of water before going to YouTube and searching for her channel. She had over thirty-two videos, many of them featuring her travels to different cities or countries and showing off her views, outfits, and the foods she ate. She had a whopping 252,000 subscribers—all people who lived vicariously through the pretty Latina girl who traveled.

Her last video was uploaded two weeks ago. A three-day trip to Dubai. Eve was a biweekly poster. If she wasn't uploading to YouTube, she was posting on Instagram. I'd previously blocked Eve on Instagram. My thumb felt heavy as I unblocked her to check her profile. Her last picture was posted five days ago and for some reason, my heart dropped when I saw where she was.

She was standing in front of the cottage from the listing. Clearly on a dock, with the home in the distance at the top of a hill, it's gold lights glowing behind her like halos. It was autumn, so the leaves behind her were vibrant hues of saffron, yellow, and brown.

Supposedly she'd checked into the cottage five days ago. She was smiling on the dock with her hands raised in the air like she was the happiest girl in the world. It annoyed me for a split second, thinking about how she might've been holed up in that marvelous home, ignoring everyone and doing God knows what.

The annoyance passed the more I thought about who my ex–best friend truly was.

I came to the solid conclusion that Eve was a woman who talked too much, shared too much, and wanted too much. A person like that doesn't just ignore the rest of the world. They don't shy away from attention. They *embrace* it. Eve may have been on a getaway to disconnect, but she would still be vocal about it somewhere.

I went back to the listing and searched for the owner's number. When I found it, I typed it into my phone's keypad. As I brought the phone to my ear, I glanced out the window of my office that revealed the hallway, and spotted Herbert walking with two cups of coffee in hand. The phone rang as he set my cup down on the desk.

"*Thank you*," I mouthed.

"*You know I got you*," he mouthed back, then he disappeared again.

I took a sip of the coffee that was still warm and creamy.

The ringing on the phone was replaced by a deep voice. "This is Alex," a man said.

"Oh—hi, Alex! Alex Reed, right?"

He hesitated before saying, "Yes?"

"Great. I was just calling about your listing for the 'Gorgeous Two Bedroom Lakefront Cottage in Sage Hill.'" I read each word from the listing carefully.

"All right. You interested in booking it, or what?"

Okay, rude asshole.

"If so, you know you can just book online," he added sarcastically.

"Yes, I'm well aware," I returned, clinging to politeness. "I was actually calling to see if you have someone staying in the cottage right now who goes by the name of Eve? Her last name is Castillo."

The line went dead silent. So quiet, I thought he'd hung up. "Hello?" I pulled the phone from my ear to check the

screen. The digits were still ticking away as the call rolled on.
"Mr. Reed?"

"I don't know anyone by that name."

"Oh, okay. I believe she booked your rental a few days ago but—"

"I can't share our tenants' information with strangers over the phone. Look, I have to go. All the info you need about the place can be found online." He hung up before I could squeeze another word in.

"The hell?" I muttered. Right. So, this Alex Reed was a stickler.

I clicked on the profile link for Alex on the bottom of the listing page and he only had one property under his name. And it was *that* cottage Eve booked. How would he not know her name if her stay was that fresh?

Call it the investigator in me, but that feeling in my gut was heavier now. Sure, I could've been overreacting. For all I knew, Eve was doing all this just so I would talk to her again. She was pretending to run off and be sad, ignoring her own sister, just so I'd reach out to her. She'd done something like this before. After an argument, she performed a disappearing act just to see if we cared enough to come looking for her.

A part of me wanted to let it go. Eve would come back. She'd call Zoey. She'd tell her that she broke her phone or accidentally dropped it in the damn lake while trying to take a selfie. Whatever the case was, I was sure she was fine.

She *was* fine... but that little voice in the back of my mind whispered otherwise.

She can use her laptop to reach out to Zoey.

Nope, spotty Wi-Fi, I thought.

She could drive somewhere else to find service and check on her sister if she needs to.

Not if she's high, I thought.

Worst case scenario, she can bail on the trip and drive back home.

Not if something happened to her.

I drummed my fingers on the desk, telling myself over and over again she was fine. Just being Eve. Reckless, inconsiderate, selfish Eve.

Eventually, I couldn't lie to myself anymore. My coffee was cold by the time I looked up how many hours it'd take to drive to Sage Hill along with more information on the small town. Then I booked a stay for Alex Reed's next available date, two days from now.

CHAPTER TEN

Concentrating at the office was futile, too many thoughts about Eve. I had a piece to write, and I couldn't do that if my mind constantly resorted to what-ifs and maybes about her. I decided to go to a coffee shop and soak up the scent of ground coffee beans and baked pastries. After ordering an iced coffee with extra caramel, I found a corner, cracked my laptop open, and dove in.

I was on a roll for a while, until I heard the door of the shop open with a chime. Quickly, I glanced up, but did a double take when I saw a familiar face. My fingers paused as I spotted Lincoln Fowler walking to the counter. His voice was gravelly and deep as he placed an order.

He wore a white tank shirt and jeans. His short dark hair appeared damp, like he'd recently showered. He'd shaved since I last saw him. The baby face didn't make him look innocent though. He looked more like a sex offender. There was a tattoo on his forearm with the name *Eve*. He waited in the pickup area, scrolling through his phone with his back to me. I was glad he didn't bother looking around. I never particularly liked chatting with him.

I stared at his tattoo a moment before flicking my gaze up to his face again. He now had his phone to his ear. With a scowl, I could hear him say, "I'm getting pissed off. Fucking call me back already." Then he slipped the phone into his pocket. The barista called his name. He snatched up his drink and slipped out of the shop.

Confusion wrapped around me. What was he doing on this side of town? And did he just call Eve? Apparently, Zoey and I weren't the only people she was ignoring.

I had the urge to chase after him but thought it would be better not to. It was good Eve wasn't answering him . . . but not good that neither Zoey nor I had heard from her. My concentration escaped me again. With a sigh, I packed up my things and left the shop to go home.

Eve Castillo journal entry

I used to think I wanted to be married when I was younger. I wanted to be the bride who wore the pretty dress and full face of makeup. I wanted my hair styled with pearls. To kiss my man. To toss a bouquet to women who wanted love too.

When Lincoln dropped to one knee and asked me to marry him, I didn't hesitate.

It didn't matter that he had a temper.

That he was always checking my location.

That he grabbed me too hard or shouted when he was upset.

It didn't matter as long as I was a bride.

But it did matter when he threw a glass cup at my sister and almost hit her. It was a crazy revelation to realize that I didn't care how much he hurt me, but when it came to hurting Zoey, I wanted to murder him on the spot.

Murder would've been the easy way out for him. Instead, I called off the engagement, packed my shit, and left. There were two things Lincoln hated: being embarrassed and being alone. Perhaps the latter is why I'd stuck with him for so long. Because I hated the loneliness too.

I'm proud to say I haven't looked back. Is it bad that I miss him though? I think about him every day. I try to distract myself, but nothing works. I even saw him eating at our favorite Chinese restaurant with some girl after we split up, and found myself getting jealous.

But I remembered Zoey. Her safety will always come first. Violence had been in our lives before and it ruined me. I'd be damned if I allowed it in again to ruin her.

CHAPTER ELEVEN

I don't understand why I even care. I stared at my reflection with an exasperated sigh, pulling my box braids into a bun. I picked up the tweezers and started plucking at my brows next. Pausing for a moment, I studied my features. The rich brown skin and light brown eyes. My small nose and full lips that I'd gotten from my mother. My lash extensions that I loved refilling every couple of weeks because they made me feel prettier and more feminine.

I wondered what it was about me that Cole didn't think was enough? Of course I wasn't the sexiest woman on earth, but I was still attractive. I didn't have a killer body, but I kept track of my calorie intake and hardly ever overindulged. I had nice D-cup breasts and full hips. A great butt—bigger than Eve's for sure.

So, what was it that steered Cole away completely? I didn't think I had a horrible attitude. I was a generally nice person . . . well, until you got on my bad side. I compromised with Cole all the time. I gave him what he needed whenever he needed it. Sure, our marriage was on the rocks, but I never rejected him. I never told him I was "too tired" or acted like he wasn't enough for me. He *was* enough . . . until he wasn't.

Sighing, I went back to plucking my brows before filling them in with my eyebrow pencil.

As much as I hated to admit it, I thought about Eve every day. I couldn't help but wonder how she's holding up. If she cared all that much about what she did. If she regretted it at all.

I think about how carefree she can be sometimes, and I envy that. I wish I was someone who didn't care—who let things roll off my back and proceeded to the next best thing. The sad part is that ever since the situation with Cole and Eve, I couldn't sleep properly at night anymore. Usually, I caught a maximum of five hours of sleep and the rest was interrupted. I'd dream about the slap. The fire. The look of pure shock on his face. Sometimes, I'd wake up sweating. Panting. Holding my chest. I would take melatonin, drink tea, even smoke CBD, all of which were temporary aids.

All of this didn't help because I continued to wake every night, and my mind would go back to that vision of Cole and Eve in the living room. I couldn't stop seeing the shock written all over his face and the panic in Eve's eyes. And it could have been my mind playing tricks on me, but I didn't see any regret in Cole's eyes. All I saw was complete and utter shock, like he hated that he'd been caught in the act.

I left the bathroom and started the coffeemaker. As the pot filled, I peered out the kitchen window. The sun was rising, presenting me with a new day . . . and I was about to waste it searching for a betrayer of the worst kind. After pouring a cup, I added creamer, collected my things, and left the apartment.

Once I'd typed in the address for the cottage on Aquilla Lake in Sage Hill, I sent up a prayer and asked God to give me patience and strength. I was going need it if I found Eve wandering around that lake house high off her ass.

Eve Castillo journal entry

I try not to do drugs all the time. I mean, I smoke weed almost every night. But only because it helps me fall asleep. If I don't smoke, I lie in bed thinking about Ma and Pa.

I think about how they used to lock me in the closet for hours. How they wouldn't feed me and Zoey for a whole day as punishment. Or worse, how Pa slapped me if I made a simple mistake, like spilling milk (literally) or having a stain on my clothes when I came home from school.

Zoey thinks that made me OCD. I hate messes. I keep all of my things organized. I can't stand a cup on the counter or a sink full of dishes. It needs to be taken care of immediately or I'll lose my mind. Trauma does that to a person, I guess.

As far as snorting coke and stuff, it's sporadic. I started doing it more with Lincoln. We'd go to his apartment, do a few lines, drink, then fuck. I swear it was the best sex of my life. Sometimes when I travel, I take a Xanax. It keeps me calm. But I'm not a druggy. Rose would say that I am, but that's because she's Miss Perfect. Nothing affects her. I'm not an addict and I think that counts for something.

There are people in the world who have succumbed to their bad drug habits. I haven't. That's what sets me apart from the rest. I may be a little fucked up in the head, but no one would ever know it. I'm good at pretending. Good at pleasing. I've had to be since I was a child. Why would I change that now?

CHAPTER TWELVE

"I don't get why you're even bothering with this." Diana's voice filled my car as I put on the turn signal.

I was thirty minutes away from Sage Hill. It was a two-and-a-half-hour drive in total.

Twyla wasn't pleased to hear that I was leaving. This story about Robert Cowan was huge and they needed a final piece for publication, stat. I told her I'd have it completed and ready to turn in by deadline.

Since it was my turn to stay at the quaint cottage, it probably meant Eve was no longer there. However, she hadn't returned home either. I went back to Eve's place last night and her car still wasn't in the designated spot, plus her townhome was vacant.

"I know, but Zoey is stressed out and her stress is stressing me out," I said.

"Alright, tongue twister." Diana laughed. "I mean you said it yourself, Rose. Eve is spontaneous. Honestly, sis, I'm surprised your friendship with her lasted as long as it did."

"Yeah, me too," I muttered. Diana was the only person I could turn to about my issue with Eve and Cole. "How's Daddy?"

"He's good. Wanna talk to him?"

"Please," I said.

There was some rustling, then my daddy's voice filled the car. "Rosette, hey." His voice was deep but friendly. Daddy was always fun, even when our mom died. It'd been eighteen years since my mother passed away in a fire. As tragic as it was, my father kept his chin up and his eyes bright. I recall him grieving deeply for about four days before finally pulling himself together. To this day I don't know how he did it.

Perhaps it was taking a toll on him now, bottling all that emotion in for so long. Arthritis was eating away at different parts of his body. Sciatica was destroying his back. He had to retire from social work because his body couldn't handle the physical demands of the job anymore. Now, he gives piano lessons and makes pretty decent money from it.

"Hi, Daddy. How you holdin' up?" I asked.

"Better than ever now that Diana done made her good chicken." He chuckled.

"It better not be fried chicken," I playfully scolded.

"Uh-oh."

I couldn't help laughing as he did.

"Daddy, I told you to watch what you eat now. More greens, fruits, veggies. That's what the doctor said."

"I know. But one leg won't hurt."

"I guess not."

"Sounds like you're driving. Traveling for another story?"

"You could say that." I glanced at the rearview mirror. It was midday. The sun was starting to set. The closer I got to Sage Hill, the more my ears began to clog from the elevation. I flexed my jaw to make them pop.

"What's this I hear about Eve not answering her phone?" he asked.

"Oh, it's probably nothing. Just Eve being Eve."

"How so?"

"She's not answering her calls or texts. Me and Zoey have been trying to get in touch with her for a few days."

"You sure she's okay?" he asked, true concern lacing his

voice. Daddy always had a soft spot for Eve. He saw her as one of his own. A daughter—a troubled one who needed love and guidance.

He was there for her a lot. He even bought her and Zoey clothes, shoes—whatever they needed when they couldn't afford it. Even though they had their abuela for a few years, they may as well have lived with us. They spent the night almost every other day, ate dinner with us, watched movies. They especially enjoyed watching Daddy grill steaks when his tax refund money came in. He only ever bought steak around that time.

"I think she's fine. Just wanting attention like always."

"Oh, come on, Rosette. She's your friend. Don't be like that."

"We're not friends anymore," I reminded him.

"You can't erase sixteen years of friendship that easily, sweetheart. She may have done some wild things; I get that, but writing her off would be like doing the same to Diana. That's hard to do. And I know you. You're not the kind of person to stay angry, Rose. You'll find it in your heart to forgive her for whatever she did. But you can't do that if she ain't okay."

"I know," I murmured. "I'll let you know when I talk to her."

A siren blared and my eyes shifted to the rearview mirror again. Blue and red lights sparked behind me and my heart dropped a notch.

"Seriously?" I muttered.

"What happened?" Daddy inquired.

"It's nothing. I'll call you guys later, okay?"

"Okay. Drive safe," he said.

"I will. I love you."

I pulled the car to the side of the road. The cop parked behind me, and I sighed, shutting off my engine. I wasn't speeding and I'd just had my car inspected a month ago, so it couldn't have been a taillight or anything like that. What the hell did they want?

After about a minute, the officer stepped out of his vehicle. I kept my face forward and my hands on the wheel, but my eyes wandered to the side mirror. He walked slowly, hands on his waist, close to his belt. Well, more like on his gun. He stopped at my window and gave it a knock. I rolled it down, making sure to keep my movements slow and steady.

I looked up at him—a white man with aviator sunglasses on and a brown cowboy hat. His mustache was thick and seemed to cover his whole upper lip. His uniform was tan. He had to be in his mid-fifties and appeared to be in decent shape for his age. I studied his sheriff's badge, surprised by the name.

"How's it going?" he asked.

"I'm great," I replied, forcing a smile. "Is there a problem, sir?"

"In fact, there is." He slid his eyes to my back seat.

"Okay. What's that?"

"Your third brake light," he said. "The strip on the trunk. I think the bulb is out."

"Is it?"

"Indeed. Wanted to let you know, in case that was important to you. Also, may help someone traveling behind you at night and all."

"Oh." I relaxed a bit, loosening my grip on the steering wheel. "Well, thanks for that. I'll have it looked at."

He said nothing in response. Instead, he looked through the window of my back seat again. This time I frowned. What was he looking for?

"Is that all?" I asked.

He turned his attention to me. I couldn't see his eyes behind the dark lenses of his sunglasses.

"Where are you headed?" he asked.

"Sage Hill," I answered, though I didn't understand how that was any of his business.

The sheriff smiled. "Ah. Heading to my little town, I see."

I gave a nervous laugh. His town? Right, of course it was. I noticed my hands were shaking and tried to control them. "Guess so."

The sheriff noticed my hands too, studying them a moment before looking at me behind those dark lenses. "What's the matter? You nervous?" he asked.

I blinked, then swallowed. "A little," I admitted.

"Well, don't be nervous now. The only reason you would need to be is if you're guilty of something, right?" He chuckled.

I forced a laugh, despite my rapidly beating heart.

"Anyway, my nephew's a pretty good mechanic if you're looking for someone local. Can give you his number if you want it," he offered.

"Oh, that's okay." I waved a hand. "I won't be here long."

He pressed his lips and nodded. "Suit yourself. Well, you have a good one. And lose the nerves. Sage Hill is a beautiful place." He gave the top of my car a rapid knock. "Drive safely."

"I will. Thank you, sir."

When he walked away, I rolled my window up and started the engine again. I watched him open the door of his truck before putting my signal on and veering onto the road. I glanced at the rearview mirror again. He was watching me go as he spoke into the walkie-talkie on his shoulder. The stop wasn't horrifying, but something about it unnerved me. I couldn't put my finger on what it was exactly.

It took another five minutes for the nerves to melt away and for me to realize what it was about the stop that bugged me. The name on his badge was Reed.

Like Alex Reed.

CHAPTER THIRTEEN

When I felt Sheriff Reed was far behind, I cracked the windows to let some air in. There was a bit of a chill now—a comforting one that screamed autumn. Fall was my favorite season. It meant getting to wear sweaters and hoodies. Cozy up in blankets. Sit around bonfires with wine and snacks. Taking strolls through the park and enjoying the foliage.

The breeze cooled my mind a bit, but it didn't keep the questions from coming at me fast and furiously. Why did that sheriff stop me for a measly LED light? Why did it matter? And most importantly, was he related to Alex Reed?

I brushed the questions aside as I turned onto another single-lane road and drove about three more miles. Before I knew it, the wheels of my car were traveling up a steep, rocky pathway. The tires dipped and bobbed as clusters of colorful trees surrounded me. Then I saw it.

According to the description, the cottage was named Twilight Oaks. Seeing it in person, I understood why. Twilight Oaks may have been swallowed in the trees, but from the middle of the pathway, if you looked up at just the right angle, you saw so much of the sky beyond the mountains of lush treetops. Above those mountains were an accumulation of thick clouds swirling with remnants of a lavender and orange sunset. Wisps of blue lingered in the sky, painting a beautiful canvas that only God's hand could create.

The view was breathtaking. I could see why Eve booked here. She lived for aesthetics and this view would've made any influencer happy.

Along the way, I noticed a house painted blue to my left. It was deeper within the trees, sconces glowing gold on the porch. As I drove by, I spotted a person standing on the left-hand side looking in my direction. I was going too fast to take in the detail of them, but it was good to know there were neighbors around. Once parked, I climbed out of the car and opened the back door to collect my overnight bag. The air smelled earthy and sweet at the same time, like a mixture of maple syrup and briny water.

I focused on the cottage again while shutting the door. Up close, I could tell its age. At least forty years old with some recent renovations. The gray paint and white shutters looked like new additions. One part of the house, the face of it, was made of stone. The wood porch and stoop glistened, as if it'd recently been rinsed off. Not a splinter or crack in sight. Planted flowers were surrounded by dark mulch and a footpath led to the back of the house.

Alex Reed certainly took care of his home.

The front of the house had trees hovering in every direction, like parents cradling a baby. They towered so high I had to tip my head back to see the tops of them. At the door, I typed in the provided code from my confirmation email on the lock and gained access. The interior was cozy. Suede sofas, wooden walls, a stone fireplace. Throw blankets in a basket in the corner. The kitchen had wooden countertops, a butcher block island, and stainless-steel pots and pans hanging from a built-in shelf above the island. The age of the house revealed itself again as I walked deeper into the house, hearing the creaking and moaning fill the silence.

Setting my things down near the four-top table, I soaked in all the details before venturing toward the rooms. The smaller room had a full-sized bed and TV. One window to the right of the bed with the curtains parted. The master bedroom was simple. Kind of tight, but tolerable for someone planning a short stay. The king-sized bed was too big for the room. On either side of the bed, nightstands were wedged in the corners and topped with lamps. Random paintings of lakes were attached to the wall, all looking like they'd been picked from a thrift shop. A sliding door was in the room. I pushed the curtain aside and it revealed a cluster of tree trunks. In between the trunks, I spotted dark, rippling water.

Right. Now to look for signs of Eve.

I checked the closet. Empty. The bathroom was spotless. Nothing but a bottle of hand soap and complimentary shampoo. Nothing under the bed. I slid the sliding door open and popped my head out. There was a single Adirondack chair to the right facing the trees and distant lake. Leaves were scattered on the cement block. No sign of her.

I left the bedroom and returned to the main area, checking the kitchen next. Nothing was in the pantries except salt and a few other condiments. The dishwasher was clear. The fridge had only ketchup and mustard inside. But when I opened the freezer, I paused. A pint of ice cream was in the door of it. And not just any ice cream. Baskin Robbins cotton candy ice cream.

There was only one person I knew personally who ate that sickeningly sweet ice cream. It was her comfort treat. Her favorite to eat when she'd had a bad day or when her period came on.

We had nights where I'd settle for a chocolate pint while she devoured her cotton candy. I'd tease her about how gross it was, and she'd stick her tongue out to show me the melted blue and pink swirl.

Eve had definitely been here. That was *her* ice cream.

I grabbed it quickly, opening it. The container was half empty. No freezer burn. Sure, it could've been anyone else's ice cream, but what were the odds someone would have selected *that* particular flavor? And likely during the same week she was here, no less.

I placed it back in the freezer and went to retrieve my phone from my purse. I had to jump on this now. After several failed attempts, my text message finally went through as a green bubble to Nico.

Eve Castillo journal entry

I met someone a few nights ago. I went to Miami with Pam, and we sunbathed and took pics for our Instas. Pam is kind of annoying, but she has a big following and a lot of connections, so I deal with her. I feel bad saying that because she is very sweet. But she talks so damn loud and is so theatrical. It just totally blows my mind.

Anyway, this guy kept looking at me when we were at the pool. He had a cabana boy drop drinks off for us. Pam said he was looking at me the most. She said it loud enough for him to hear (like I said, annoying). At first, I ignored the guy. He was cute but really not my type. I can't lie and say I didn't like the attention though. After dealing with Lincoln, it was nice to know I was still desired, still wanted, still eye fuckable.

Men always looked at me. It wasn't new. But lately, it seemed to be happening less often, or maybe I didn't care enough to notice. The way this guy eyed me . . . it was as if he practically owned me already. Like he knew he would have me, no matter what it took. For some reason, I liked that. His assuredness. His confidence.

He asked me to meet him at a club and we really hit it off. We took ecstasy. I danced with him all night long. Took shots. Fucked him in his hotel room. Then fucked him again in the shower. The night was a beautiful whirlwind. No, it was magical.

We've been texting every day since I left. He FaceTimes me when he's free. He's so fucking amazing. Like I literally can't get him out of my head. He's patient, smart, sexy, and makes really good money.

But I don't want to jinx it. The good thing is he's ten

times better than Lincoln, but I wonder sometimes what Lincoln is up to. I wonder if he misses me as much as I miss him. If he regrets letting me slip away.

Anyway, we'll see how things go with the new guy. If it feels right, maybe his name will be worthy enough for me to write it down.

CHAPTER FOURTEEN

While I waited for Nico to respond to my text, I carried my phone with me to the sliding glass doors near the kitchen and walked outside. A massive body of water was ahead, revealing Aquilla Lake. On the other side were copious lines of pine trees. By nightfall, they'd blend in with the night. Another house was on the opposite side of the lake. It had many windows and was painted white. Their lights were on, and a boat was docked in front of it. Two people milled about but were practically specks in the distance.

I stepped farther out, the bottoms of my boots sinking into the plush grass. Just down the hill, a set of wooden stairs led to a wide dock overlooking the lake. At the end of the dock, an ivory and black speedboat bobbed on the water. I remembered the mention of it on the cottage's listing. If tenants wanted to use it, they had to reach out to Alex and request it so he could fill it up and then charge a fifty-dollar fee.

I checked my phone again. My signal was absolute garbage. "Yeah, this isn't going to work," I muttered, raising my phone in the air. How the hell did Eve spend time here without a good signal? How had it not driven her crazy?

I swung my arm to the right, then the left, before finally seeing a bar appear. Just as it did, a call came in. I broke out in a smile when I saw it was Jayson. Then I cursed at myself for allowing my body to react that way.

"Hi, Jayson," I answered, walking farther down the hill.

"Hello, my Rose." His voice was smooth like satin, deep and delicious. It made my insides twist in a delightful way. "Been trying to call you for about an hour now. Everything okay?"

"Oh, yeah. Everything's fine." I waved a hand. "I'm at this cabin in Sage Hill. The cell service is terrible."

"Really? I didn't know you'd be traveling. Didn't you say you had a big article to turn in?"

"I do." I sighed. "But I had to deviate a bit."

"Oh." He chuckled. "So, you just need a getaway then?"

"I wish it was a getaway," I said, finding the stairs to the dock. "I'm looking for Eve. I booked this cottage hoping to figure out where she is or what she might be up to but—" I waved it off again. "I don't know. It's stupid. She's not here. If she doesn't want to answer her phone, then whatever, you know? I shouldn't be putting so much effort into finding a grown woman."

"Yeah," he said before going quiet. For a second, I thought I'd turned him away with my mini rant. "But that's not like you. Forgetting about your friends. That isn't the Rose I know."

"You've only known me for a couple of months." I laughed, feeling heat coil in my belly. I cleared my throat, forcing my body to rinse the feeling away. The last time I felt like this was when I met Cole. Now look at us.

"They've been an amazing couple of months though," Jayson said. "What can I say?"

I laughed again.

"I was hoping to see you today, sit at the end of your couch and rub your feet while you bang out some words on your keyboard. Maybe even *bang you* afterwards."

I threw my head back to laugh. "Smooth, Jayson. Real smooth."

"You know me."

I caged my bottom lip between my teeth, studying the lake. I was going to spend the next two nights here. Alone. If Eve wasn't here, there was no point in staying in Twilight Oaks by myself. Plenty of space. Lots of counters. A plush bed. And it would probably help to be in a quiet place to get my article written up.

"Why don't you join me?" I suggested, my heart beating faster. "Sage Hill is only two hours away. There's lots of room in the place I'm renting. I'm having some groceries delivered . . ." I let the sentence fall short, waiting to see what he'd say.

That was the thing with Jayson. We weren't supposed to get too serious. We'd agreed early on that sex was the focus. It would be the thing we sought each other out for to scratch that itch.

He'd just gotten out of a toxic relationship a year prior and . . . well, we knew my situation. Committing to anyone else was not in the cards for us at the moment.

However, a cozy cottage on a lake, just the two of us, sounded extremely romantic—like, next level romantic. I wouldn't have blamed him for making an excuse.

But to my surprise, he said, "Sure. Shoot me the address."

Once again, I grinned as I felt that naughty tug in my belly.

CHAPTER FIFTEEN

I met Jayson Daniels on a rainy night in his bar called The Drop. I'd decided to do a casual piece for my boss on the best places to stop for a drink while in Charlotte and his bar was number three on the list.

That night, he served me the best cocktails to taste-test. I didn't miss the way his eyes connected with mine as he poured the liquor. Or the way he licked his bottom lip and held my gaze as he mixed everything together. The way he teased and joked, shooting his game, was flattering.

That same night, he led me to his office to conduct the interview in a "quieter" space. Before I knew it, my knees were parted and he was between my thighs, his tongue colliding with mine and my fingers threading through his dreads. I like to blame it on the drinks, but truth of the matter is I wanted him—pure and simple.

Jayson was unlike any man I'd ever met. He could be greedy but not selfish. Dominant but never overdid it. He made my toes curl the first time we had sex in an uptown hotel, and things hadn't been the same since. To put it simply, being separated from a cheating husband wasn't so intolerable with a snack like Jayson around. How we acted in that hotel the first night was exactly how we were now. My ass planted on the dining table, panties removed, his boxers lowered so he could bury himself deeper inside me. As soon as I swung the door open when he arrived, he cupped my face in his large hands and kissed me. Passionately. Thoroughly. And with our lips still locked, he shut the door and picked me up to place me on the dining table. I mentally apologized to Alex Reed and any other person who had to eat at that table because we didn't care about the mess we made or what might get broken in the process.

"Damn, I missed you," Jayson breathed in the crook of my neck. We panted raggedly, both of us having reached our peak.

I smiled, unsure what to say to that. If I expressed how much I missed him, that would take things a step further. I *did* miss him. But saying it out loud was risky considering how fragile my trust was. Not that I didn't trust Jayson in a sense. He seemed like an honest man. In fact, the first night we slept together, we'd lain naked under the sheets afterward, discussing personal tidbits about our lives.

When my emotions had gotten the best of me, I told him about my separation and how I'd found my husband cheating on me with my best friend in our house. Then I got on the topic of losing my mom when I was fourteen because of a fire, and that's what truly bonded us: the loss of our mothers. He'd lost his mom in 2009 to cancer.

When he pulled himself free and stepped back, I climbed off the table and picked my panties and leggings up from the floor. "So are you going to stay both nights or just tonight?" I asked, side-eyeing him.

"Just tonight." He slipped into his boxers as I tugged my panties up. "Wish I could stick around both nights, but the bar needs me. Big corporate party tomorrow. They rented out the whole place and I have to make sure they don't destroy my shit."

I laughed. "I get that."

He smiled down at me with those warm brown almond eyes. His hair was freshly tapered at the edges, his dreadlocks bound in two strands with rubber bands on the ends. His skin was light brown, the hair above his lips lined precisely. Curling a muscled arm around me, he reeled me close and kissed me.

I kissed him back, moaning softly. "I should shower," I said when our lips parted.

"Can I join?"

I laughed behind the next kiss. "If you want."

Our mouths drifted apart but his hovered above mine.

He smirked. "I'll let you have a moment," he murmured. "I'll make us something to eat while you shower. That cool?"

"I would love that." I stood on my toes and kissed him once more before pulling away and going for my bag. "I didn't order much though. Just a few things."

"All good." He pulled his basketball shorts on. "I'll work with what you got."

I drifted around the corner as he made his way to the kitchen, digging through the groceries still bagged on the counter. Still shirtless. Damn, that man was fine.

Once I was in the bathroom, I took everything I needed out of my toiletry pack. I was grateful for the clean folded towels on the rack built into the wall. As I stuffed my braids into a shower cap, I stood in front of the mirror and my eyes shifted up.

I hadn't realized it before, but there was a rectangular window just above the shower. I twisted back around, not liking that at all. I hated bathrooms with windows. Not that anyone could see through a window that high or with opaque glass unless they were ten or eleven feet tall, but still. It was the principle.

Ignoring it, I undressed and stood beneath the stream. As the minutes passed, I kept thinking about the ice cream in the freezer. Where was Eve now? Had she returned to Charlotte?

Was she staying at some other friend's house that I didn't know? Or was she with Cole? Had he been lying about *not* seeing her?

That could've been a possibility. Cole could've stopped by and pretended to be concerned about her whereabouts so I wouldn't figure out they were together. *No.* That was stupid. She wouldn't go that low . . . *would she?*

Something slammed into the glass above the shower. I screamed, clutching myself as if that would save me from whatever was trying to break in.

"Rose?" Jayson's deep, concerned voice carried all the way to the bathroom. He barged in, peering around with wide eyes. "What happened?" he asked.

"I—think something hit the window!" My voice shook as I pointed up. Suds clung to my chest and water poured over my shoulder.

"The window? You sure?" he asked, a frown taking hold of his features.

"Yes! It sounded like someone hit it or threw something at it! Shit, I need to get out." I turned around and rinsed the suds away.

"Hold on, hold on. Let me see what it is." Jayson left before I could speak again.

I swallowed hard, shutting off the shower and reaching for a towel on the rack. I wrapped the towel around my body and left the bedroom to get to the living room. The front door was cracked open, so I stuffed my feet into my shoes and walked out.

It was pitch-black outside now. Minus the porch lights and solar lights planted into the ground to reveal a trail to the cottage, there was hardly any visibility. Just trees, darkness, noisy cicadas, and croaking frogs.

"Jayson?" I called out.

"Over here." I followed his voice to the right side of the cottage and spotted him and the rectangular window belonging to the bathroom illuminated with light. A sconce attached to the house was pitched next to the window with insects swarming around it. Something dark was flapping around at Jayson's feet.

"What is that?" I asked.

"A bat," he said, frowning down at it.

"That's what hit the window?" I breathed a sigh of relief as Jayson stepped back.

"Yeah, looks like it. Probably tried going for the moths. Might be injured now."

He walked my way and we both watched the bat thrash around. The left wing appeared a bit crooked. There was no way we could really help it though. Bats could carry rabies and all sorts of diseases.

"I'll find something to use so I can move it. Come on." Jayson wrapped an arm around my damp shoulders and led me back to the porch.

I couldn't help peering over my shoulder at the bat.

The way it thrashed.

Squeaked.

Begging for help.

Begging for more out of life . . .

Just like Eve, the voice in the back of my head whispered.

Eve Castillo journal entry

I'm feeling too emotional today. For some reason I can't stop thinking about a situation that happened when I was younger. I ran away from Abuela's and went straight to Rose's house. I burst into her room and had a panic attack out of nowhere.

It was the first of many to come.

She asked me what was wrong, what had happened, but I couldn't give her an explanation. I remember feeling so overwhelmed. Something had triggered me. After calming down, I realized what it was. That morning, Abuela told me my mom was being let out of prison early. When she told me over breakfast, I shrugged it off and told myself I didn't care.

But I think I glossed over my emotions. I swallowed it down and pretended it didn't matter. The truth is that throughout the whole school day, I kept picturing my mom showing up to the building and dragging me out of the classroom by my hair right in front of my peers. I pictured her yelling at me, berating me, slapping me, mocking me. Blaming me for her problems.

Then I wondered if my dad would get out too. Would he find me? Punch me in the stomach again? Lock me in a room? Force me to get into the trunk of a car? Starve me for hours? That's all I could wonder when I got home after school.

As I thought about it all, I only wanted to be comforted by Rose. I wanted to hear from her that I would be okay, then I wanted to hear from Rose's dad Ben that they would never hurt me again. My parents lost custody of me and Zoey. They couldn't just show up and take us away, and if they did show their face, the police would be called.

Ben reminded me of that constantly and didn't stop

until it was planted deep in my brain like a rooted tree. Rose hugged me tight and cried with me that day. Then she brought me Oreos and cold milk. We talked about it a little more as we dunked the cookies into the cold white liquid. We liked it when the Oreos got just a little soggy on one half but stayed crunchy on the other.

We started giggling about this boy named Bradley with braces who was dying for an invitation to Rose's pool party. Both of us had black crumbs and cream in our teeth and we looked ridiculous as tears of joy left the corners of our eyes.

Rose and I had known each other for three years then. We had been friends in middle school, but became even closer our freshman year of high school. I ate alone at lunch on the first day. Back then, I was wary of everyone and preferred being alone.

Rose sat right next to me and said, "I enjoy eating alone too."

I remember looking at her and smiling. She smiled back then offered me a pack of fruit snacks. Our friendship started out simply. First there were sporadic dinners at her house that Ben would invite me to, then later laughing together in middle school PE. At the start of high school, we began to trust one another more and began walking together in the hallways, meeting at our lockers, and sitting together at lunch every day.

When I ran to Rose's house that night, it was the first time I'd been truly vulnerable with her. I knew before that I loved having her as a friend, but that night she became my best friend forever. I also knew that I would do anything for her . . . and she'd do anything for me.

Friends like her don't come around often. But friends like me are a dime a dozen. I'm cheap. Selfish. Hard to deal with. I don't deserve her. I never have.

CHAPTER SIXTEEN

I couldn't sleep.

Jayson lay right next to me on the bed, one arm draped over my torso, his soft breaths skating down my arm. We'd just had BLT wraps and fries along with some wine. I pointed the ice cream out to him and told him it was Eve's favorite.

"So, she *was* here," he said.

"Yes, she was," I answered back. The question was where was she *now*?

I gently peeled Jayson's arm away and grabbed my phone from the nightstand before leaving the bedroom. I turned on one of the lights in the living room and went for my laptop.

I couldn't help looking out the patio doors in the back along the way. The moon was shining on the lake, revealing gentle ripples bathed in silvery white light.

After logging in, I went to my emails, refreshing constantly until the stupid Wi-Fi cooperated. There was a new email from Nico.

> Shouldn't be sending this via email but my text to you keeps failing.
> Details on Castillo attached.

I clicked the doc.

Of course it took forever to download. When two minutes passed and the thing still hadn't finished, I got up and went to the kitchen to pour a glass of wine. Walking back to the table, I took a careful sip and allowed the flavors to marinate on my tongue. The file was almost done downloading. I tilted my gaze and looked toward the fireplace. The brick and wood design was gorgeous, and I could tell the mantel was a recent addition. There was no TV in this place at all. Probably the best for someone who wants to escape the real world.

My eyes lowered, and I paused on my next sip of wine when I noticed something sparkling in the fireplace. I set my glass down, making my way across the room to grab a poker. I pushed some of the ashes out of the way. When the object became clearer, my chest tightened.

It was a necklace, silver, with a teardrop-shaped sapphire pendant. The chain was charred and the sapphire was damaged.

"Please, no," I whispered. I picked it up and raised it in the air with shaking hands. A name was etched on the back of it, one I was hoping *not* to see.

Eve.

"Oh, shit."

Eve never took this necklace off—*ever*. Not even when she showered. She'd never have left it here either. It was a gift from her abuela, the only relative she and Zoey had who actually showed them love and kindness. She'd never leave something this cherished and valuable behind. For years, Eve and Zoey had lived with their grandmother, even as she grew ill. Their parents were no longer around and she was the only real family they had left.

My throat thickened as I clutched the necklace in my palm. This couldn't be. How was this here? Who tried to burn it? I rushed for my phone, trying Eve's cell again. Just as it had the four or five times prior, my call went directly to voicemail. My legs felt liquid as I sat down in front of my laptop again. The download for my document had finally finished. I gave it a click.

I'd asked Nico to figure out the last time Eve had made a phone call. It was on September 5th at 6:24 PM. That had to be the night before she checked out of the cottage. Zoey said she'd tried calling Eve several times that night. I didn't start calling until the sixth. According to the location provided, she was still in Sage Hill at the time.

So why the hell didn't she answer her phone?

CHAPTER SEVENTEEN

The curtains draped in front of the sliding doors in the bedroom were sheer. All the lights were off inside and out of the cottage. However, the moon was bold, bright, and beaming right down on it.

I'd finally crawled back into bed after reading the document. The wine had soothed me just enough to yearn for sleep. I flipped onto my side, eyelids heavy, and that's when I saw it. A shadow passing right by the door. One minute it was there and the next it was gone.

I lay there a moment, blinking slowly, waiting to see if it would appear again.

A deer? I thought.

But deer didn't walk on two feet.

"Are you sure you can't stay?" I asked, faking a pout as Jayson slung the strap of his backpack over his shoulder.

"You know I would if they didn't need me, my Rose." He stood in front of me with a warm smile. I loved it when he called me that.

"I know, I know. I'm messing with you. I should do some digging anyway."

"Yeah, about that," he said, his smile slowly slipping away.

"Be careful, aight? You don't know how people are around here."

I'd told Jayson about the necklace when we woke up. I didn't mention anything about the shadow though. I still wasn't sure if it had been a figment of my imagination or not.

"That's why I carry," I said, shrugging. "It's fine. I do this kind of stuff for a living. I know how to tread carefully."

He studied me closely, looking deep into my eyes. Worried. That's what he was. I could tell it took everything in him not to voice his concern. Instead, he gripped my chin and lowered his mouth to place a deep kiss on my lips. That kiss did something to me. It stirred me up, stole the breath from my lungs and made mini-Roses do somersaults in my belly.

After one last kiss, I walked him to his car and watched as he climbed inside. When he backed away, he waved before turning the steering wheel and driving down the main path. When I no longer could see his car, I drank in my surroundings again. I listened to the wind ruffle the trees and the soft trickling of the lake in the distance.

To my right, I heard something snap, like a twig breaking. My heart sped up a notch. *Snap.*

There it was again. My body went rigid as I looked toward the noise. I waited, holding my breath. A bunny scurried from a bush, pouncing along the gravelly trail.

"Good Lord, Rose." I huffed a laugh, relief sinking in. "Get it together."

I shook the creeps away and headed inside again to collect my purse and keys. According to Nico, Eve's phone had also been connected to the Wi-Fi in a diner called Flip Stack. I didn't know how he'd discovered that, but with how much he knew about technology, it didn't surprise me.

I locked the door and went to my car, backing out just enough so I could turn the wheel and drive down the trail. It was a steep drive, one that had me cautiously using the brakes.

When the trees cleared a bit to my right, I spotted the blue house again. In broad daylight, I could see the shutters were painted black and four rocking chairs were on the porch. A large and burly man was in the front yard with an axe. He had deep brown skin and a thick neck. He swung the axe down and split a chunk of wood. Then his eyes snapped my way as I passed.

I waved.

He didn't wave back, just frowned.

"O-kay," I mumbled, releasing the brakes a bit so the car would move faster.

When I finally made it to flatter ground, I made a right and followed the GPS instructions to Flip Stack. It was just like any other diner in a small town, with neon-red signs, red and white paint, wide windows revealing patrons hovering over cups of steaming coffee and food. I parked before unlocking my phone and sharing my location with Nico.

At this point, Eve's disappearance was starting to feel like some of the other crime cases I'd investigated. Not that I thought she was dead or anything, but something was clearly going on with her and I needed to get to the bottom of it. Finding her special necklace in the fireplace proved as much.

The aroma of coffee and pancake batter wrapped around me as soon as I walked inside the diner. A blast of AC also hit me, and I fought a shiver. Seeing as it was fifty degrees out, the cold air wasn't necessary. Security cameras were pitched in two corners at the far end of the diner. It was a relief seeing them, but that feeling didn't last long. A lot of times, security cameras were only for show, and they didn't actually record anything.

I spotted a heavy-chested Latina woman behind the counter in an all-black uniform with a red apron. She eyed me as she ran someone's credit card, chomping hard on a piece of gum. Her name badge read: *Luisa*. The word *manager* was typed above it. I made my way to the bar, sitting about two seats away from where she stood on the opposite side. She glanced at me again before pursing her lips and pulling out a menu.

"Flapjacks are on special today," she said, sliding the menu my way. "Three for four bucks. Ten for six."

"Oh. Thank you." I smiled while trying to figure out who in their right mind would order ten pancakes for just themselves. "I'll just take a coffee for now, if you don't mind."

"Sure, honey." She had a monotone voice, yet somehow it was comforting. "Let me just take care of the gentleman over there."

She plucked a receipt from the till, then wandered around the counter to reach a man seated in a middle booth. She handed him his credit card back with a warm smile. When she was behind the counter again, she poured my coffee, slid it across, then placed a bowl of creamer packets next to it.

"You must be new around here," she said, setting a glass container of sugar down in front of me too.

"I am. Just visiting."

"Perfect season for a visit. Nice car you've got." She gestured toward the windows, likely at my Mercedes. It was a 2006 CLS500. It had formerly belonged to my mother. She'd bought it the same year she died.

"Thanks."

"You don't strike me as flapjack kind of girl," Luisa said, her eyes narrowing a bit as she chomped on her gum again. "What you *really* in here for?"

I figured this was the best time to bring it up. Cut straight to the chase. "You got me." I laughed, glancing at the man frying an egg behind her. "I'm actually looking for someone." I dug into my bag for my wallet, pulling out an old photo of me and Eve. Both of us were twenty-six years old, fresh-faced, young, and hopeful. We'd taken the picture at a photo-booth in the mall. For some odd reason, I never removed it.

I slid the photo toward Luisa and pointed at Eve. "Have you seen her around here?"

Luisa frowned a bit, studying the image, before tilting her gaze to mine. "Can't say that I have."

"Are you sure? It's just—I only ask because she'd mentioned coming here to eat one night." Granted, this was a lie. But a lie helps when you need answers.

"Oh, that must be why I haven't seen her. I don't work the night shift." She backed away when the man behind her rang a bell. She picked up two plates stacked with flapjacks and carried them around the counter to two truckers in the back.

When she returned, busying herself with wiping the menus clean, I looked from her to one of the cameras. "Do those work?" I peeled one of the creamer packets open, nodding my head at the camera.

She gave a bored glance over her shoulder before wiping the menus again. "Depends on the day."

"Do you think I can take a look at the footage you have? From three nights ago?"

Luisa planted a hand on her hip. "Are you some kind of food reviewer or something?" she asked, eyeing me suspiciously. "Because if so, we've told y'all a million times that we are a *clean* restaurant. You can see our health code right there! Whoever put up that review about the roaches was lying."

"No, no. I'm—" I forced a laugh, tossing up a hand. The truckers looked our way. The last thing I needed was attention on me. "I'm not a food reviewer. I'm just worried about my friend and hoping to get a lead on where she might be."

"Oh." Luisa softened a bit, chewing slowly as she mulled that over. "Well, why didn't you just say that to begin with? Beating around the bush won't get you nowhere with me."

"I don't know." I shrugged. "I figured you wouldn't really care."

"Fair point," she said, about to turn away.

"Wait." I held up a hand for her to stop, then dug into my

purse for my wallet. I plucked out three twenties and slid them across the counter. "I'll pay if you give me a chance to look at the footage." I internally cursed, always the one paying for Eve's fuck-ups.

She stared at the money, then raised a brow.

Drawing in a breath, I pulled one more twenty out.

This time she reached for the money with a smirk. "Fine. But I'm not all that good with the cameras and stuff. Freddy can help. He's in the back. Come on."

CHAPTER EIGHTEEN

Freddy was an oily-haired twenty-something who was now sitting in front of a desktop. Acne had not been kind to his face and there were thick lines of dirt underneath his fingernails.

"What date are you looking for?" Freddy asked me.

"Can you go back to September fifth?"

Freddy let out a long breath. I was clearly an inconvenience to his day. He'd been lying on a couch in the break room playing a Nintendo Switch when Luisa and I walked in.

"Alright. This is the fifth," he said, boredom lacing his voice.

"Great. Can you fast forward to about six that night?"

Freddy tapped a button on the keyboard, sending off a loud *clack*. Then he clicked the mouse.

"Right there." I pointed at the screen, and he gave the keyboard a clack again. "Go back a bit."

Clack.

"Right there," I murmured.

He paused the video, revealing a still of Eve entering the diner in a brown hoodie, leggings, and Uggs. Her hair was pulled into a loose bun, her face pale, hands tucked into the hoodie pocket. She looked exhausted. She stopped at a table where someone was already sitting. This person had a hood on, their back to the camera and the diner entrance.

Who is that?

"Is there an angle where I can see the person sitting with that woman?" I asked Freddy as I pointed at Eve.

Clack.

Click.

Freddy switched to another angle of the diner, went back to September 5th, and stopped the time at 6:04 PM, just like the previous still. He paused it, but even from this angle I couldn't see the person's face. They had their head down, hood pulled low, only the bill of a hat poking out, completely aware of the cameras.

Eve sat with this person for no longer than six minutes. Throughout the entire six minutes, she appeared visibly upset, slapping her hands on the table, throwing them in the air with exasperation, before finally hopping out of the booth, flipping the person off, and leaving the restaurant.

I tried following her to see which direction she might've gone outside of the building but had no luck.

"Are there cameras outside the diner?" I asked.

"Only in the back," Freddy said. "The rest are CCTV, and I don't control those."

"Right." I gave the screen one more look. The person sat at the booth in their hood, watching Eve go. They sat for three minutes before finally standing up, pulling the hat lower with leather-gloved hands, and exiting the diner too.

"That's creepy as shit." Freddy chortled.

Yeah. It *was* creepy, not only because I had no idea who this person was, but because whoever it was, they'd clearly done something to Eve. Judging by the build, this was a man. Unless there was some buff, broad-shouldered woman wandering around that I wasn't aware of.

"Thank you for your help, Freddy. Have fun playing with your Switch."

"It *is* fun, actually," Freddy retorted.

I left the back room with more questions than I'd gone in with. On my way out the diner, I checked my phone, and my signal was ten times better here than at the cottage. I searched for Nico's name again but bumped into someone along the way.

A large pair of hands caught me before I could stumble. Gasping, I looked up at the familiar older man with ivory skin, a graying mustache, and large cowboy hat atop his head. He wore the same sheriff's badge I saw yesterday but he didn't have the aviator sunglasses.

"I'm so sorry." I collected myself as Sheriff Reed released me. "Wasn't paying attention."

"Nose stuck in your phone," he said, but he didn't smile. It was weird. His eyes were beady and dark, blending in with his irises. I was glad I hadn't seen them when he pulled me over or I would've been even more unnerved. I didn't like the way he looked at me either, like I was a pest he wanted to squish with his foot.

"Yeah," I said before walking away and hurrying to my car. Once inside, I locked the doors and watched the sheriff make his way inside the diner, stopping at the counter in front of Luisa. She poured him a coffee as he said (or asked) something, then she spoke.

Sheriff Reed looked back at me with narrowed eyes as Luisa mouthed away, waving her hands in pure nonchalance. When he held up a finger at her and marched toward the exit, I started my engine, put the car in gear, and drove out of the parking lot.

Eve Castillo journal entry

I was supposed to meet Rose for a movie last night. I wanted to vent to her about how this new guy had upset me. I bought my favorite ice cream, and she asked me to grab butter pecan for her. When I got to her place, Cole said she'd left really quick because Ben had called her. His arthritis was getting worse so I understood why she left but I wish she'd told me in advance.

It was just me and Cole. I didn't like it. We'd kissed before. Now we were alone again. It wasn't safe. He could sense that I was about to leave so he made up some stupid question and asked me for advice on a logo he'd hired someone to design. He had two options, and both were ugly, but I told him to go with the blue one. He could tell I was upset about something so he asked me about it but I shrugged it off.

I sent Rose a text and told her I would catch her another time. She replied quickly and begged me not to leave—said it shouldn't take her too long to get back. She wanted to vent to me too, most likely about Cole. She'd been hinting at how they were having issues and were arguing a lot more. But then Cole came up to me. He wrapped his arms around me from behind and reeled me backwards. I asked him what the hell he was doing, and he started kissing my neck.

I don't know how he managed it, but somehow, he'd guided me to the couch. He took off all my clothes and I just . . . let him. He kept saying we needed to finish what we'd started and that's when I knew I had to end this.

I told him to get off. He didn't. He just held on tighter and kept kissing me, even when I tried pushing him off. He continued spreading my legs so he could make it easier for himself to enter me. I was triggered. I realize that now. And when I'm triggered, I have the tendency to freeze.

For some reason, while this was happening, I thought about my dad and how sometimes I had to just take the beating so it would end sooner. Don't fight back. Just let it happen, let him get it out so he can move on and leave you alone.

It was called being in survival mode.

That's what my mother always said.

I remember just . . . letting it happen.

Letting Cole suck on my nipples and moan as he rolled his tongue around my piercings. Letting him palm my breasts as he grunted in the crook of my neck. He kept saying how much he missed being inside me. How he wished I was in Rose's place. I was glad he had a condom on because he came fast.

Then Rose came home, and she saw us together. I don't know what to do. She won't answer me. It's been hours and I can't sleep because I feel horrible. I need to explain to her what really happened and tell her I never wanted that with Cole.

I think because the act was forbidden, Cole wanted me more. He knew he'd never be able to have me again with Rose in the picture, and he couldn't live with that. He also knew he'd never leave Rose for someone like me. To him, I was forbidden fruit and despite the issues it would bring, he wanted to devour me. Now I understand why my parents named me after the first woman who sinned.

CHAPTER NINETEEN

Eve had officially been MIA for four days with no new YouTube uploads or Instagram posts. As a travel influencer, this was *highly* unlike her. I scrolled through her Instagram as I sat on the sofa in Twilight Oaks, trying to find a clue as to where she might be or what she could be doing.

It was all to no avail and, eventually, I gave up and finished eating my dinner. Going to the diner was a bust, and after seeing Sheriff Reed there, I wasn't sure I wanted to visit again anytime soon. My phone buzzed on the counter while I was washing my dishes. Zoey was calling. *Again.* She'd called twice in less than an hour.

I groaned.

It wasn't that I *didn't* want to speak with her. I just wasn't sure what to tell her. I was also worried that it would slip out that I definitely thought Eve was missing and in some kind of trouble. The last thing I needed was for her to overthink and panic.

"Hi, Zoey," I finally answered.

"So, I'm at Eve's apartment," she said, ignoring my greeting. I sat back down on the couch. "Why aren't you at school?"

"Because my sister is missing and no one else seems to be doing a damn thing about it."

"That's not true. I found out Eve was staying in a cottage in Sage Hill. Did she mention this place to you?"

"No. Never," Zoey answered.

"Well, there's a cottage here on Aquilla Lake that she booked for four nights. I'm sitting in it right now."

"You are?" She gasped. "Is she there? Did you find her?"

"No. But there are signs she was here. I found her favorite ice cream in the freezer and her necklace . . ." I couldn't tell her it was in the fireplace, burned, likely meant to be destroyed.

"The one Abuela gave to her?" asked Zoey.

"Yes." I sighed. "That one."

"Rose, she *never* takes that off."

"I know."

"She'd have died with it on."

I smashed my lips together. It was not the time to be talking as if Eve was already dead or to reveal that, after inspecting the necklace a bit more, the chain was broken, as if it had been snatched off her neck.

"I see her old laptop," Zoey said as distant clicks of a keyboard sounded off. "I know her password. She used this laptop as backup. But all of her uploads and files sync to this one. If she's uploaded anything new, I can see it here. See if maybe she's active but ignoring us?"

"You can try," I murmured. I seriously doubted that was the case.

The line went quiet for a few seconds. I peered around the cottage, from the portrait of a fish on the wall to the refrigerator in the kitchen. The tall walls and wide windows covered by curtains that blocked out a foggy view of the lake. Last I checked, it was drizzling outside.

"Oh, wait!" Zoey's voice filled the silence again. "I'm in her emails. It says she booked a flight to Thailand on the night of September eighth."

"Wait—*yesterday?*" I mulled the information over. "That's . . . random."

"She wouldn't book a trip abroad and not tell me. Sage Hill or whatever is one thing. But *Thailand?*"

"Yeah." Now my worries were increasing.

First the broken necklace. Then the hooded stranger she met at the diner. Now a booked trip *thousands* of miles away from home? Eve would've bragged about a trip like that. If not to us, then to her followers.

Zoey let out a defeated breath. "Something happened to her, Rose. I can feel it in my gut. I hate to even consider this, but what if she went hiking and she's hurt? Or she's been kidnapped?"

I frowned. "Why would anyone want to kidnap her?"

"Well, she used to tell me about this fan she had online. She was a superfan, you know. Eventually it got to a point where she started showing up at Eve's gym and then to her chiropractic appointments the same day. She followed Eve in her car once and that's when Eve filed a restraining order."

"Wait . . ." I raised a hand and closed my eyes for a second. "When was this?"

"Like, last year sometime, I think."

Back when we were still somewhat friends. "Why was I never informed about this?"

"It was around the time you were in New York. Remember you went for like a month in July? Around then, I think. It slipped my mind, I guess. As for Eve, well . . . there's a lot she didn't tell you. Probably because she was worried you'd judge her."

I scoffed. "I don't judge people."

"You criticized her *all the time*, Rose."

"Polite criticism and judging are two very different things. I only did it because I wanted her to take care of herself and stop doing dumb shit all the time. I criticized *sometimes* because I cared."

"I guess." Zoey paused. "It does get frustrating looking after her. I never understood why she couldn't just be *normal*, you know? Live a regular life. Focus on herself. Not live a life that alters everyone else's."

Because your sister is self-centered, attention-seeking, and obnoxious, I wanted to say.

"Anyway, I'll keep digging around, see what I can find," Zoey went on.

"Okay."

When she hung up, something she said hit me again. Eve did like to go hiking. Perhaps she'd taken a trail leading to the mountains and was hurt. The problem, though, was that I *hated* hiking. I grumpily went to my bag, plucking out a pair of leggings and a long-sleeved shirt. After grabbing my phone and gun from my purse, I left the cottage and took the trail to the right of the house.

There was an easy footpath to follow. According to the welcome binder, this particular trail led to a four-mile hike that gave you the sweetest view of the mountains. The air was cooler now and I was swallowed in mist. The smell of rain was powerful. A downpour was on the way. The deeper I walked into the forest, the stronger the scent of wet bark and leaves became.

"Really got me out here hiking," I grumbled, swinging my arms faster, my gun knocking against my hip.

A fork in the path appeared. One trail led to the lake. I could see the water in the distance. Another led deeper into the forest. The middle carried on, but there was a bend farther along, like it wrapped around to the other side of Aquilla Lake. I decided to check the path leading to the water. Other than a bench built into the ground facing the lake, an old grill full of ash, and several geese, nothing was there.

I returned to the path, deciding to move forward and take the trail that wrapped around the lake. Thunder rumbled in the sky now. Leaves rustled and tree branches groaned from the light breeze. I swung my gaze to the right, focusing on the empty spaces between the tree trunks. It was so quiet out here, not even the birds tweeted. Maybe they were hiding from the oncoming storm. The rustling of leaves grew louder. Then again, maybe it wasn't the leaves.

Footsteps.

I hitched a breath, spinning around and facing a vacant path. Tree branches hovered inches above, the dirt stamped with my own tracks. No one was there. My fingers twitched for my gun anyway. I paused, letting my heart settle while breathing in deep.

I wasn't some extreme gun lover. In fact, I hated them . . . until I was attacked one night after work. I'd left late and a man was standing in the lobby. He was in front of the desk with his back to me. I thought he was an employee or our hired security. As it turned out, he was never meant to be in there. He was a squatter. The man heard me coming and turned around, ripped my purse out of my hands, then shoved me to the floor. A woman appeared right next to him and punched me square in the face before kicking me in the ribs. They stole everything of value I had on me.

The security guard on duty had run off to the bathroom. No one could figure out how they'd gotten into the building. Many assumed they snuck in during business hours somehow and just waited for the right opportunity to strike. I was shaken after the attack. My eye was swollen and blackened for days. My rib had been fractured. My confidence was gone with all of my valuables.

After the assault, I had to go to therapy to deal with the trauma. There were moments I never wanted to leave home. Others where I wanted to sink into the floor and be swallowed whole. How could two people do that? Attack a defenseless woman for no reason? Ruin her in the short span of thirty seconds? Because that's all it took for them to do a psychological number on me. Thirty seconds.

I'd read a lot of forums about what happened after people were attacked, women raped or assaulted, or others almost being kidnapped. This led me down a rabbit hole where I found a community of victims who swore that taking defense classes and buying a gun made them feel more secure. So that's what I did. I started with the classes. Learned how to fight. Then, eventually, I walked into a gun store and bought one. That quiet community was correct. I felt much better walking around this world knowing I could protect myself no matter where I was.

Regaining a bit of confidence, I started up my walk again. I was being really paranoid. Attacks like that didn't happen often. My community reminded us of that, every chance it could. I was just at the wrong place at the wrong time. It could've happened to anyone.

Relief sunk in when I reached a clearing in the forest. Off to the right was a view of the lake again. I took the right, hurrying toward the nearest bench and sitting. I glanced over my shoulder, just to be sure no one was following me.

No one was.

I faced forward, closed my eyes, and drew in a breath. *Inhale. Exhale.*

Just like my therapist had taught me.

When I felt well enough, my eyelids fluttered open. There was a dock nearby. I hadn't noticed it before in my haste, but someone was sitting on the edge of it. The mist was thicker, so the person looked more like a dark blob in the distance. I frowned as they looked my way. The mist made it difficult to see them clearly. I stood up and stepped closer to make sure my mind wasn't playing tricks on me.

Slowly, their details became visible. The figure was wearing an all-black T-shirt, jeans, and had short hair.

"Hey," the person called out, pulling their legs up and rising to a stand.

I stumbled backwards as they walked in my direction.

CHAPTER TWENTY

Once again, my fingers twitched, ready to grab hold of my gun. But grabbing it was unnecessary. It was only a girl. Her skin was deep brown, and she had a buzz cut. She wore glasses and looked so thin it seemed she was malnourished. Her feet were bare and wet as she approached me with a wide smile. She couldn't have been any older than sixteen or seventeen.

"Hey—oh, sorry!" She glanced at the gun holster attached to my hip, throwing her hands up. "I didn't mean to scare you." She shifted on her feet like she was ready to bolt. Clearly, I was the dangerous one to her.

"That's alright." I forced a smile at her and cocked my hip left a bit, so the gun wasn't as threatening.

She forced a smile back at me, glancing at the gun again. "You know, it's smart to carry these days. You just never know sometimes. I want one when I'm older."

I pressed my lips together.

She focused on the lake again. "It probably looks weird that I'm just sitting out here while it's all gloomy looking. Like the start of a horror movie or something, right?" She giggled.

"No, that's your business." I laughed. "It's none of mine."

"I've never seen you around here before. Are you renting the cottage?" she asked. "Twilight Oaks?"

I nodded. "I am."

"So, you're Rose, then."

I hesitated and it took everything in me not to frown. "How do you know that?"

"I saw your name in the confirmation emails. Nothing weird or anything!" She threw her hands in the air, feigning innocence. "I live with Alex. He's the one who rents the place out. We stay in the blue house along the main path."

"Oh, okay!" I lowered my guard. So, Alex Reed lived in that house. Interesting. "That makes sense. What are you doing all the way over here?"

"I dunno. Just wanted to take a walk. Needed some air. Things have been weird at home. When it gets like that, I like putting my feet in the water and pretending I'm on vacation or something." She gave me an uneasy smile. I sensed that wasn't all she wanted to say.

I waited to see if she'd provide more.

She twisted her fingers in front of her, chewing on her bottom lip instead, like she knew better than to keep talking.

"I understand." I paused. "I have a question for you. Hopefully you can help me out."

"Sure!"

"Did you happen to run into the person who rented the cottage before me, by any chance?"

"Oh. Um . . ." She avoided my eyes and stared at the grass. "I don't think so."

It was obvious she was lying.

"It's just . . ." I lifted my phone and swiped to unlock it. I scrolled through my photos until I found the most recent image of me and Eve. "This is my friend Eve. She was staying here for a few days."

The girl stared at the picture for a lengthy amount of time. Her face seemed go pale. After ten more seconds, I wasn't sure if she'd gotten lost in thought or what. Finally, her eyes swooped up to mine and she shook her head. "I don't remember seeing her."

"Okay." I pulled my phone away with a defeated sigh.

"I do remember seeing her name when she booked though," she tossed in. "I help Alex clean the cottage sometimes and with the background work."

"That's very kind of you."

"Thanks. Anyway, I should get back. They don't like me being gone for too long, especially on days when I have an appointment."

"Appointment?" I repeated.

"Oh—um, yes. I had leukemia."

"Oh . . . I'm so sorry," I murmured.

"But I'm in remission now, so yay! You shouldn't be sorry. It's not your fault it happened," she chimed, as bubbly as ever. "I guess God just hates me."

I gasped. "No. Don't say that. He doesn't hate you."

"Then why would He allow me or anyone else to be diagnosed with a disease that can end a life at any given moment?" She stared at me with her deep brown eyes, tears accumulating at the rims.

I wanted to hug her. She looked like she needed a hug, but I didn't know her, so I kept still.

She sniffed. Blinked the tears away. "I'm Rory, by the way." Another one of her smiles appeared, despite the sheen in her eyes. "I would shake your hand but my immune system sucks ass right now."

Poor baby. Smiling through the heartache.

"It's nice to meet you, Rory."

"Hey, maybe while you're here I can bring you some of my brownies. My brothers love them. Is it okay to bring some tonight?"

"Yeah, of course. That's really nice of you." And a perk for me. If she swung by, I could ask her more questions. I could get her to spill the truth. She had to know *something* about Eve. She had to have seen her at least once.

"Great! I can't wait for you to taste them! See you soon!"

I smiled at her as she twisted around to walk off. As she drifted away, swallowed in mist, I couldn't help thinking how odd the encounter was to begin with. What was a girl who'd been sick with cancer doing outside alone?

I tilted my gaze and noticed the house across from the cottage was several yards away now. It was stark white with black trimmings. Massive windows took over the back side of the home, likely giving the owners a crystal-clear view of the lake. I hadn't realized it before, but there was another house on this side of Lake Aquilla too. It was deeper within the trees, making it much harder to see from a distance. There weren't any lights on inside that one. It seemed so small compared to the white one.

Someone walked along the dock in front of the white house to reach a boat. I made my way in their direction and didn't slow down until I found a set of stairs that led to the wooden platform. Leaves were scattered around, the wood slick and wet. It smelled like salt and fish.

As I moseyed along, I found where the fishy scent was coming from. An open cooler with four fish lay across ice. Fresh catch?

A man was on the boat, bent over and searching for something.

"Uh—hi! Excuse me!" I called, keeping a safe distance.

The man jerked backwards but ended up slamming his head into the seat above. "Ow. Damn it!" he yelled, wrenching himself out and clutching the back of his head.

"Oh. Yikes," I cried, pressing a hand to my mouth.

He scowled as he looked my way. Then his face relaxed as curiosity stole its place.

"I'm so sorry. I didn't mean to scare you." I held out both hands as if apologizing with them. "Are you okay?"

"Yeah, yeah, I'm fine." The man stood. He was a few inches taller than me, light brown skin, hazel eyes, and neatly cut hair. He wore a button-down polo shirt and jeans with a pair of Sperrys. I wanted to say he was in his late forties or so.

"Uh, who are you?" he asked, still rubbing his head.

"I'm Rose Ho—Gibson. Rose Gibson." I smiled wider as he gave me a funny look. "Sorry. Just um . . . going through a stupid divorce and still getting used to not using his name."

He stepped off the boat with a nod. "I understand that. Marriage is tricky sometimes."

"Ha. Yeah, it is." I glanced over my shoulder at his house. Up close, I could see more of the details. The table on the patio. Sliding doors. Fancy pendant lights in the kitchen. A slide and swing set was off to the left, along with a sand pit.

My eyes swooped right, to the darker house tucked deeper within the trees. The lights were now on in one of the downstairs windows. If I wasn't mistaken, the curtains shifted, like someone had been watching but let them drop when I looked.

"So, uh, what can I help you with?" the man asked, wiping his hands on his pants.

"Right." I whipped out my phone again and turned the screen his way. "I'm just going around the neighborhood and hoping someone can help me. Have you seen this woman?"

He studied Eve's picture, looking down his nose at it. "Hmm . . . no. Can't say that I have. Why? Who is she?"

"Her name's Eve." I lowered my arm. "She stayed in the cottage across the lake from here."

"Oh—the rental?" he asked, then scoffed.

"What?" I gave a wary laugh.

"Nothing. It's just the boys who own that rental. Don't like 'em."

"Why not?"

The man peered over his shoulder like someone was around who could hear.

"Long story. Would you like something to drink?" he asked. "I'll have to bring it outside. My daughter is napping right now."

"Um . . . sure. That would be nice. Water, please."

"Of course. I'm Eddie, by the way. Be right back."

CHAPTER TWENTY-ONE

I sipped from the glass of cold water as Eddie sat down with a mug of coffee.

"I get wary about visitors," he confessed. "Especially around here."

"Why is that?" I asked.

"I don't know." He waved a dismissive hand. "This town has great views, but the people here are just... *weird*. I'm telling ya. They all just stare at you. Look at you like you're an alien if they haven't seen you before."

I could understand that, especially after that random run-in with Rory and bumping into Sherriff Reed.

"Well, if it helps, I'm only here temporarily. I'm actually staying in the cottage we just spoke about. The one those guys own?"

"Oh, right. Yeah. The *Reeds*." He made a noise of disapproval, sipping again. He said their name like it was a disease. "They're too quiet for me. And not a good quiet, you know? They ain't neighbors who respect the peace. Like the Abbots over there." He pointed to the dark house a few yards away. "The Abbots are pretty good people. Well, Mrs. Abbot is. Haven't talked to Mr. Abbot much but he seems like a decent man.

"But the Reeds have that eerie quiet going on, like they're hiding something. I always catch them on this side of the lake looking at my house. I don't understand why they do it. Like they own the whole damn area or something. You should've seen them when we had the place built. They were pissed about all the noise, which I understand, but it still wasn't any of their business. Plus, the Abbots said they catch them sometimes too, just milling around, looking at their house. If either of our houses are ever robbed, we'll know who did it. I'll tell you that much."

"Have you ever spoken to the Reeds personally?" I asked.

"Just once. To the one named Damian. And I wouldn't exactly call it a conversation. He's a strange one."

I shifted in my seat. "How do you mean?"

"Dunno. There's just something off about that kid. He has that look in his eyes—the kind you see and are immediately skeptical of. Get this: I saw him fishing one day, figured I'd say hello. We'd just built the house, and I wanted to get to know the lands. I approached him, waved and asked how he was doing, and he just stared at me." Eddie narrowed his eyes, focusing on the lake. "For a while I thought something might've been wrong with him. Maybe he was deaf or mute. But he's not."

"Oh, wow. Yeah, that is strange. I waved at one of them earlier and they stared at me too. Didn't bother waving back."

Eddie sipped before saying, "It was probably Damian then."

"So, when did you officially move here?"

"Well, we bought the land about three years ago and had the house built last year. We moved in 'round April, so a couple of months now."

I sipped again. "And do you like it here?"

"I do. It's quiet. Like I said, the people can be a little weird, but we just have things delivered or order groceries for pickup if we don't want to be bothered."

"That sounds really nice. I'd probably be doing the same." I laughed.

"See." He tipped his mug my way. "You get it."

I looked up as a bird squawked. "Have you ever met the owner of the rental? Alex, I think."

"Haven't met him, no," Eddie answered. "But I hear he's civilized enough. His uncle is the sheriff. James Reed. I see his face plastered all over the town. The people love him."

"Mmm. Yeah, I've met the sheriff. Twice, actually. He pulled me over when I was on the way here."

"Seriously?" Eddie scoffed. "My wife got pulled over by him about a month ago. He claimed she was speeding but she swears up and down she wasn't."

"I can imagine the cops here are extremely bored."

"Oh yeah. No doubt about that." He took a brief pause, then switched gears. "So, what's all this about your friend?"

"Well, she booked Alex's cottage a few days ago but I haven't heard from her since she checked out. When I call, her phone goes straight to voicemail. I figured I'd come to Sage Hill and check things out, but I haven't had much luck."

"Damn. I'm sorry to hear that. Did you ask them if they'd seen her?" he asked, gesturing across the lake.

"Not yet. I don't want to alarm too many people." I swallowed hard while shaking my head. "The thing is, Eve is the kind of friend who is spontaneous. I don't want to assume she's missing or anything if she's just booked a trip to Hawaii or something." I laughed.

Eddie laughed too. "Hawaii sounds like a dream right about now."

"Right? So . . . who knows, you know? Only thing is it's not like her to *not* be in touch."

His brows dipped. "No?"

"Not at all."

"Well, I'll tell you what." Eddie placed his coffee down on the nearest surface and leaned back, folding his arms. "I wouldn't put anything past those boys. I'd go and ask them if they have seen her. Wouldn't even beat around the bush."

"Daddy?" a small voice came from the left and I craned

my neck to see a little girl standing on the dock with a pink dress on. Her coily dark hair was unruly and her feet bare. She had beautiful beige skin and eyes just like her father's. Couldn't have been any older than four.

"Oh, baby girl!" Eddie stood and walked off the boat to scoop her up. "I've told you about coming down here all by yourself."

"Sowwy," she said in a soft voice.

"That's alright." He bounced her on his hip. "How was your nap?"

"Good." The little girl laughed.

I took that as my sign to get up and stop interrupting this man's day.

"What's her name?" I asked, joining them on the dock.

"Go on, baby. Tell her your name," Eddie encouraged.

"Emily," she replied bashfully, placing her head on her dad's shoulder.

"It's so nice to meet you, Emily," I cooed. "Well, I'm going to get going. Thank you for the water and for taking time to speak with me, Eddie. I really appreciate it."

"'Course. No problem."

"I'm thirsty, Daddy."

Eddie smiled at Emily, then gave me an apologetic look. "I'm sorry I couldn't be much help, but I hope you figure things out. If you need anything else, I'm only a knock away."

"Thank you. I'll keep that in mind."

I walked away as Eddie started asking Emily if she was hungry too.

I thought about going back to the cottage, but I gave another glance at the house in the trees. The Abbots. Though I doubted they'd be of more help than Eddie was, I walked in the direction of their home anyway.

Eve Castillo journal entry

I've been having weird dreams.

Last night, I dreamt I was under water. For some reason, I'm not in my own body. I can see myself . . . all of me. I'm under water and my leg is caught on something and I can't free myself from it. I look up where the sun is shining. I see people splashing around. I hear them having so much fun. Someone leans over a platform and looks right at me, pointing. I open my mouth and bubbles come out as I try to call for help.

I try to swim up but whatever is wrapped around my ankle is holding on tighter and dragging me down. Then I panic because I can't breathe. I flap my arms, wanting to reach the surface but I never do.

I've had this dream two nights in a row. I can't help wondering if it means my life has become too much—or that I've become too much. I ask myself if it's because I feel like I'm drowning now. Could this mean that when people see me struggling, they don't care enough to save me?

I don't blame them.

I can't even save myself.

CHAPTER TWENTY-TWO

The Abbots had a lovely home made of wood with cream shutters and a metal roof. It was hard not to notice how well-kept it was. Their house appeared nearly as old as Twilight Oaks, and it too seemed to have gone through a few renovations over the years. A maroon Buick was parked in the driveaway to my left. Another car was beside it, concealed with a gray covering.

I took the rocky footpath that led to their front door. The stairs of the porch creaked with my weight. Wind chimes let off a gentle tinkle as I gave the wide porch a once-over. Two wooden rocking chairs, potted flowers, random ceramic figurines that never made any sense to me. Why did people need gnomes, frogs, and angels around the outside of their houses? To each their own, but I just never understood it.

I ignored the thought and stepped on their welcome mat, giving the doorbell a ring. There were a few thuds, rapid footsteps, a pause, and then the locks on the door clinked. The door opened halfway to reveal a petite woman with weathered brown skin and gray, shoulder-length curls. She wore a sky-blue dress with tiny black flowers on it and a pair of house slippers with winking eyes. Her hands shook as she pulled the door open a bit wider.

"Can I help you?" she asked. Her voice wavered but was also meek, like she was the shyest person on the planet.

"Hi, Mrs. Abbot. I was just at Eddie's house next door. He told me your name. I'm Rose Gibson. I was just wondering if I could ask you a few questions."

She glanced past me, blinking her glassy eyes a few times before asking, "What kind of questions?"

"I just want to know if you've seen a certain person recently. She was staying in the rental across the lake."

She stared at me.

I shifted on my feet.

"I can show you a picture," I offered, breaking the silence. "Of the person I'm looking for."

She seemed to hesitate, but then nodded and opened the door a little wider. I pulled out my phone once again to show her the image I'd just shown Eddie.

She grabbed her glasses hanging from a string around her neck and placed them on the bridge of her nose. "Oh, yes." She smiled and her whole face seemed to light up. "I saw her a few days ago. She was a really nice girl."

"You did?" My heart raced a bit faster. "Do you know how many days exactly since you've seen her?"

"I saw her Thursday morning," she said, nodding. "Thursday, September fifth."

I made a mental note that was the day before she stopped answering her phone.

"I remember because I grocery shop on that day every week. She helped me pick up my groceries when I dropped one of the bags."

That sounded like Eve. She could be selfish, but she was also attentive. She cared for others but had a weird way of showing it sometimes. One thing I knew about Eve was that she respected her elders the same way I did.

"Why are you looking for her?" the woman asked, eyes sliding up to mine.

"Because I haven't seen her in a few days. I'm going around to gather information so I can figure out where she is."

The woman studied me a beat before looking past me again. What was she looking for?

"You can come in for a cup of tea. I'll try and answer any questions you have but we'll have to be quick. Okay?"

"Of course, yeah. Thank you."

I wanted to ask why we had to be so quick, but judging by the way she kept peering past me, like she expected trouble, I figured it was best not to. The last thing I wanted was to get mixed up in the crossfire of someone else's drama. The faster this happened, the better.

CHAPTER TWENTY-THREE

"I saw her when I parked, and I remember wondering why she was on this side of the lake." Selma placed a teacup on a saucer in front of me with unsteady hands. She'd told me her first name while heating the kettle. Her shakiness wasn't from fear or worry. It came with age, as something she couldn't control.

"But she was wearing the gear all the young girls wear now," she went on. "You know, with the sports bras and leggings that make their behinds look bunched up and bigger?"

I huffed a laugh. "I know exactly what you're talking about."

She slid a bottle of honey my way, sugar packets, and a small dish topped with chocolate chip cookies.

"Why do girls wear things like that?" she asked, smiling a bit and revealing dentures. "My mother would have flipped in her grave if she'd seen me in something like that at her age."

"Fashion trends, I guess," I said, shrugging.

"Anyway, I think your friend Eve was taking a walk that morning. She saw me when I was collecting the groceries from the back seat of my car. One of the paper bags was a little wet at the bottom and the groceries fell everywhere. Fortunately, it was packaged and boxed things, not my good fruit from the farmer's market." She cleared her throat before sipping her tea.

I drizzled honey into my teacup. "Did she seem happy when you first spotted her?"

"I'm not sure. I couldn't really tell from where I was. Up close she seemed perfectly fine, though. She smiled and helped me pick everything up and carry it into the house. I offered her some water because her cheeks were flushed, and she looked a little hot. She thanked me for it." Selma's face changed then. Her brows strung together, and her eyes became cloudy as she smoothed down the napkin on the table in front of her. "Griffin came home while she was in here. He wasn't very happy."

"Who is Griffin?" I asked.

"My husband."

"Oh. Why wasn't he happy?"

"He doesn't like having guests over. I'd invited Eddie and his daughter once during Easter. I told Emily I wanted to make an Easter basket for her when we met them and that she should stop by. Griffin came home from work while they were around, and I knew he was upset. Fortunately, Eddie didn't pick up on his bad mood. I haven't invited them over since."

"Oh." I fidgeted in my chair and looked over my shoulder to the front door. "Where is Griffin now?"

"He's at work. He'll likely be off in an hour or so."

It was none of my business and I didn't want to ask but . . . "Does he . . . *hurt* you?"

Her eyes expanded as she pressed a shaking hand to her chest. "Oh, no, dear! Not at all. He's just protective."

It sounded like more possessive than protective.

"I have lapses in memory sometimes, so he worries. He doesn't want people taking advantage of that. I never know when an episode will happen, but I tell him often that I'm a good judge of character . . . or I like to think so. Your friend

Eve seemed like a nice young woman. But Griffin got one look at her and immediately dismissed her. He told her we'd be having dinner soon and that she needed to go."

"Did she seem bothered by that?"

"A little. She was more confused, if anything. But she left. That was the only day I saw her." Selma tried to smile but was battling it with a frown.

"Is there something else, Mrs. Abbot?"

The kitchen fell silent as she kept smoothing the napkin out and avoiding my eyes.

I leaned forward and placed a hand on top of hers to stop the action. "Mrs. Abbot?"

She tilted her chin, eyes connecting with mine. "He called her a whore," she whispered.

My heart slowed in rhythm. "Your husband?"

"Yes. When she left, he came back to me and told me to never invite a *whore* in his house again."

Good grief. Griffin sounded like a straight up asshole. I'd have never called Eve that. It was too harsh a term. But she did have a high body count. She took sex wherever she could get it. It worried me how often she gave herself away to random men. Men she knew nothing about. Men who could've carried sexually transmitted diseases.

"On the same day I saw her, I was sitting on the back porch knitting. It was getting darker, had to be around dusk. But I heard a scream or a screech of some sort across the way."

"Across the lake?" I asked, my chest tightening.

"Yes. But I thought it was just kids being kids, you know? Lots of young kids rent that cottage out and make use of the lake."

"I don't think so. Eve was supposedly by herself." I studied the tea that I still hadn't taken a drink of. "Was Griffin home with you?"

"Yes." She bobbed her head. "He heard it too. When he did, he insisted that we needed to get in the house."

"So, he was spooked by the scream?"

"Somewhat. I was too, but only when I saw him locking all the doors and windows." Selma's lips pursed as she looked past me and at the door. *Again.* "When I think about it now, the scream didn't sound like a joyous one. It sounded fearful. And it was definitely coming from a woman."

I really hoped it wasn't Eve. If that were the case, the Reeds would have heard it too. I needed to ask them about it. Maybe something had happened. Perhaps Eve had hurt herself. There was a possibility she could've slipped and fell into the lake and now her body was in there somewhere. My heart thumped harder as I thought about all the horrible things that could have happened to her. I started to ask something else, but I heard a car door shut in the distance.

Selma let out a sharp gasp and stood so quickly, she knocked over her teacup. She rushed out of the kitchen to peer out the window in the living room. "Oh no. He's home." She twisted around with wide, panicked eyes. "You have to go, dear. I'm so sorry, but you have to go. He can't know you were here."

"Oh—um, okay." I stood and pushed my chair in as she took my full teacup and dumped the amber liquid down the drain. "Go through the back door, if you will. I—I'm so sorry. I just don't want him to see you. He has his moods, my Griffin. He's a good man, but he's just . . . *please.* Go."

"Yeah, yeah. Of course." I unlocked her back door and peeled it open.

She gave me a half-hearted smile before placing the teacup on a drying rack and then grabbing a rag to clean her spilled drink. I closed the door behind me and rushed across their back patio, taking the stairs down and rounding the house.

There was a window on the right side. From there, I could see a man entering the house. I paused and hid behind a tree to see the man who was likely tormenting his wife. He was tall, broad-shouldered, with a slight pot belly. He snatched off his hat and tossed it on a table. A tool bag hung from a strap on his shoulder, and he had a plastic bag in his left hand. It looked like a case of beer was inside it. He peered around the space before walking deeper into the house.

One of their windows must've been open because I heard a deep voice ask, "Why is the back door unlocked?"

I could hear Selma providing a response, but it wasn't clear enough. The man spoke again after a brief pause. "I don't like this dress on you, Selm. You know that. Go on and change, then hurry up and get lunch started. Gettin' hungry."

I took that as my cue to get the fuck up out of there. I ventured through the woods and didn't slow down, even as I passed Eddie's house. I power walked my way ahead, relieved when the side of Twilight Oaks appeared. I wish I could say that talk with Selma brought me relief. Instead, it left me feeling even more confused . . . and afraid.

CHAPTER TWENTY-FOUR

"Rose. Come."

I walked along the grass barefoot, the cool dampness on my soles. The sky was hazy, a thick layer of fog hovering over the lake. From here, the water appeared black, like it'd swallowed all the shadows around it. Behind me, Twilight Oaks was pitch-black. No lights on inside or out.

Cobwebs clung to the exterior.

The flowers were dead.

The floorboards creaked quietly.

Bats with crooked wings flapped around it.

"Keep walking. You're close," a voice whispered.

I walked faster, making my way down the hill. Someone appeared, standing on the edge of the platform dock. She was facing the water, her curly hair flowing down her back. She wore all white and had her arms out, like she was trying to keep her balance.

"Eve!" I called. She didn't answer.

"Eve!" I called again, hurrying down the stairs and taking the path leading to the dock.

She finally turned her head a fraction. I kept walking, ready to meet up to her, to demand to know where she'd been all this time. As I approached and she'd turned fully to face me, her eyes were dark, hollow gaps and her lips were stitched together and bloody.

Eve dropped to her knees and stretched her mouth just enough to moan. Her face was tight and exhibited pain. Blood spilled down her chin as the flesh on her lips ripped apart. She tilted backwards and fell into the dark water. I peered over the edge, wondering how the water had become so silent after the splash. How not a single ripple was there.

But as I did, a withered, gray hand shot out of the water, grabbed my ankle, and snatched me down with it.

A sharp gasp split the air as I sprang up on the sofa. My phone clattered on the floor and my laptop careened to the left. I caught it before it could fall too, and set it down next to me. The cottage was darker now. My laptop screen was pitch-black. I picked up my phone and it was nearing six o'clock in the late afternoon.

"Shit." How long had I been asleep?

I had come back to the cottage, had Nico run a check on Eve's superfan that Zoey told me about, then decided to dive into my article about Robert Cowan. The rain was coming down hard outside, lightning strikes exposing parts of the interior. Thunder rumbled as I stood and stretched. I flipped a light switch on, opened the fridge, and reached for a bottled water.

As I cracked it open, someone pounded on the front door. I froze, listening to heavy footsteps thunder off the porch. Hurrying to the window, I saw someone in jeans and a black T-shirt running toward the main path, then disappearing between a line of trees.

What the fuck?

I immediately went for my gun and then my phone to punch 911 into the keypad. I took careful steps to the door, rising on my toes to see through the peephole. I didn't see anyone, but there was something on the porch floor. With my hand holding the phone, I managed to twist the doorknob.

The door creaked on its hinges and a strong gust of damp wind sprayed me.

I peered through the crack with my gun raised as I studied the surroundings. When I caught no one, I looked down. My breath hitched as I stared at the object. I yanked the door open wider before lowering to a squat in utter disbelief. It was an oversized beige Michael Kors bag. And not just any bag.

"Eve's," I whispered.

CHAPTER TWENTY-FIVE

Eve's purse contained her wallet, a camera, an older model iPhone that she used for backup, and worst of all: *her passport.* How could she travel to Thailand without a passport? Or even her ID, which was still tucked away in her wallet. There was no more denying it now. Eve was in trouble. The biggest question though, was who the hell left it on the porch? Who was the person that'd just run away?

I tucked everything back into the purse and went for my gun again, clipping the holster to my waist before tossing on a cardigan to cover it. Outside, the rain had finally settled to a light drizzle. Water dripped from the copious number of leaves, landing in fat drops on my head and shoulders as I walked.

To my left, I spotted groves of trees. Mountains of them going farther than the eye could see. When I spotted the blue house ahead, I noticed the main door was open with a screen door attached. Three stairs led to a wraparound porch and if I took about five steps to my left, I could see a partial view of the lake.

Gathering the courage, I walked up the stoop and gave the doorbell a ring. It'd been a while since I went around knocking on people's doors asking for things. My job should've allowed the act to come naturally, but ever since the attack, I'd found myself wanting to make less contact with people, seeking them out digitally first.

Footsteps thundered on the other side of the door and the broad-shouldered man who was chopping wood earlier appeared. He had mahogany skin and coarse, dark hair braided into cornrows that stopped at his collarbone. He was tall, and being your average five-six woman, I had to incline my chin to keep steady on his eyes. His gray shirt was sweat stained, brown eyes glaring at me through the screen.

Was this Alex?

"Help you?" he asked on the other side of the door. A dish towel was in his hands, and he used it to dry them.

"Hi—actually, yes. I'm sorry to bother you. I'm Rose Gibson. I'm currently staying at the little cottage a short walk away. Twilight Oaks?"

I expected the man to open the door and step out, be a bit more welcoming. Instead, he glared at me with his lips pinched tight and his brows furrowed.

"Just wondering if you have a moment to talk," I said.

"'Bout what?" he grumbled, eyes swinging left, then right as he looked past me.

"Did you happen to meet or see the last person staying at that cottage? Maybe in passing?"

Right after asking those questions, I noticed the subtle change in his face. The grimace almost melted as a bolt of fear appeared. But just as quickly, he was grimacing again. "I wouldn't know anything about who stayed there. I don't handle that stuff. My brother does."

"Oh. So, you're not Alex Reed?"

"No."

"Is he around?"

"I sure am," a deep voice said behind me.

I twisted around, spotting another man in a white tee that had black stains on it, and faded jeans. His hair was blond and cut short on the sides, tousled at the top like he'd been running his fingers through it all day. He was lean, tall—but not as tall as the guy on the other side of the door.

"Hi," I greeted as he joined me on the porch. "I'm Rose Gibson. I'm currently staying in Twilight—"

"I know who you are." I was relieved to see him smile, considering how serious his tone was. He offered me a hand and I took it, giving it a quick shake.

He laughed nervously before looking to my left. The other guy was gone. "That's Damian," Alex said, jerking a thumb at the door. "He's not much of a talker. Likes keeping his head down. Not much of a people person either."

"But I assume you are?"

Alex smiled in response. "What brings you this way, Ms. Gibson?"

"I was wondering if you stumbled upon the person who stayed here last, or had any kind of encounter with her."

"I don't usually share details about my tenants with other tenants, Ms. Gibson," Alex said, inclining a brow. He gave me a thorough once-over before pointing a knowing finger. "Wait a minute. Someone called a few days ago asking the same thing. That was you, wasn't it?"

"It was," I admitted.

"Well, I'm sorry, Ms. Gibson, but just 'cause you booked the property doesn't mean I can tell you anything about the previous tenants."

"I understand that, but this situation is delicate. See, the whole reason I booked your *beautiful* cottage"—*gotta stroke the ego*—"is because my friend stayed here. Her name is Eve Castillo."

Just like Damian, Alex's eyes held a flicker of panic. And just like Damian, he recovered quickly. "Yeah, I can't say that I really saw her." He scratched the back of his head. "We try not to bother the tenants unless they need us for emergencies. Makes people feel like they're at home and all that. I'm sure you get it."

"Of course." I nodded, but what I really wanted to do was grab his shirt, yank him forward, and slap him until he gave me answers.

Alex and Damian were hiding something. That much was clear. Eddie wasn't wrong about Damian either. He was a bit off-putting. I had the urge to ask about the scream Selma mentioned, but something told me to hold off on that nugget of information for now.

"Well, if you remember anything at all, will you contact me? I can leave you my number."

"Nah, that's alright." Alex raised a hand that was stained with black smudges similar to his shirt. "I can find it on your application."

"Oh." I huffed a humorless laugh, walking toward the steps. "Right. Well, thanks for your time."

"Sure thing."

I walked away, making sure not to look too suspicious or panicked. When I finally rounded a thick-trunked tree, I released the trapped breath in my lungs. With one last glance at the blue house, I saw Alex storm inside and slam the main door behind him.

CHAPTER TWENTY-SIX

Back at the rental, I closed the door behind me and locked it. This house was so quiet compared to my apartment. I always heard the people walking upstairs, neighbors shutting their doors, or dogs barking. The quietness here was deafening. Removing my gun, I checked to make sure the safety was still on, then placed it on the dining table.

Eve's purse was where I'd left it, the contents laid out on the table as well. The iPhone and camera were what I was interested in most. Eve used both to record her content. Sometimes she used them to take pictures and record random events happening in her life.

I picked up the phone first. It was dead. "Of course," I grumbled.

I searched for my charger in the bedroom and plugged it in. While it was soaking up juice, I returned to the table and grabbed the camera. After powering it on, I noticed right away that there wasn't much battery left. I didn't have the proper USB to charge it, nor was there one in Eve's purse. I sat at the table, going to the camera's gallery and hoping it wouldn't die on me.

Images of the lake appeared. Some during the daytime and others when the sun was setting. The last photo she'd uploaded to her Instagram was there as well, followed by a slew of about ten more. Each had her striking a different pose. Forever the girl needing the perfect picture. I clicked and a video was next.

After hitting the Play button, Eve's voice filled the room. "So, I swore I wasn't going to make any content during this trip," she said in a cheerful voice, "but you guys know me. Even when I need time to myself, I want to share my experiences with you. And even if I'm feeling kinda blah and—*oh, crap!*"

Eve's laughter filled the room. It made me stir in my seat hearing it. She had a contagious laugh—one you'd never expect to come out of her. Almost like a hyena, but on steroids.

"Oh, my goodness. Did you just see that? I almost busted my ass tripping over my umbrella. Good grief." She bent down to pick the umbrella up and chucked it someplace else. "Anyway, let me show you around. This is the living room. It gives pretty views of the trees and the front of the property. Over there is the dining area and I opened the curtains so you can see some of the lake. The kitchen is over there. That's where the best view is. Kind of backwards though. You'd think the living room would have the better view but that's what I like about this place. Things are switched up here. Those are the patio doors," she said, pointing ahead. When she approached the door, she slid it open and let out a dramatic gasp. "Guys. Oh, my Godfrey. Look at that view."

I huffed a laugh at the name Godfrey. It was a thing we made up because my dad would get upset about us using God's name in vain.

The footage revealed Eve walking farther outside and stepping onto a familiar grassy hill. "Here, let me just . . ." She removed the camera from what I assumed was a tripod and held it up so only the lake was in sight. From where she stood, you could see the top of the stairs leading to the dock, as well as the massive body of water.

"Oh, there you are!" Eve shrilled as the top of someone's head appeared near the stairs. The video ended abruptly.

"Shit," I hissed. I rewound the video to study the top of the person's head. It was hard to tell who they were. The sunlight behind the person made them look like nothing more than a dark smudge. I wanted to pinch zoom, but that's not how Eve's camera worked.

I clicked to the next video. This was one of her *get ready with me* videos. She didn't talk, but I admit it was awkward seeing live footage of her getting ready. I saw videos like this all the time online, but it's different when there's music, editing, and the video is sped up twice the regular speed.

The time stamp showed it was 7:21 in the morning on September 3rd. She was setting up the camera at first, staging it just right. Then she climbed back into bed and pulled the covers on top of herself. She sprang up and faked a yawn as she twisted her legs to hang off the side of the bed. Her arms stretched above her head before she stood, wearing shorts and an oversized T-shirt.

I groaned. This was painfully awkward to watch. There was noise in the background as she made the bed then rushed to the camera again to pick it up from the stand. She held the camera, tossing an outfit on the bed for all to see.

Then the video ended.

I clicked to the next one.

In this one, the camera was set up behind her and she was washing her face, brushing her teeth, going through her whole morning routine, but not without intentionally raising a bottle of face moisturizer for the camera. Likely from a company that'd paid her to feature it. The video ended there.

I clicked to the next one and pressed Play.

She was fully dressed and standing in front of the floor-length mirror in the hallway while holding the camera. "Here's my outfit," she said. "What do you think? Let me know in the comments."

After a few more poses, she carried the camera with her and rounded a corner. The noise in the background grew louder. It was the sound of dishes clinking, glass tinkling. Someone else was in the cottage with her. I waited to see if she'd turn the camera to the kitchen but she didn't. She kept it straight and walked to the patio doors to step outside.

"Guys, I'll never get tired of this view." She sighed, zooming in on the lake.

"Me neither," a guttural voice rumbled behind her.

Mid-giggle, Eve ended the video.

That voice. I knew that voice but couldn't place it. Where had I heard it before? Something chirped and I jolted. When it chirped again, I rushed to the bedroom. Eve's iPhone. It had powered back on. I picked it up while it was still on the charger and there were multiple notifications from Instagram. A passcode was required to unlock the phone.

Zoey's birthday. It was always her birthday.

I typed in the digits and the screen unlocked. There were hundreds of notifications, most of them likes and comments from followers. I opened the app and scrolled through them. I went to her DMs and checked a few she'd responded to. Most of them were to her followers, thanking them or responding to a question they had. There wasn't much luck there.

Her text messages were dry, and that didn't surprise me. She didn't use this phone to text or call people. In fact, it didn't have any service unless connected to the Wi-Fi. It obviously had been automatically connected to Twilight Oaks's.

I went to her photos next, spotting selfies of her on the dock, a few of her on the hill while sitting on a blanket with a book. Photos of the sky and the trees above. Then I saw a picture that made my heart drop. A selfie she'd taken with a man holding her from behind. Suddenly, it became very clear who that familiar voice I'd heard in the background belonged to.

Kissing her cheek as she smiled and held the phone in the air was Lincoln Fowler. Eve's ex-fiancé.

Eve Castillo journal entry

I just got back from Cancún. It was soooo damn hot. My gosh! Zoey came with me, but she didn't want to do anything. She stayed in the room most of the time, reading. I wish she'd come out of her shell more. She tells me I do entirely too much, but I tell her she does entirely too little.

I don't understand what's so wrong with having a little fun in life. Why does everyone take everything so seriously? I feel like I'm the only person who just goes with the flow and travels where I'm needed.

Lincoln has been constantly texting me. He actually sent my favorite chocolates before I left for my trip. I think he's changing. I wish I could talk to Rose about him, but she hasn't answered my calls or texts in weeks. I went to her job, hoping to catch her and apologize, but she had security kick me out. Now that I think about it, that wasn't a smart move. I could've embarrassed her, then she'd have been even more pissed.

I went to Ben's and spoke to him. I hoped her dad could get her to make an appearance. I wanted to surprise her when she showed up. She'd have come too, if Diana hadn't opened her big mouth and told her I was behind it.

Ben kept asking what was going on between us. I couldn't bring myself to tell him the whole truth. Ben had been good to me. He was the closest thing I had to a trustworthy father figure. Telling him what I'd done would've betrayed his trust too. The fact that he didn't know proved how good of a person Rose was. Even when she was hurt, angry, and sad . . . she never let me take the brunt of her emotions.

She's kept what I've done a secret. Rose refuses to

let me suffer, even though I deserve that and more. It frustrates me to no end because sometimes I want her to just spaz the fuck out on me. I want her to blow up and lose it. At least then I'd know she still cares. At least I'd know there's still hope. But that'll never happen again. I have a feeling she's cut me off for good.

It's time to swallow the truth.

Time for me to accept that I've lost my best friend forever.

CHAPTER TWENTY-SEVEN

"Hey, Herbert. Have you spoken to Nico today?"

"Not at the moment," Herbert answered. "Why?"

I held my phone to my ear as I sat in my car. I was parked next to Flip Stack. This place had the best cell service in all of Sage Hill that I could find so far. It's too bad that I had to drive six minutes just to use it.

I glanced at Eve's purse and her belongings on the passenger seat. "I need him to look into something for me but he isn't answering. It's important."

"Okay, don't worry, Rose. He's probably sleeping or something. You know he's a night owl."

That was true. Nico had once been in the military. After a bad accident that he doesn't like talking about, he was honorably discharged but left with a minor case of PTSD. He stayed home most of the time. He hardly ever left his chair or all those monitors in his room unless he needed food or some other human necessity.

I hadn't heard from him since he gave me the update on Eve's stalker-ish superfan. That was a dead end. Turns out that fan of hers moved to New Mexico shortly after Eve filed the restraining order. From what Nico could find, the woman was married and currently seven months' pregnant. I seriously doubted a pregnant woman was behind this. I relaxed a bit, knowing Herbert was right about Nico. I needed to get a grip.

"Is everything okay?" Herbert asked.

"Honestly . . . no." I closed my eyes when I felt the burn behind them. "It's Eve."

"What about Eve? What happened?"

"I think she's in trouble. Like, deep trouble, Herbert. I—I found her purse with some of her stuff in it. Zoey said she saw an email that indicated Eve booked a flight to Thailand, but her passport is still in the purse. No one has seen her for the past four days. She's missing and I think someone kidnapped her." *Or killed her*, a voice whispered in the back of my mind.

The nightmare I had before waking up on the couch came to mind. The sunken eyes. Stitched, bloody lips. The hand grabbing my ankle and dragging me into the water with it.

"Whoa, are you sure?" Herbert asked. "You know how Eve is. How do you know she's not just *being Eve?*"

"This time is different. I can *feel* it. Something is off about all of this." I drew in a breath to combat my tears. "I booked the cottage she stayed in last and there's a weird vibe in this town." I glanced at the diner, spotting a waitress moving through the aisle holding plates in both hands. "And about an hour and a half ago, someone knocked on the door, then ran away. That's how I found Eve's purse. They left it there."

"*What?*" Herbert shrieked. "Why haven't you called the police?"

"I was going to, but when I thought about it, it struck me that this person isn't trying to hurt me. I think they're trying to help or *warn* me. Why else would they give me her purse? This is evidence."

"Well, why wouldn't they just speak to you like a normal person?"

"Probably because they don't want to be involved."

My mind reverted to Rory. The absent stare she gave

when she saw the picture of Eve on my phone. The way her face grew pale. The fact that she was so clearly lying. Was she covering for Alex and Damian? Had they been holding on to Eve's belongings all this time? If so, why would she sneak it to me? What did she want me to know?

"This is a mess, Rose." Herbert's voice pulled me back to the present. "You can't possibly think something happened to Eve. I swear she's always stressing you out."

"I don't know." I bit my bottom lip. "I looked through her camera. She took pictures. One showed her with *Lincoln*."

"The guy who gave her about five black eyes? Is she fucking crazy?"

"If anyone is behind it, it's probably him. That's why I need Nico. I need to know where Lincoln is now. I know he does all our searching stuff, but he can do . . . *other* stuff too."

"Yeah, but he hasn't done that *other stuff* in a while," Herbert countered.

"I need him for this."

He sighed. "Okay. I guess. If I hear from him before you do, I'll let him know. So, what are you going to do now? You don't plan on staying there, do you? Need I remind you about your deadline? Twyla needs that article on Cowan soon. She's been sniffing around my desk all day."

"I know, I know. But I can't leave until I know what's going on." I went to the search engine on my phone, typed something in, then started my car and drove out of the diner's parking lot. "In the meantime, I'm going to the police station. I need to put in a missing person's report for Eve."

Eve Castillo journal entry

I can only write this here because if I tell anyone they'll judge me. I went to a festival to see the fireworks uptown with Lincoln for the Fourth of July. I expected to be scared. I mean I was nervous to see him after so much time apart, but he looked great. He was dressed well. His eyes were softer. He held my hand and wrapped his arm around my shoulders. We shared a funnel cake and ate kettle corn. He smelled really good. I just wanted to curl into him and sniff forever.

That was one thing I missed most about him. His smell, especially when we had sex and he'd sweat. I'd breathe him in as he buried himself inside me and groaned in my ear. I wanted to merge with him, become one. His kindness could be a front. He's done this before—buttered me up just to rope me back in and then punch me square in the face or grip my upper thigh so hard he left a bruise.

The sad thing is, I'm not afraid of Lincoln. Yes, he hits me. Yes, he's abusive. But I'm not afraid. Maybe that's why I keep going back. No one can protect and hurt me like he can.

The pain and pleasure are a powerful combination. I'm thinking about seeing him again. We'll never get married like we'd planned, but we can have fun . . . until one of us gets bored.

CHAPTER TWENTY-EIGHT

Sheriff Reed's office smelled like damp wood and stale cigarettes. It was about the size of a closet, with a wide desk crammed inside. A wide window overlooked Sage Lake, and the entire building was built on stilts, but the place had to be close to one hundred years old.

The sheriff's office itself was dry. I'd only seen a handful of deputies. Some were seated at their desks. Others sipped coffee while reading papers. On my way back, I saw a man playing darts in what I assumed was the break room, while another had his feet propped up on the table and his eyes closed for a nap.

"We just keep running into each other, huh?" Sheriff Reed said when I was escorted to his office. There was no humor in his tone of voice. It was dryer than the desert. I really did not get good vibes from this man.

I refrained from clearing my throat as Sheriff Reed sat on the other side of the desk, studying the photo I'd given him of Eve. "And you say she's been missing for how many days now?" he asked.

"Four, I believe."

"And no one's heard from her at all?"

"The last time anyone heard from her was on September fifth."

"Strange." He gave me that beady-eyed stare as he slid the

photo across the desk. "This friend of yours. What's her last name?"

"Castillo," I answered as he plucked a small notepad from his shirt pocket. He picked up a pen and clicked it, letting out a deep, guttural sigh.

Good Lord! He was no better at hiding his boredom than oily Freddy. You'd think he'd be excited for some action around here.

"Castillo," the sheriff repeated. "Two *l*'s or one?"

It took everything in me not to roll my eyes. "Two. I'm sorry. Do you not have a detective here? Shouldn't they be doing this?"

The sheriff barked a laugh. "Sage Hill is a small town with a population of four thousand and forty-seven people. I *am* your detective, Mrs. Howard."

I held back a cringe hearing that last name again. He'd seen it on my ID, and though I'd corrected him, he proceeded to use it.

"Right. So, you haven't heard from this friend of yours, Eve, in four days." Sheriff Reed went on. "Why do you assume she's still *here*?" He folded his fingers on top of the desk.

"Because this town was the last location she booked a stay in."

"How do you know that?"

"Because I looked with her sister through her emails once we noticed she wasn't answering her phone." A white lie. "And she isn't home."

"Her sister?" He quirked a brow. "Is she here too?"

"No."

"Okay." He scribbled something down. "Where are you currently staying while you look for your friend?"

"In the same cottage Eve was in. Twilight Oaks."

Sheriff Reed froze for a split second, just like Damian and Alex had. His eyes flooded with panic before quickly being erased. "That's interesting," Reed responded. "My nephew rents that place out. It used to be his mother's before she died. He grew up there with his brother and sister."

"Are you talking about Alex?"

"Alex is my nephew, yes. Damian and Rory are his adopted siblings."

So why was he calling them Alex's brother and sister? Why not call them *his* nephew and niece too?

I tried hard not to think it, but maybe he was prejudiced. Perhaps he didn't want to claim Black kids as his family. Alex was as white as a white boy could get with his blond hair and blue eyes.

"Have you personally met Alex?" he asked.

"I did. Earlier, actually. I asked if he'd spoken to or seen Eve in person."

"Why would they have spoken in person?" he asked rather defensively. "They only communicate with their tenants online or by phone."

"I don't know. They could've seen her in passing. Eve is a wanderer. She likes looking around. Hiking. Taking pictures. One of the neighbors, Mrs. Abbot, said she bumped into her while she was here and she's all the way on the other side of the lake."

"You can't trust anything Mrs. Abbot says," he told me. "Her husband says her mind ain't right. She forgets things. Imagines stuff."

"She seemed perfectly fine to me." I officially did not like Selma's husband now, talking about his own wife to others, making her sound delusional. I didn't get the impression that she was a woman out of her mind.

Reed blinked twice before asking, "What did my nephew say when you asked if he'd seen her?"

"That he hadn't."

"And Damian and Rory? Did you speak to them too?"

"Yes."

His shoulders tensed up. "And what did they say?"

"They hadn't seen her either."

He seemed to relax a bit, the hardness melting from his shoulders.

"Sheriff Reed, is there something I should know about that cottage or even your nephews?"

"Like what?" He leaned back and folded his arms tightly across his chest.

"I'm not sure. Just seems like you all are being very careful with what you say to me."

Sheriff Reed's jaw ticked before settling. "Not sure what you're implyin' there, Mrs. Howard."

"Call me Rose." I scooted toward the edge of my chair, clearing my throat. "And I'll break it down for you. Not even two hours ago, someone pounded on the door of their rental while I was there, and ran off. I don't know what they wanted, but there is only one other house on my side of the lake, and it belongs to your *nephews*." I made sure to put emphasis on the *s*.

The sheriff's throat bobbed. He dropped his arms to pick up his pen and notepad. "Did someone threaten you?"

"No." I wasn't about to tell him I'd been given Eve's purse, or that I suspected it was Rory who left it.

"Did you catch a description of the person?" he asked, pen still in hand, ready to scribble.

"I didn't."

He sighed and dropped the pen.

It was best to shift the focus before he became too frustrated. "The thing is, Eve was engaged once to a guy named Lincoln Fowler. I found out he was staying in the cottage with her."

"So, how do you know she hasn't just run off with him?"

"She wouldn't. He abused her. *Constantly*."

Reed pressed his lips, glancing at his notepad. *Why not write that down?*

"I see." He grabbed the mouse to his desktop and sighed. "I'll file the missing person's report. But I've gotta tell ya, this Eve Castillo sounds like she doesn't want to be found."

"Yeah, well, you don't really know Eve." My attitude was on full display, and I wanted him to know it. He was taking this situation much too lightly.

"No," Sheriff Reed said, cutting a glance at me. "I don't. And I doubt anyone else around here does either."

What is that supposed to mean? I almost asked him. That wouldn't have made things easier though, so I smashed my lips together and remained quiet. The office fell silent, minus him typing away on his keyboard.

"I'll need a photo of her," he said after a while.

I unlocked my phone and scrolled until I found a good, clear image of Eve from a few months ago. She always stole my phone to take selfies, flooding the camera roll with her face.

So you'll always see me pop up in your memories, she'd say. It was cute before, seeing her pop up. Now, it irritated me. Despite it, I couldn't find the gumption to delete them all.

"I can email a single portrait to you."

Sheriff Reed plucked a business card from a tray and slid it to me. "Email address is on there."

Once the photo was sent, Sheriff Reed took five or so more minutes before releasing the mouse and standing. "The report is in and I have your number. I'll let you know if anything comes up."

"Thanks," I murmured.

He escorted me out of his office and through the building, but not without offering me a coffee.

I declined.

When I stepped outside, the mist was thick. The fog was back. Thunder rumbled in the sky, a bolt of lightning flashing in the distance. The storm was continuing.

"Drive safely now," Sheriff Reed called after me.

I forced a smile at him before hurrying to my car just as droplets of rain began to descend. Before leaving the parking lot, I spotted Sheriff Reed still standing by the door. He wasn't looking at me, but he did have his phone glued to his ear.

Who was he in such a hurry to call?

CHAPTER TWENTY-NINE

Before returning to the rental, I stopped at Flip Stacks again to take advantage of their cell service. Nico had finally called me back.

"Nico, hey!"

"What's up, Rosette? Herb said you needed me."

"Yes. And you're going to hate me for asking, but I need *two* favors?"

"You act like needing favors from me is new." He laughed.

"I know. Don't hate me."

"Could never hate a woman with the name Rosette. What's going on now?"

"So, my friend Eve, the one I told you to look into. I'm about ninety-nine percent sure she's missing and that someone is behind her disappearance."

"Oh. *Shit.*"

"Yeah. But get this. I have her camera, and I saw that she was last seen with her ex-fiancé. This guy is an asshole, Nico, but I need to know where he is. For all I know, he's kidnapped her or something. I was hoping you could look into him, find his location. And . . . I was also hoping you could pay him a certain type of visit when you do?"

Nico went silent.

"I'm sorry if I triggered you," I added quickly. "But you know I wouldn't ask for this if it wasn't urgent."

"Damn right I'm triggered," he mumbled. "I don't do that stuff anymore, Rosette."

"I wholeheartedly understand." I stayed quiet, waiting him out.

I could tell he was contemplating it. "The last time I did something like that, I almost killed that guy."

"I know, but that guy deserved it. He was hurting your cousin. And *this* guy? If I don't get to him sooner rather than later, I'll never know where Eve is. He was abusive, Nico. He beat on her every day until she finally got out. I can't figure out why she let him back in, and I don't want to get into a whole domestic abuse spiel, but... he doesn't deserve to walk free. Just like your dad didn't deserve to walk free."

Nico poured out a long sigh. "Fuck."

"Think about your mom, Nico. Think about how you helped her and Caitlin. Your sister is so much happier now. If you hadn't gotten there in time, Caitlin would've died."

"Fuck. *Fine*, Rosette. Fine!"

I released a sigh of relief. "Thank you, Nico!"

"Don't thank me," he grumbled. "Always striking where it hurts. You're too good at that shit." He sighed again. I bet Nico hated that Herbert had told me all about his past. "If I do this, it'll be the last time I ever do it. Understand?"

"Yep, I understand. Trust me, I'll never ask you for something like this again."

He huffed and I heard him tapping away on his keyboard. "What's the fucker's name?"

"Lincoln Fowler."

"'Kay. On it."

"Thank you so much. Call me when you find out where he is."

"I want free Chipotle for a month," he grumbled.

I busted out laughing. "You do this for me, and I'll buy you Chipotle for a year."

CHAPTER THIRTY

When I parked in front of Twilight Oaks and stepped out of the car, my phone vibrated in my hand. A text from Diana came across.
Zoey just told me you guys still haven't heard from Eve. What's going on with her?
I walked into the cottage, locked the door, then texted her back.
No one has heard from her. Just filed a missing person's report. Not like her to just disappear. Not only that but I found her backup iPhone. She has recent pics with Lincoln.
I tapped send but the message failed to go through. "Oh, come on."
This wasn't going to work. If I didn't have service, how was I going to hear from Nico, or even Sheriff Reed if he discovered something? I went to the patio doors and slid them open to walk along the top of the hill and hold my phone in the muggy air. Now that the rain had passed (for now), it was humid. When I hit send again, it took a few seconds, but the text went through.
Then Cole's name appeared on the screen. I swear I was going to punch that man in the throat. Just one good time so he'd leave me alone.
"What do you want, Cole?" I answered with a snap.

"I just got off the phone with Herbert."

"Why were you talking to Herbert?"

"I was trying to figure out where you were. Wanted you to know in person that I signed the papers."

Was I supposed to clap and sing his praises?

"He told me you're in some place called Sage Hill and that you're looking for Eve."

I was going to throat punch Herbert too. "Why does it matter?" I asked, exasperated.

"Did you find her?"

"Again, *why* does it matter?"

"I'm just asking."

"Are you pretending you don't know where she is?" I asked. "Is she with you? Because I swear to God if she is, and I'm doing all of this, I will—"

"No, Rose. *What?*" Cole's voice raised a notch. "Why the hell would I be with her? I don't know where she is. I was going to say that I don't think you should be in that town alone. I looked into it, and it seems kinda bigoted. I should drive there, right? Someone needs to look out for you."

I inhaled then exhaled. Was he really trying to use this as a way to get on my good side again? Or to win me back, as he put it.

"I don't need you looking out for me."

"I worry about you, Rose."

"Look, I have to go."

"Rose?" he called.

"Bye, Cole."

"Rose?" he called again.

The call failed.

I stood there a moment, crossing my arms and staring at the lake. The flashbacks punched me right in the gut.

Cole with his pants around his ankles.

Eve completely naked.
Cole's face dropping. Eve's hands going up, begging me to wait before she'd even spoken. Eve running toward me, pleading.
A slam of the door.
It took everything in me not to cry. I was so conflicted as of this moment. I wanted to hate Eve for what she'd done. I shouldn't have been at this damn cottage looking for her. I shouldn't have cared about her at all. Maybe it was a good thing she was missing, then she wouldn't ruin anyone else's life. That was a foul thought though. She shouldn't have been missing. Her safety was still important.

Jayson had been right, before. It was impossible for me *not* to care about her. This was a person who'd been in my life for almost two decades. A person I shared so many of my secrets with—things about my husband that I'd never voiced to anyone else. Things about my childhood that only she knew. You can't just write something like that off in the span of three months.

A text rolled in from Cole: **Be safe Rose. Plz.**

He was pathetic.

Both of them were.

Snap.

I gasped, twisting around to face a line of trees. There it was again, just like this morning.

This time the snap was louder. And it damn sure didn't belong to a rabbit. I stepped back, keeping watch of the area. Then a foot stepped out. A black and white Converse followed by another. Jeans. A gray shirt this time.

"Rory?" I called, clutching my chest.

"I keep scaring you! Sorry!" Rory apologized as she approached. She had a Tupperware container in one hand. "I promised to bring you the brownies. I really hope you like them."

She offered the container to me.

I accepted. "Why are you coming from behind the house?" I asked.

"There's a path back there that leads from my house to this one. I actually snuck out. Alex is in one of his moods again."

"Is he?" *The lying jerk.*

"I can show you the path if you wanna see it," she offered.

"Oh—no. It's fine. I believe you."

She grinned, twisting her fingers together.

"Would you like to come in?" I asked.

"I'd love to."

CHAPTER THIRTY-ONE

Rory sat at the dining table, legs crossed on the chair, eyes bright as I placed the container of brownies in front of us. "They're still warm," she said as I removed the lid. "Double chocolate too. I use the Ghirardelli chocolate bars and cut them into chunks. It's so freaking good."

"Well, come on. Have one with me," I insisted.

"I'd love one," she said, laughing. "I shouldn't though. I had, like, three sugar cookies yesterday and my doctor says I should watch how much sugar I eat right now. I've been in remission for five months, so he's all strict and serious about my diet."

"Well, now I'll feel guilty for eating them in front of you." I laughed.

"Please don't! I made them for you. Plus, you can give me your opinion on them. I'm actually thinking about selling them. We could use the money."

That surprised me. "Are you guys not making enough money from renting this place?"

"It got booked, like, four or five times last year. Mostly at the beginning of fall. And so far this year, maybe about three times, including yours. There's this writer who comes and stays for, like, two weeks so he can finish a book. I've never spoken to him, but I've always wanted to ask him a thing or two about writing."

"What about your brothers? Do they work?"

"Yeah. Alex is a mechanic, but I mean, come on. We're in a small town. Business isn't exactly booming for him. Plus, he has a minor record."

I frowned. "A record? For what?"

"Sexual assault, I think. But he swears that girl lied. They were at a party and both of them were drinking and stuff. She told the cops he took things too far. I don't know. I was super young when it happened."

"Oh." That sent a cold shiver through me, but I kept my expression neutral.

"As for Damian, he works on the farm with Mr. Klinebek sometimes," Rory went on. "Helps with the animals and at the farmer's market on Saturdays. He brings fresh eggs home for us." She pointed to the brownie I was about to take a bite of. "I actually used some of the eggs for that batch."

I bit into the brownie. It probably wasn't wise to eat a brownie from a suspect. But there was something about Rory that was innocent. Kind. If anyone were to poison me, it would likely be Alex or Damian.

"Oh wow," I garbled around a mouthful. "These are *really* good, Rory. And you said you make these from scratch?"

She beamed proudly. "Sure do."

"Wow. You're gifted."

She couldn't contain her grin.

"Do you want something to drink? Some water? Juice?"

"Water is good," she said.

I grabbed two bottles from the fridge, then joined her at the table.

"This place is really nice," I said, looking around. "More people should book here."

"Alex thinks they will. He's only just put it up as a listing last year. He and Damian renovated a lot. They swapped out some of the furniture. He took out a loan to do it, actually. Gotta spend money to make money. That's what he always says."

"Hmm. You guys sound really close."

"We are."

"What's the story, if you don't mind me asking? I mean, how did you come to live with Alex?"

"His mom took me and Damian in as foster kids. Ended up adopting us. Couple years later, she was in a car accident." Her face crumpled as she lowered her eyes to the table. "She um . . . she died instantly."

"Oh, Rory. I apologize for asking. I didn't mean to upset you." I placed a hand on top of hers as she blinked, trying to get rid of the tears.

"It's okay. I actually *want* to talk about her. Alex and Damian never want to. They act like it never happened and I hate it. She was so nice to me. The perfect mom. Having someone like her in my life was all I ever wanted."

Hearing her say that reminded me of Eve. It was all she ever wanted too.

"I can't say that it didn't push us closer though, me and my brothers. We started looking out for each other more. We were actually living in this house before she passed. The one we're staying in now used to be my uncle's. It was paid off a long time ago. This house was pretty much falling apart so we moved. This place sat around for years before Alex decided to finally do something with it."

"Do you like living here? In Sage Hill, I mean," I asked.

"It's all I know." She shrugged. "I do want to travel one day. My immune system is kind of crap right now, so I've been homeschooled. Damian helps with that and sometimes a tutor will stop by. It works for us for now."

"My friend Eve—the uh, the one I asked you about earlier. She *loves* to travel. She's actually an influencer. People pay her to stay in their rentals and make videos or whatever—I'm sure you know all about that." I laughed like it was stupid, but I didn't miss the way Rory tensed.

She avoided my eyes, picking up her water bottle instead and opening it.

"It's just weird not hearing from her," I went on, plucking off a corner of another brownie. "She's my best friend. Like a sister, actually."

"Yeah. I get it. Um, I—I should go before my brothers notice I'm missing," Rory said, dropping her legs.

Before she could stand, I placed a hand on top of hers and she halted, staring down at me. She was shaking now, her eyes watery and swimming with fear.

"Rory, if you know something, *please* tell me," I pleaded in a whisper.

Her throat bobbed as she continued a stare, looking from my eyes to my hand on top of hers. "They told me not to say anything," she whispered back.

"Why would they ask you to do that?"

"Because they..." She clamped her mouth shut then snatched her hand away. "You have her purse now. Just... keep looking for the answers."

My heart dropped as Rory dashed for the door.

"Wait—Rory!" I called, but she'd already yanked the door open and run out. "Rory!" I shouted.

I trundled down the porch steps, but Rory was already near the main path.

Watching her run reminded me of the person I'd seen earlier. The same one who ran away after knocking on the door. I'd suspected it before, but there was no doubt about it now.

Rory had left Eve's purse.

Eve Castillo journal entry

Victor called earlier.

I was at the gym, so I ignored his first call. He called again when I got home. I almost paid no attention to it, but a part of me wanted to hear what he had to say. He said he missed me. That he wants to meet up. I'm not sure I want to. Me and Lincoln are on better terms now. Besides, the last time I spoke with Victor, he made me feel like shit. He can be so toxic . . . but he promised to make it up to me.

Am I dumb for considering it? I feel like I should reject him, but we have such good sex. And when he's in a good mood, he really is kind. I might meet him for lunch just to hear him grovel. Who knows what'll happen after that.

CHAPTER THIRTY-TWO

I dug around in one of the kitchen drawers until I came across a flashlight, then hurried out the front door. I clicked it on, swinging the beaming light forward, and went in the direction Rory had come from when she first arrived.

The path within the woods was easy to find. I walked rapidly while trying to keep my breaths and heart steady. The water of the lake trickled, and damp leaves swished. Heavy branches groaned and twigs snapped beneath my feet, but I didn't slow until I spotted the lights on the Reeds' house.

"What the hell is wrong with you?" a deep voice growled.

I clicked the flashlight off and rushed behind a tree. Peering around the corner, I saw Rory standing next to a set of stairs on the side of the house. The stairs led to a side door. Probably the one she'd snuck out of to get to me. She stood next to an unlit firepit, quivering as Damian glowered at her.

"We told you not to go over there, Ro! You aren't supposed to be talking to her!"

"I—I didn't tell her anything!" Rory exclaimed.

"It's not about that! Damn it, Rory! You never fucking think!" Damian whirled around and stormed off.

Rory sniffled, then she turned her head and let out a startled gasp. For some reason, my heart dropped when I spotted a silhouette standing in front of the side door.

"Alex," Rory breathed.

"Where is the bag, Rory?" His voice sent a chill down my spine. It was eerily calm.

"W-what bag?" Rory asked.

"You know what *fucking* bag."

She flinched as he stormed down the stairs. He gripped her upper arm and wrangled her close to him. "The bag the girl had," he snarled.

Rory was still shaking. Whimpering. "I—I don't know where it is."

"It was in my room and now it's gone, so where is it?"

Rory didn't respond and her silence clearly pissed him off. He gripped her arm harder, and she cried out as he started dragging her toward the door.

"Let her go, Alex!" Damian appeared again, chest puffed up as he glared at Alex's back. "Don't hold her like that."

"She's fucking lying, Damian!" Alex shot back. "Who else was in the house to take that girl's bag? I'm sure it wasn't you, was it?" He released Rory and practically shoved her away so he could walk in Damian's direction.

It was strange to see a person as large as Damian shrink at Alex's approach. Damian had way more muscle and could've taken him down easily.

"She's recovering," Damian said in an even voice. "Her body is still weak. You can't just grab her like that."

"She's not too weak to talk to the fucking tenants," Alex spat.

Damian looked from Alex to Rory, but Rory was scurrying into the house. Alex stepped closer, getting in Damian's face. His chin dropped to avoid his brother's eyes.

"You can defend her all you want," Alex said. "But I'm not going to prison because both of you want to act like fucking idiots."

To prison? What would cause him to go to prison? I

shifted, trying to hear what more he was saying, and a branch snapped. Both men looked in my direction.

Shit.

I hid behind the tree again, lowering to a squat. They couldn't see me here. It was too dark. I peeked around the edge of the tree, then cupped my mouth to refrain from gasping. Someone stood at the edge of the woods, peering into the darkness. They were only a few steps away. I wasn't sure which brother it was, but I could hear him breathing. My heart drummed an uneven beat. If he walked any closer, he'd catch me.

"Just get in the fucking house," Alex snapped. His voice was distant.

I took another peek, and the men were rounding the house to reach the front porch. Once they were out of sight, I made a dash for it back to the rental. Without the flashlight on, it was tricky sticking to the trail. I got caught in a few branches and nearly tripped over roots but, eventually, I found the cottage lights.

I made it back to the front door, breathing raggedly as I shot up the porch. Once inside, I slammed and locked the door. I stood there for a moment, panting as I replayed the situation with the Reeds in my head.

I'm not going to prison because both of you want to act like fucking idiots. What did Alex mean by that? Go to prison? For what?

He'd obviously taken Eve's purse, but why would he do that unless he had something to hide? I pressed my forehead to the door and squeezed my eyes shut.

What did they do to Eve?

CHAPTER THIRTY-THREE

The smartest thing for me to do was call the police. Any sane person would've done it. But the sheriff was the Reeds' uncle. There was no way in hell he was going to believe me enough to investigate them. I had no proof that they'd done anything to Eve other than having her purse, which was an easy out. Eve's purse could've been anywhere. They could easily lie and say they'd never seen it.

The charred necklace was also an easy out. Eve could've been distraught and tossed it into the fireplace out of anger. They'd probably not find any fingerprints on it other than mine now. I stood in the bedroom with all the curtains closed as I paced back and forth.

It wasn't safe to stay in this house anymore. Not when they could access it so easily. What did that family even have to do with Eve? I had no clue who those men were. I'd never seen them before, not a day in my life. Eve knew a lot of people, but I had reason to believe she didn't know the Reeds before her visit to Aquilla Lake.

Her camera was still on the bed. I picked it up and powered it on again. The battery was at an even lower percentage. I turned it off, tucked it into my overnight bag, then started packing up all my shit. I'd be damned if I stuck around just to go missing too.

I carried everything with me to the living room where my purse and keys were. After double checking that I had everything (including my gun), I left the cottage and jumped into the car. Screw cleaning up and emptying the trash as a courtesy. They could do it themselves. I turned the key fob to start the car but the unexpected happened.

My engine stalled. I tried again. The engine sputtered.

"*What?* No. Come on."

I tried once more to no avail. A knock sounded on my window and I shrieked.

"Oh shit! Sorry!" Alex took a large step back with his hands raised. "I didn't mean to scare you!"

My hands shook as I blew out a breath. "It's . . . it's fine. What, um . . . why are you here?"

"What?" he cupped his ear.

"Why are you here?" I repeated in a louder voice.

"Oh. You told me to come and check in with you if I remembered anything. About Eve." His voice was muffled but I could make out what he was saying.

"Okay?" What was he playing at? I glanced at my purse, where my gun was tucked away. I had every urge to take it out and place it on my lap, just so he wouldn't try anything reckless. I resisted though.

"Are you coming out of the car?"

"No. I'm good in here."

He gave me a funny look. Then he put on a crooked smile, huffing. The smile was charismatic, almost boyish. A deceptive display.

"Um, okay. Well, like I told you. I didn't personally run into your friend," he said loudly, "but Damian just told me that he saw Eve hanging out around the lake with some guy. I remember now because Damian was so pissed about it. He said he caught the guy peeing in the water or something."

"What did he look like?"

"He said he was tall. Short, dark hair. Native American or Hispanic maybe?"

I swallowed. That sounded just like Lincoln. He was of Native American descent. God, I was so confused now. "Great." I forced a smile. "Thank you for letting me know."

"Sure." He paused. "Is everything alright?"

"Yeah," I lied. "Everything's fine."

He glanced at my bag on the seat. Eve's purse. There was a mild twitch to his right eye. "Are you leaving?"

I scoffed. "I don't think that's any business of yours."

"I was just asking." He threw his hands in the air again. "I know your check-out is in the morning." He stepped back some more, shrugging. Then he gestured to the car. "Do you want me to take a look under the hood?"

"That's okay. I'll call triple A."

"Oh, please. They'll take forever to get here. I'm happy to look. I work with cars all the time."

"Alex, really, that's okay. I've already called."

Alex blinked with his lips pressed. Then he stepped back again, swinging his arms forward and clasping his hands together. He appeared to be praying as he brought his hands in front of his chest. This man was no saint.

"Alright. Well, if you need anything at all, feel free to reach out."

I nodded. "Sure."

He turned away, hesitant at first, like he was trying to make sure that *I* was sure. When he finally put some pep in his step and found his way around the bend of the path, disappearing into darkness, I sucked in a breath and dug into my purse for my phone.

I sent another text to Diana.

If something happens to me, tell the authorities to look into Alex and Damian Reed.

It was dramatic, sure. But it was better than nothing. Even if the message wasn't sent now, it would eventually . . . I hoped.

Besides, I didn't need Alex's help checking under the hood. My dad was all about teaching us girls how to be independent. If a tire needed changing, I knew how to swap it out. Battery dying? I knew exactly how to replace it. He didn't want us roaming this world helpless or relying on a man to rescue us. He wanted us to be our own saviors.

I popped the hood and then climbed out of the car after taking a visual sweep of the area. The culprit became very clear when I checked the engine. One of the spark plugs was loose.

I fixed the spark plug, slammed the hood, then climbed behind the wheel again. The engine started with ease, and I drove away, but not without thinking that someone had *purposely* loosened my spark plug. Probably because that same someone didn't want me leaving.

Eve Castillo journal entry

I think about my mom a lot. Sometimes I catch myself feeling guilty about what I did to her.

The problem with Ma is that she was so easy to manipulate. To me, she was like a lump of clay: easy to mold and shape into whatever you wanted.

I remember a time when she was actually nice to me and Zoey. I recall her braiding our hair, and even taking us to Cici's Pizza so we could eat however much we wanted and then play arcade games afterward. The cinnamon rolls were her favorite. She used to bring some home with her and eat them while she watched telenovelas.

The thing is, Pa left her for another woman when Zoey was born. We were okay for a few years. But that other woman he was with kicked his dusty ass to the curb. When she did, he came running back to Ma. And Ma took him right in. At first, it didn't bother me that he was around. Pa worked and helped her with the bills. He ate dinner with us most nights but avoided me and Zoey for some reason.

Then something changed. It started with the slamming of doors. A quick beer that led to two, three, four, five even. Punching holes in the wall after a bad day at work. When I was eight, I remember him coming into my room, grabbing one of my braids, and yanking me off of the bed. Zoey was on her bed, sound asleep.

Pa looked down at me with his fists clenched and said, "Why the fuck didn't you wash the dishes?"

I was too stunned to speak. He'd never hit me before, never been rough with me. He took my speechlessness as disrespect and hauled me up, just to steer me out of the bedroom. Ma came out of her room with a robe on, her hair all over the place, and bleary eyed.

She worked the third shift, and it wasn't time for her to get up yet. She asked what was wrong.

"She didn't wash the fucking dishes!" Pa yelled as he stormed into the kitchen with my arm in his tight grasp. I cried for him to let me go. I kept telling him that he was hurting me. He didn't care.

He shoved me forward to face the sink. It was already full of water and suds. There was only a bowl and a spoon next to it. Zoey had cereal when she got home from school. We didn't even eat dinner that night at the house. We went to McDonald's.

After taking out a wooden spatula from one of the drawers, he stood beside me as I started crying and said, "Pick up the bowl and wash that shit."

I grabbed the bowl and washed it, then the spoon. I rinsed both and put them on the drying rack. He took them back off and placed them in the soapy water again.

"Wash it again."

"But I—"

I couldn't even protest. He raised the flat end of the spatula and smacked my behind with it so hard, it felt like it was on fire. I cried harder and picked up the bowl, washed it again, rinsed it, then put it on the drying rack.

He took it back off and dropped it into the soapy water again.

"Amor," Ma called, staring at him with pleading eyes. I hated that she referred to him as love. He was filled with nothing but hatred.

He ignored her and continued staring at me, all vicious and angry. I was glad Zoey was still asleep. I didn't want him hurting her too.

"You're going to wash that bowl as many times as I tell you to until you get it through your thick fucking skull that you don't leave dirty dishes in my sink." I'm paraphrasing here, but that's how I remember it. Then he said something like, "You're the oldest. We work too hard for this shit. Take care of your fucking house."

I was only nine at the time. I was just starting to learn how to take care of myself. He made me wash the bowl five more times. Ma stood and watched the entire exchange. I hated that she didn't stop him, that she didn't at least try to intervene. When Pa grew bored, he stepped away from me and took her by the arm, heading to their bedroom.

My hands shook as I wiped the counters. I checked to make sure no other dishes were around, then went back to my room. Along the way, I heard my parents in their bedroom making noises. They were having sex. I knew what that was, even at the age of nine. I knew a lot of things I shouldn't have. I guess that's what happens when you're forced to mature ahead of time.

I lay in bed and cried for hours. When I think about it now, I assumed he probably got off on that—being in control. Abusing others and shouting at them. It made him feel bigger than he was and that's why he'd dragged my mother with him to their room and had his way with her. He had a sick, twisted mind.

You'd think as I grew older, I would've done the opposite of my mother. Instead of giving myself to a man who'd hurt me constantly, I would run. However, as you get older, you realize that you aren't too far off from being your parents. There's always some part of them inside of you. You can't fully escape what you were once surrounded by. That noise that took up a large portion of your life will always linger in the back of your mind. That's why I hate my brain sometimes. It feels like a prison.

When I was nine, Ma started hitting me too, just to

see Pa nod and praise her for disciplining their kids. They found a thrill in hurting me. I told them I'd tell someone what they were doing but they constantly told me that if I said anything, Zoey and I would be separated from each other, and we'd never see one another again. I didn't want that. I love Zoey so, so much.

Soon after, they were going after Zoey too. I couldn't stand to see her get hurt, so I bit the bullet. At that point, I didn't care if we wound up separated. It was better than seeing her cry with welts on her legs. At eleven, I had the courage to tell Abuela. I showed her the marks from the spatula and the bruises on my arms. I begged her to make sure me and Zoey stayed together, and she promised me we would. That same day, Abuela called the police and our parents were investigated. She couldn't believe her own daughter could hurt us that way.

Ben was assigned to our case and I remember thinking he was a really nice person. And it turned out he lived only a block away from Abuela. He invited us to his place often for dinner. That's how I met Rose. Ben made sure he had enough evidence to have them arrested.

When I think about that short era when Ma smiled, hugged us, kissed our foreheads, and shared cinnamon rolls with us, I couldn't believe it either. It's astounding how much a good woman's whole life can change because of one bad man.

CHAPTER THIRTY-FOUR

"Just one night?" The hotel clerk smiled wide with lips covered in burgundy lipstick. A tiny smudge of color was on the corner of one of her front teeth.

I looked away, digging through my purse for my wallet. "Yes. Just tonight."

I'd found the best hotel closest to Sage Hill in another small town called Green Pines. It was sixteen minutes away. And the perk? There was great cell service and Wi-Fi here. After the clerk handed me my key card, I boarded the elevator and watched the digital floor numbers climb. As soon as I'd made it to my room, I sighed with relief.

I changed into pajamas, washed my face, tied my braids into a bun, then sat on the bed with my purse. I dug through it until I found my phone and Eve's camera. I wanted to contact the police of Green Pines, but if they were this close to Sage Hill, they probably knew James Reed personally.

I didn't trust James.

I didn't trust anyone in that damn town.

Instead, I sent a text to Nico: **Anything?**

Not yet

I typed up another text, this time to Zoey. **Have you gone back to school?**

No. Took the day off. I can't concentrate knowing Eve is gone.

Eve is gone.

Something about those words haunted me. I didn't want to believe she was gone either. She could still be out there somewhere, waiting for someone to rescue her. I chewed on my lip, debating on what to tell her next. If I told Zoey what I'd discovered so far, she'd panic. Zoey had *really* bad panic attacks. If she was alone, no one would be able to console her. I had to let her know the truth though.

Do me a favor and go to my dad's house. There's something I need to tell you, and I want to make sure you're not alone.

Zoey replied almost instantly. **WHAT? ROSE! WHAT IS GOING ON? WHAT DID YOU FIND OUT. SERIOUSLY I NEED TO KNOW. NOW**

She didn't even give me the chance to reply. Her name appeared on the screen. It wasn't a text, but a call this time.

I answered. "Zoey, I'm not telling you anything until I know you're safe."

"Why do I need to be *safe*?" she asked, her voice laced with apprehension.

"Because I don't want you to freak out too much and have another panic attack. You need someone to keep an eye on you."

"Okay—fine. Fine. I'll go. But—just stay on the phone, okay?" I heard keys jingling in the background and then a door slamming.

"Rose?" she called.

"I'm still here."

"'Kay."

Her car door closed. I could tell she was driving by the steady whooshing noise in the background.

"Make sure you're driving the speed limit, Zo."

"I am, I am." She released a heavy breath. "Was I right? Was she kidnapped?"

I hesitated before answering. "I'm not sure."

"Oh Godfrey," she whined.

"But I don't think she's hurt," I added. A lie, of course. "So don't work yourself up."

"Did you guys get into an argument or something?" she asked. "I mean, before all of this? Maybe that's why all of this is happening. She's been so sad because you guys aren't as close anymore."

I swallowed, swinging my gaze to the dark curtains. "Eve and I aren't on good terms anymore for good reason, Zoey. I haven't talked to her in in about three months, so I don't think that's why she's missing."

"I don't get why you're avoiding her," she said.

"Because she . . . she did something unforgiveable."

"What could she have possibly done for you not to speak to her for that long?"

I paused before saying, "She slept with Cole."

The line went quiet. The seconds ticked by, one after another, until Zoey spoke up again.

"She wouldn't do that," she muttered, finally.

"Well, I'm telling you she did. I literally saw them with my own eyes."

"What the fuck," Zoey breathed. "WHAT THE FUCK!" she screamed this time. "Why would she do that?"

I refrained from crying and instead squeezed my eyes shut. "I don't know."

"I don't get it," she whispered. "I—I really don't get it. That's why she was acting so weird. She kept saying something about how she needed to forgive people for their mistakes because she was always making bad ones."

I had no idea what that meant, and right now I was too tired to care. "Are you close to Dad's?" I asked.

"Just a few minutes away."

"'Kay. When you get there, don't tell him what I told you about her and Cole, okay? He doesn't know but Diana does."

"Okay."

She didn't speak much until she'd made it to Dad's. I heard him in the background asking her *what in the world* was she doing home. I heard Diana shrilling, some rustling, and then it was quiet.

"I'm in your old room," she murmured. "Now tell me what's going on with Eve."

I broke it all down for Zoey. Every single event that had happened since arriving at the cottage. I explained the knock on the door, the purse, and having gone to the sheriff's office to file a report. I told her how little I trusted the only sheriff there and explained to her who Alex and Damian were. The spark plug thing definitely shook her.

"So, you think one of those guys did something to her?" she asked.

"I can't say for sure, but I do know they're hiding something."

"Why would someone just leave her purse on the porch? Who do you think had it?" She was breathing faster, on the verge of hyperventilation.

"I think it was their sister, Rory. I met her when I was taking a walk through the woods and looking for a sign of Eve."

"Do you think she knows something?"

"I *know* she does," I said, thinking about the last thing Rory said before fleeing the cottage. *Just keep looking for answers.*

"What about Eve's main phone? Was it there?"

"No. I had Nico track her last location and she was at was a diner in that area. The night before she stopped answering her phone."

"Oh God," Zoey moaned. "She's dead!" She was breathing raggedly now. "She's dead, Rose! She's *dead*!"

I knew this was coming. I sent Diana a text as I told Zoey to calm down and breathe.

The next thing I knew, I was hearing my sister's concerned voice. She was soothing Zoey, telling her to count down from ten.

"Rose?" Diana called out as Zoey wept in the background. "You okay?"

"I'm okay. I'm in a hotel right now." My eyes welled with tears. "I don't know what to do, Diana."

"Come back home." Her words were final. "Wherever Eve is or whatever she's got going on, that's on her. You did your part, sis. So just . . . come back to Charlotte. We'll figure things out from here."

I swiped at my eyes and nodded. "Okay."

"Okay. Let me take care of Zo. I love you."

"I love you too."

I hung up and sniffled, wiping my eyes again.

Tears dripped on the bed, some landing on my pajama pants and turning the cotton a darker shade. I drew my knees to my chest and rested my forehead on them, sinking into darker thoughts about Eve. If she was dead, what were we going to do? I should've forgiven her. Maybe if I had, she'd have never gone to that damn lake. I wasn't sure how long I sat that way, curled over and crying, but when my phone rang and I saw Nico calling, I swiftly dried my face and answered.

"Nico." I sniffled. "Hey!"

"Hey. What's wrong?"

"Nothing. I'm okay." I wiped my cheek with the back of my hand. "What do you have for me?"

"I'm at Lincoln's apartment right now," he said. "Place is a shit show. He's got coke everywhere. Pretty sure he's selling it."

That didn't surprise me. "Is he there? Did he let you in?"

"Not willingly. But yeah, he's here. His lip is busted a little bit but he can still talk. Wanna speak to him?"

"Uh. Sure. Yeah."

My heart drummed faster as I heard Nico say, "Get the fuck up."

A deep groan crackled through the receiver. Then came Lincoln's familiar voice. Definitely the one from the camera.

"Rose, I already told your guy everything." He groaned again. "I—I don't know where Eve is."

"But you were at that cottage with her? In Sage Hill?" I asked.

"Y-yeah I was, but it was only for the first two nights. She said she was staying for two more nights or something. I left the next morning 'cause I had to work."

"Did she invite you there?"

"Yes. She said she . . . that she wanted me to be there. She said she missed me. She . . . *fuck*, I think you broke my nose, man."

"Keep talking," I heard Nico growl.

"That's all I know. For real," Lincoln said.

"Was she drinking?" I asked. "Did you have her doing coke?"

"I don't make her do lines, she willingly does it. But no, she wasn't doing any of that. She kept telling me she wanted to change. That she wanted to be a better person. I didn't hurt her, I swear. We had a good time, and she wanted me." He paused to groan. "When I left the next morning, I saw someone driving to that place, though."

"A man or a woman?"

"I don't know. The windows were tinted so I couldn't really see. Could've been multiple people."

"Well, what kind of car were they driving?"

"An Aston Martin," Lincoln answered. "It was like . . . like a metallic red color or some shit."

The next question I asked was highly unlikely, but I went for it anyway. "Did you happen to see their license plate?"

"No. I—I didn't really care to look. Please, I promise you I didn't do shit to Eve! I don't know where she is! I've been calling her for days and she hasn't picked up!"

I sighed. Lincoln may have been an asshole, but he was a *stupid* asshole. He wasn't smart or calculating enough to be behind this. Oddly enough, I believed he was telling the truth.

"Fine," I muttered. "You can let him go, Nico."

Eve Castillo journal entry

I miss Rose.

I don't know how to make things up to her. I feel like I should reach out to Cole and have him do something to win her back. Then maybe she'll forgive me? I don't know. Rose is a sucker for romantic gestures. She likes being surprised. If she restores her marriage there's hope our relationship can be salvaged too.

It was Ben's birthday yesterday, but I didn't get invited. Zoey went and asked if I was coming. I had to tell her I was busy and wouldn't make it. I hate lying to Zoey. But I'd rather lie than have her find out the truth—that I'm a shit friend who can't reject her best friend's husband.

Here's the crazy thing though. I started seeing a therapist and she thinks I'm envious of Rose.

She believes that, deep down, there's a part of me that is jealous of her life—that secretly a part of me blames her for my struggles. I couldn't say that I've ever felt that way, but my therapist broke it down for me.

"It's not blatant envy," she said. The way she explained it is that I have this friend who has lived a decent life. Meanwhile I've lived a shitty one. We became friends at a young age, so I watched her grow with me, year after year, getting better and better while I'd practically remained stagnant.

Rose's boyfriends were always really into her. All the boys who were into me only wanted me for sex. She had loving family members to throw surprise parties for her, or to buy her a car. I had no loving family other than Zoey and Abuela. Rose was considered family, but I'd never ask her to throw me a party. They would cook for me. But as far as having a car . . . yeah, I had to buy my own and I wasn't even able to do that until I was twenty.

Rose going to college while I couldn't afford it. Rose graduating while I was stuck working at H&M. Having a dad who was proud of her every step of the way and not one like mine, who beat me, cursed me out, and made me feel less than human.

Then she married the guy I once had to myself. My therapist made me question that aspect of it. She asked me if I had purposely stayed around Cole without Rose being present because, subconsciously, I was upset that he'd chosen her over me. She also asked if I was harboring anger because he didn't try harder to keep me. If I was troubled because he treated Rose ten times better than he'd ever treated me, prior to his cheating.

Was I seeking attention?

Wanting Rose's life?

Was I truly envious and oblivious to it?

In a way, I wanted what she had. I longed to be loved and appreciated too. That's a sad, bitter pill to swallow. Without even realizing it, I was throwing blame on my best friend. One of the only people in the world to truly love me for me, despite my flaws, my rebellion, my lust. One of the people who would have loved me unconditionally had I not betrayed her.

I silently blamed Rose because I'm miserable. And, according to my therapist, I wanted my misery to have company . . . Even if it cost me everything.

Eve Castillo journal entry

The summer was a whirlwind. My trip to Cali was really good but I'm glad to be home. I'm getting a little tired of traveling so much. I like recording videos, but I think I'm burning out with social media. I might take a break and go somewhere quiet. Have some me time. I just hope my followers stick around and don't go anywhere else.

The truth is I need to feel wanted—Loved. I want to be held by someone for hours and hours. I could call Lincoln and have him meet me.

Or Victor.

Maybe both.

CHAPTER THIRTY-FIVE

I'm not sure when I fell asleep but when I woke up, it took me a moment to remember where I was. The AC rattled to my right. My phone, Eve's camera, and my laptop were next to me on the bed. The screen of the laptop was dark, revealing my dim reflection. According to my phone, it was 12:17 AM and there was a missed call from Jayson.

I sat up, rubbing my eyes with one hand while giving my laptop's keyboard a tap. After signing in, my latest document appeared. *Right.* The article for Robert Cowan. I'd added one measly paragraph to the document. Twyla was going to kill me . . . well, if she was able to beat Herbert to the punch.

Sighing, I climbed out of bed to use the bathroom. My best bet was to listen to Diana and go home. Honestly, I should've been home by now but something in my gut told me not to leave. Not until I knew for sure where Eve was.

After rinsing my face with cold water, I called Jayson back.

"Baby?" he answered.

My stomach fluttered hearing him call me that. Flutters were not supposed to be happening between us like this. "Hi, Jayson."

Music pulsed in the background. "Hold on. Let me get to a quieter place." The music slowly faded, then I heard a door click shut. "Hey, my Rose," he crooned in that warm, sultry voice of his.

"Hey." I bit back a smile.

"Called you about an hour ago. You avoiding me?"

"No." I laughed. "I was sleeping, actually."

"Oh, okay. You still at the lake?"

I hesitated. "Sort of."

"Sort of?"

"I'm close by. I couldn't stay in that cottage another night."

"Why not?" he asked, his voice growing serious. "What happened?"

I contemplated telling him everything. The last thing I wanted was to drag another person into this situation, but at the same time I needed to vent to someone who wouldn't judge me. I needed someone to know what was happening and what I was facing so I wouldn't drive myself crazy trying to find out where Eve was.

I sat on the edge of the bed and with a quivering voice that eventually shifted into sobs, I told him *everything.* Jayson was quiet the entire time as he absorbed the details. When I was done, he finally released a long breath.

"I'm coming to you," he said.

"What? No, Jayson. You don't have to do that. I'll be going home soon anyway."

"Well, I'll be coming there to make sure you get home safely. I told you something was off about that town, Rose. I didn't even feel right leaving you there but didn't want to protest because I know we aren't in a place where I can tell you what to do."

I wish he had. Then maybe I wouldn't have been so worked up and paranoid.

"Just stay put at the hotel. I'll have Pete close for me tonight and I'll call someone in to help him."

"Are you sure?" I asked.

"Positive. Now send me the hotel address and your room number."

Nearly three hours later, Jayson was knocking on my door. I opened it quickly and wanted to cry at the sight of a familiar face. I'd only been away from home for a day and some change, but I felt so lost, like I no longer belonged in this world. What next step do you take when your friend is missing and no one in town is willing to help? Who do you reach out to? What can you do? You can't just let it go. Quitting was a reasonable option, but I was Rosette Gibson. I didn't quit.

"Come here," Jayson said, roping me into his arms. He let the door shut behind him and I sighed with my cheek pressed to his chest, holding him just as tight. He smelled like sweet pine body wash and a hint of spiced cologne. He planted a kiss on the top of my head and a soothing warmth coursed through me. We were pushing our boundaries at this point, but I didn't care. He felt good—safe.

Safety was what I should've felt with Cole. Even with Eve. Instead, I found it here, in the arms of a man I never expected to meet.

Eve Castillo journal entry

I've made up my mind. I'm going to Lake Aquilla. There's this gorgeous house there with a nice view and great hiking trails. They call it Twilight Oaks. I just booked the place, so I'm leaving in the morning.

It'll be good to get away. To think.

Lincoln says he'll join me at the lake but won't be able to stay long. That's okay because Victor will swing by. Truthfully, after everything, I'd rather be with him.

Eve Castillo journal entry

Lake Aquilla is gorgeous and the little cottage I'm in is like a dream. I told myself I wouldn't make content, but there's no way I can't share this place. My followers are going to love this. I normally announce my upcoming trips, but this will be a nice surprise. People love quiet getaways, and my followers love when I surprise them.

I actually spoke to the owner of this place when I arrived and told him who I was. He saw my following and said I could really help him get the word out about his house. I wasn't going to record a ton of footage, just a few tidbits to post on Instagram. The guy agreed to give me a discount in exchange for me posting all about it, so I'll take it.

He's kinda sexy too. I'm not usually into white boys but there's something about this one. It's like he's pretending to be this sweet, charming guy but there's a rough beast hidden within.

Alex.

Wonder what I'd sound like saying his name while he shows me who he really is.

CHAPTER THIRTY-SIX

"I'm sure Alex is behind all of this." I bit off a piece of bacon as Jayson rubbed a triangle of pancake in a puddle of syrup on his plate.

We were sitting in the hotel café. I'd decided last night, after hashing things out a bit more with Jayson, that I was going home. There was nothing more I could do here. Plus, I was in danger now. If I showed my face to Alex or any of his family again, there was no guarantee I'd make it out a second time.

"You should've seen the way he talked to his sister." I shook my head with a scowl. "It looked like he was going to hit her or something until Damian intervened."

"And Damian is the other brother?" Jayson asked.

"Yes. Damian is Rory's biological brother. Rory and Damian are Black, but she says they were adopted by Alex's mom, who I'm sure was a white woman."

"Oh." He took a gulp of orange juice. "It just doesn't make sense though. If Rory knows something or assumes her brothers are behind it, why would she be talking to you and feeding you information?"

"I don't know." That's what I was trying to wrap my head around. It was obvious Rory loved both Damian and Alex, despite how gruff both men were. She seemed like the type to protect her loved ones. Then again, I didn't know much about her and could've been reading her all wrong.

"Well, fuck them." Jayson set his fork down. The metal clattered on the plate. "I can drive over there if you want me to. Ask which one of those motherfuckers pulled your spark plug."

"My God, no." I laughed. "Let's just get back to Charlotte. I'm tired of being here."

"Alright." Jayson nodded, then pushed back in his chair. "Let me hit the men's room and we'll get outta here."

I watched him go as I picked up my coffee to polish it off. My eyes dropped to Eve's purse next to my belongings. I grabbed it by the strap and placed it on the table, shuffling through it again. I don't know why I bothered. It wasn't like anything new was going to magically appear overnight. I looked through the inside pockets, finding a variety of lip gloss and some coins. The bigger pocket had a strawberry scented hand cream, a pack of gum with only three pieces left, and hand sanitizer.

I grabbed her wallet and unzipped it. Her ID was still inside along with a few credit and debit cards. Old coupons were in one of the small pouches, a crumpled car wash receipt, and more coins. I slid each card out of their slots. One of them made me pause. This one didn't have her name on it. Instead, the name was Victor E. McDonnell.

My mind circled back to the night before, the call with Nico and Lincoln. He said someone else had driven to the cabin. Could that have been this Victor person? I grabbed my phone and sent Nico a text, asking him to look into this person next. He was likely asleep and wouldn't see my message for another couple hours. I hoped he wasn't sick of me at this point.

Jayson returned just as I pushed Eve's wallet back into her purse. "Ready?" he asked.

"Yeah." I stood, about to collect my bags until Jayson scooped them up, slung them over his shoulder, and winked at me. I couldn't fight my smile.

Sunlight streaked through thick clouds as we left the hotel, presenting me with a slightly brighter day. Brighter day, new beginnings. Perhaps I needed to take that as a sign to leave since it'd been so gloomy the day before.

Jayson walked with me to my car and placed my things on the back seat. Once I started the engine and checked the dashboard, I cursed.

"What is it?" he asked, one brow inclining.

"I need gas," I muttered.

"Okay. No big deal. I'll follow you to the nearest gas station."

I drove away from the hotel to the station across the street. Once again, Jayson swooped in, this time with a credit card and a hand on the gas pump next to my car. "I got you, baby."

I blushed. At this point, I think he really *was* trying to win me over. To busy myself, I removed some trash and gum wrappers from my car to toss them in the nearest trash bin. Jayson was still pumping when I climbed back into the driver's seat and closed the door behind me.

I looked to my right at two men chatting in front of the station. Then my heart dropped. It was James and Alex Reed. Alex was frowning as James spoke. I couldn't tell what they were saying, but it was clearly a serious conversation happening. When James pointed past Alex, he nodded and turned around to march to his vehicle. I watched him drive away, then turned my gaze to James again, who now had his phone pressed to his ear.

My door swung open, and I gasped as Jayson said, "Full tank. Let's roll." He frowned when he saw how startled I was. "You okay?"

"No—that's the sheriff I was telling you about," I told him, pointing ahead.

Jayson pulled his head back out to look where I was pointing. When he spotted the sheriff in his cowboy hat and uniform, he ducked to put his head in the car again.

"Let's just leave it, Rose," he insisted.

"I can't just *leave it*," I told him, watching as James made his way to his marked truck. "Why are they meeting *outside* of town? A person only does that if they're hiding something."

"Yes, you *can* leave it," Jayson countered. "Let's just get back to Charlotte like you said. Whatever is going on here is out of our control."

I looked at Jayson as James's truck rumbled to life. There was desperation in Jayson's eyes. He wanted to get out of here as soon as possible and he wanted me to make this easy.

I gripped the steering wheel. "I think I should follow him."

"*Follow him?* Rose, you're trippin'. You can't follow a fucking cop."

"Why not? They follow people all the time."

"Rose, come on. You can't be serious."

I gave him my most serious face yet and he shook his head. His brown eyes flicked to the left, at James's truck that was now reversing.

"If you don't want to come, that's fine. I can meet you back here in an hour or so."

"Fuck, Rose. Fine, but we aren't taking your car. They've probably seen it too many times. Come on." He slammed my door, and I hopped out to follow him to his Lexus.

He started the ignition and put the car in gear, trailing behind the sheriff's truck. "Can't believe you got me doing this shit," Jayson grumbled.

"He's hiding something," I said as Jayson pulled onto the main road. "Stay about three cars behind him."

There was a brief silence.

"You've done this before, haven't you?" Jayson asked.

I watched as he gripped the steering wheel. "What?" I asked. "Tailed someone?"

He eyed me before nodding.

"Yeah. A time or two. Comes with the job."

"Figures." Jayson dragged a hand over his face just as James took the ramp that led to Sage Hill.

It was trickier trailing the sheriff now. We were on a single lane road and no cars were between us. Jayson stayed back a good distance. It was smart using his car. James wouldn't recognize it. James's left signal flickered and he turned into a neighborhood.

"Keep driving ahead," I told Jayson. "You can circle around."

Jayson glanced at the rearview mirror, driving about twenty seconds more before making a U-turn.

"There," I said.

We entered the neighborhood, but I couldn't find James's truck anywhere. There was no outlet on this road, though, so he had to be around. Jayson drove slowly, passing several homes where people did yardwork, and children rode scooters and bikes on the sidewalks. Then I saw the familiar truck. James was parked in front of one of the houses on the cul-de-sac.

Jayson spotted it too and pulled to the curb. We watched as James climbed out of his truck and made his way toward the garage. The garage gate lifted slowly. The sheriff peered over his shoulder.

"Shit," I whispered, ducking my head. We were a few houses back and I don't think he saw me, but still . . .

"He's gonna put our asses in jail," Jayson hissed, eyes ahead. "You better be glad he looked away."

I took a peek over the dashboard and James was walking

through the garage. Two vehicles were parked inside it. One was a green Ford pickup truck. The other a black Honda Civic with a custom license plate.

"Oh my God, Jayson," I breathed as the garage gate started to close. I gripped the sleeve of his shirt, hands shaking, body trembling.

"What, Rose? What is it?" he asked, clutching my hand.

"That's Eve's car in his garage."

Eve Castillo journal entry

Forget what I said before.

Alex is sexy, but his brother just came to fix the bathroom faucet, and THAT man is fine. I caught him looking at my butt a few times. And don't get me started on Alex and his terrible way of flirting. He's cute though. They both want me, that's clear.

After Lincoln leaves, I might invite them over for dinner. See which one of them wants me most.

Don't judge me. I need the escape.

CHAPTER THIRTY-SEVEN

"Nico, I need another favor."

"Alright. I think it's about time you start paying me now, Rosette." Nico's mouth sounded full as I sat behind the wheel of my car. We'd driven back to the gas station in Green Pines to pick it up and leave. "Besides, I'm still working on your last request."

"Right. You can keep looking into that, but this one is more urgent. Can you go through the Sage Hill Sheriff's Department roster and find me a deputy who isn't up the sheriff's ass?"

"You really think that's a possibility?" he asked.

"I don't know. Maybe. If not, I'll think of something else."

"Let me look now." I heard Nico typing and glanced to my left. Jayson was parking his car next to mine, his head visibly shaking. He'd said it himself that this situation was a mess.

It didn't make sense to him that Eve's car was in the sheriff's garage, and he agreed something twisted was happening. He still thought we needed to get the hell out of Sage Hill and let matters play out themselves . . . but I just couldn't let this go. Just when I was ready to pull the plug, something else popped up and sucked me right back in.

"Maybe she's fucking him too," Jayson suggested when we'd left James's neighborhood.

"Not her type," I'd mumbled absently. My mind was too busy reeling, trying to piece it all together. I knew there was a reason I didn't trust that man. Seeing her car there solidified it for me.

It was Eve's car. I'd know that license plate anywhere. TRVLGRL. Once she'd asked me if I thought it fit her. I told her ordering custom license plates was a waste of valuable time. She didn't like that response. In fact, she didn't talk to me for two days after I said it.

"I think I have something," Nico said, still typing.

Jayson was getting out of his car.

"There's a woman who works there, Kennedy Windsor. She's the only Black female deputy working in Sage Hill." Nico paused. "There's an incident report under her dad's name. Says here he filed an assault charge on Sheriff Reed. It happened a few years ago and doesn't specify what happened exactly, but the following week, Kennedy is hired to work with Reed and the charge is dropped."

"Hmm."

"He has her doing petty shit," Nico goes on. "Writing up parking violation tickets in town, directing traffic when signal lights are out, that sort of thing. Weird though, because she aced it at the academy. If anything, she should be deputy chief or something. Instead, they have some doofus working as deputy and he is *definitely* licking Reed's asshole."

It amazes me how quickly Nico can tap into these things. Completely illegal, but amazing. I was so glad I'd met him four years ago at Herbert's birthday dinner. Nico was Herbert's boyfriend's cousin. Herbert was originally the one who'd ask Nico for tech favors. Then he suggested I reach out to him when I was working on a piece, and we've been in touch ever since.

At one point, I wondered if he thought I was using him. Nico confirmed that he didn't feel that way and said he liked doing this stuff. It kept his mind busy.

"Do you see a cell number for her in there?" I asked as Jayson opened the passenger door of my car and climbed in.

"Texting it to you now."

"Thank you so much, Nico."

"Yeah, yeah." He hung up and not even a minute later my phone chimed with Kennedy's number.

"Nico?" Jayson asked, quirking a brow. "Who is that?"

"A friend," I said, tapping the number and pressing call.

"A friend I should be jealous of?" Jayson leaned in and kissed my neck.

"Not at all." I laughed, playfully waving him off.

"This is Kennedy," a light voice chimed on the other end of the phone.

"Kennedy, hi! I'm sorry to bother you. Do you have a moment?"

"No problem. Who is this?" she asked.

"My name is Rose Gibson." I paused and swallowed. "So, this is going to sound a bit crazy, but I was wondering if you could help me with a missing persons case."

"I'm afraid I don't handle those, Rose," she responded. "You can reach out to Deputy Henn or Sheriff Reed. They usually know what to do."

"Right but . . . that's the thing. I think Sheriff Reed is part of the reason this person is missing."

The line went quiet. I thought she hung up on me at that point. I sounded like a madwoman calling her randomly and making wild accusations about her boss. She didn't know me. Why would she take my word for anything?

But, to my utter shock, she said, "I'm listening."

CHAPTER THIRTY-EIGHT

Deputy Windsor met us in a French-themed restaurant in Green Pines. When I saw her, she wasn't at all what I was expecting. Kennedy Windsor was petite with voluminous curly hair that she had pulled into a soft puff atop her head, and false lashes. Her lips were naturally plump, her eyes deep brown, her sepia skin beautifully moisturized, and she wore acrylics on her nails with an elaborate style that I wouldn't have been bold enough to rock.

She sipped coffee from a mug as she looked between me and Jayson. "You're one hundred percent sure it was your friend's car you saw in his garage?" she asked.

"One hundred percent," I said, head bobbing. "It had her license plate."

"How close are you to Eve Castillo?" she asked.

"Really close. She might as well have lived with me growing up."

"When's the last time you spoke to her?"

I lowered my gaze to her teal and black nails. "About three months ago."

She quirked a brow. "That's a long time to not speak to someone you're close to." She sat up taller. "Did something happen?"

"It's personal," I responded, glancing at Jayson. "But that doesn't mean I stopped caring about her."

"If you haven't spoken to her, how did you notice she was missing?" Windsor asked.

"Her sister called me and asked if I'd seen or heard from her. This was almost a week ago. When I told her I hadn't, I said I'd look into it. I did some digging around and found out she was staying in the cottage Alex and Damian Reed rent out."

"Alex and Damian are pretty good guys." Windsor sat back and folded her arms. "I grew up with them, actually. We went to the same schools. They've never really been the violent type."

"Maybe you didn't really know them," I offered, and she frowned. "Alex has a charge against him for sexual assault."

"Yes, by the daughter of the previous sheriff who *hated* Alex. He did two weeks in jail and was released because evidence wasn't sufficient. That charge was scrubbed from his records but of course it still pops up through a deeper background check." Kennedy shrugged. "Hate to say it, but no one believes he took advantage of the town ho."

"Okay, regardless, all I'm saying is something fishy is going on. Rory, their little sister, is the one who left the purse for me to find. I overheard Alex talking to her and he was pissed that it was missing. Why would he have Eve's stuff in the first place?"

"Perhaps she left it behind," Windsor said. "Not uncommon for a rental owner to hold on to someone's belongings if they've forgotten it."

"Highly unlikely," I countered. "What woman do you know leaves anywhere without her purse? Eve never left without it. Not only that, but her sister found out she booked a trip to Thailand. She'd never book a trip that far away without telling one of us. And her passport is still in the bag. Look." I shuffled through Eve's purse until l found it and offered it to her.

Windsor studied it. "I shouldn't touch it. If something has happened to her, that's evidence."

"Oh. Right." I reeled my arm back.

She polished off her coffee. "Normally, I wouldn't believe stories like this," Kennedy said with a sigh. "Women around Eve's age drop off the face of the earth often, and most times it's because they want to be left alone or they've run off with some guy who's promised her the world."

Defeat settled in my gut.

"Before I arrived, I went to the station to check the recent missing persons reports. You say you spoke to Sheriff Reed yesterday and he filled one out. I didn't see a report for her in our system."

My eyes widened. "I fucking knew it."

"But that doesn't mean he's behind this."

"How isn't he if he never filed the report and her car is in his garage?" Jayson asked, mildly confused.

"Because, for all I know, Sheriff Reed is waiting to see if something turns up before filing the report. And I don't know for sure that it is her car in his garage. I have no proof, and I can't just go onto his property to look. I'd need a warrant for that."

Once again, defeat struck me.

"But I have a friend who works with the DA. I don't trust Sheriff Reed. Never have. Alex and Damian were always decent guys, but their uncle isn't, and it seems he's rubbed off on them over the years." She tapped an almond-shaped nail on the table. "I'll get in touch with my friend and have her speak to the DA, see what I can do."

"Okay, great." I nodded, breathing a sigh of relief.

"In the meantime, I *highly* encourage you to go home. If you don't feel safe in or around Sage Hill, it's best not to stick around in this area. Not until we figure out what's really going on."

When she slid out of her chair and stood, I followed her lead. Jayson moved to my side.

"Thank you, Deputy Windsor."

"Call me Kennedy," she insisted. "And it's no problem. Better to be safe than sorry, right? I'll call you if I find anything."

She left the restaurant, and Jayson and I sat again in silence. I felt somewhat hopeful now that Kennedy knew what was going on. The fact that she didn't seem to care for Sheriff Reed was a bonus. There was someone in the department not willing to look the other way, and that mattered. Without a good cop like Kennedy, I'd have been back to square one.

"So, are we *finally* going home?" Jayson asked.

"Yeah." I met his eyes. "Let's get the hell out of here."

Eve Castillo journal entry

Holy shit! I didn't expect last night to happen the way it did.

One minute I'm eating dinner with Alex and Damian and the next Alex is kissing my neck and Damian has his face between my thighs. I've only had one threesome before. I was nineteen and it was horrible. It happened with two frat boys I met at the liquor store.

But Alex and Damian... there are just no words. Who knew small-town men were so good?

They took turns with me. I knew Alex was more than he revealed. He was perfectly rough, hands around my throat as he fucked me like he owned me. Damian was gentler... but he accidentally came inside me.

I wish I could say I regretted it, but I don't. In fact, they made me feel better after talking to Victor yesterday morning. They made me forget the things Victor promised me. They made me forget that he would never, ever choose me.

Just use me. Lie to me. Fuck me over.

Victor McDonnell is an asshole.

I hate him and wish him a shitty life forever.

CHAPTER THIRTY-NINE

As soon as I made it to my apartment, I collapsed on the bed and buried my face in the comforter. For a few seconds, I couldn't breathe. I was okay with letting the breath dwell in my lungs. It gave me a chance to listen to my thudding heart, to feel my face being covered, and for the darkness to consume me. Gave me a chance to remember I was still *alive*.

When I couldn't stand another second of not breathing, I flipped onto my back and stared at the ceiling fan, gasping. Jayson had followed me home, making sure that I arrived at my apartment safely before returning to his bar. Now, I was all alone with racing thoughts. I showered, changed clothes, then went for my laptop. It was hard not to glance at Eve's purse on the dining table.

A memory struck me. We'd gone to the Michael Kors store in the outlet mall. She couldn't decide between beige or black for her new purse. She'd gotten a huge check from some deal with a yoga company and wanted to splurge.

"I always get black stuff," she'd griped, putting the darker purse back. "I think it's time to lighten it up. And here, I'll get you one too."

My eyes shifted left to the other Michael Kors purse hanging on the coat rack with the tags still attached. I have yet to use it... and probably never will after what happened between her and Cole. I didn't need the reminder. I figured I could give it to Zoey or Diana instead.

Thinking of my sister and Eve's made me want to talk to them. Be around people I loved and trusted. I abandoned the laptop to go to my bedroom and slip into an olive-green hoodie and white sneakers. I collected my purse as well as Eve's, my keys, and was in my car again before I knew it.

CHAPTER FORTY

Dad's house always smelled like cinnamon. Not an overwhelming amount, but a subtle hint, like someone was sprinkling bits of it in the corners of the house every week. It was a comforting, nostalgic scent. Pair that with being seated around our six-top dining table with a bowl of freshly made chicken soup, and there was nowhere else I wanted to be.

"I can't believe any of this." Zoey stared at Eve's purse in the center of the table as I slurped my soup. Daddy was biting into a hunk of sourdough bread while Diana topped off our sweet tea. "Why would they have her purse? It doesn't make any sense, Rose."

"I don't know. That's what I'm trying to figure out." I placed my spoon down to take a sip of my drink. "The whole town is shady."

"Yeah, well, you're lucky you aren't missing too." Diana pursed her lips as she sat back and folded her arms. I could tell she'd just gotten her hair done. Two-strand twists that curled at the ends. She and I had the same complexion. Her eyes were a little bigger than mine, but other than that, we looked very much alike. "What if Eve is just messing with us? She always liked playing those dumb games where people have to find her."

"Like the time we went to Carowinds, and she disappeared out of nowhere," I said.

"Right. We were all in line, ready to get on the roller coaster, and she just disappears on us. Doesn't show up again until the amusement park is closing. Didn't answer her phone, didn't respond to our texts." If Diana could've folded her arms any tighter, she would have. "She's so extra—sorry, Zo." She gave Zoey a sympathetic glance.

"No, I get it." Zoey lowered her gaze to Eve's purse again. With shaking hands, she grabbed it by the strap and placed it on her lap to dig through it. When she pulled out the charred necklace, her eyes filled with tears. "But if it is one of her disappearing acts, she wouldn't have done *this*." Zoey placed the necklace on the table. It offered a gentle clatter.

"That's the one your grandmama gave her?" Daddy asked, leaning forward and studying it.

"Yes. She would never try and burn it. She never took it off."

"Yeah, I remember," Daddy murmured.

"I'm with Zoey on this one, Diana," I said. "Even though we know how Eve is, this feels different. Not answering her phone is one thing, but booking a trip to Thailand and not having her passport? Her favorite necklace in a fireplace? Her car in a random sheriff's garage? No, this isn't like her at all."

"No, it's not," Zoey insisted, her eyes welling with tears. She started breathing heavily but I slid my chair closer to hers and began rubbing her back to calm her down. She did . . . only a little.

"But the good thing is I spoke to a good deputy there," I said, looking into Zoey's eyes. "Her name is Kennedy. I think we can trust her to look into this. She said she would speak to a friend of hers who knows their district attorney. Hopefully that will help figure this out."

Zoey's glossy eyes swam with a pinch of relief.

"Now district attorneys are getting involved?" Diana's

eyes expanded as she dropped her arms. "How crooked is this sheriff?"

"Very," I answered. "I don't trust him. He seems more like someone who hurts more than he protects."

"Well, it's a good thing you have the good cop helping you." Daddy wiped his mouth with a napkin.

"I probably shouldn't have left," I said.

"You absolutely *should* have left," Diana countered with furrowed brows. "We can't have two people we know in trouble. You were smart for coming back."

"Hopefully this is all just one big misunderstanding," Daddy offered. "Hopefully Eve is fine but really needed time to herself and decided to leave everything behind. Maybe she knew you all would see that trip she booked to Thailand and take the bait. I never said it, but I worry about her mentally. Eve isn't well. We all know this."

That was true. Eve had a lot of mental issues—things that I told her she needed to seriously look into. She'd always shrug off the way she acted, saying things like *This is just who I am*, or *Gotta love me or leave me, right?*

But being as attention-seeking as she was, wasn't normal. Coming to my house crying because she felt lost and heartsick for no apparent reason, wasn't normal. Waking up in the middle of the night because of night terrors about being abused wasn't normal. Sleeping with your best friend's husband *wasn't normal*.

Eve needed help, whether she wanted to admit it or not. It wouldn't have surprised me if perhaps she did suddenly just snap and said *fuck it all*. But if she did, that made this situation even more dangerous. A woman going through a mental crisis wasn't safe. And if that were the case, we needed to find her as soon as possible.

Of course, I didn't voice this to my family. Zoey would've freaked out. Diana and Daddy would've told me to let it go. As badly as I wanted to drop it, I couldn't. "I think I'm going to head back home," I said after we ate some of Diana's apple pie. "I haven't been sleeping well and I miss my bed."

"I can imagine you haven't." Daddy stood when I did. After delivering hugs to Diana and Zoey, Daddy walked me to my car. "Rosette," my father said when I was seated in the driver's seat. The door was still open, and he was clinging to it, looking right at me.

"Yeah, Daddy?"

"I know how your mind works better than anyone else." He looked me deep in the eyes with his warm brown gaze. "Promise me that whatever you decide to do, you'll be careful." His features were hard, unwavering.

My throat thickened as I nodded. "I'll be careful. I promise."

CHAPTER FORTY-ONE

I needed to keep myself busy while in my apartment. Daddy was right. I had ideas churning in my brain, but I wanted to leave Eve's disappearance to the professionals. Kennedy was looking into it and there was only so much I could do as an average citizen.

I sat at the dining table and opened my laptop. As soon as the home screen lit up, I returned to my document on Robert Cowan and proceeded to work on the article. I had one more day, and Herbert was going to grill me if I didn't get it in. He hated missing deadlines.

I typed about three more paragraphs with ease before my mind reverted to Eve again. Something was bugging me about all of this. Something just wasn't adding up with the Reeds. I glanced at her purse on the sofa before standing and walking toward it. I dug through it again for her wallet, reading the name on the credit card again.

Victor E. McDonnell.

I tried thinking of all the times Eve spoke about the men she dated. I couldn't remember a time when she talked about anyone named Victor. She must've met him recently, while we weren't talking. That, or she didn't take him very seriously and was just using him.

I returned to the table and checked my phone as if a text or call from Nico would be there. Nothing. "Just let it go, Rose," I muttered, going to the kitchen to make tea.

When I sat down again, I glanced at Eve's purse one more time. An object in my house that didn't belong, full of personal things my former best friend was meant to be carrying. Objects she'd touched. Things she *needed* to navigate this world.

In the back of my mind, I could hear her voice. The same one from my nightmare. Whispering. *Demanding.* Telling me to do something and not just sit on my ass. To get up and figure out what the hell happened to her.

I'm missing, Rose, I could hear her saying. *I need your help. Please. I know you hate me right now, but I need you.*

I polished off my tea, went for my shoes and hoodie, and left once again.

Eve's house looked exactly the same as the last time I'd visited. I couldn't even tell Zoey had been around. The kitchen was still clean. The table scarce with material. It even smelled like a hint of bleach. Her bed was made with the same comforter, no clothes missing from her closet. There were no signs that she'd been here to grab a few things and dip off again. The only difference in the bedroom was that her laptop was open.

I gave the spacebar a tap and sat in the chair at her desk. After entering her password, I sifted through her emails. There wasn't much there except that confirmation flight to Thailand Zoey had mentioned, contacts from companies, and emails from her fans.

Any new videos this week? someone asked in an email.

Eve, I miss you! Please get back on IG!

Just want to let you know that no matter what anyone says, your videos are amazing.

I left the emails and clicked on her files. Nothing much there. I went to her photos next. Most of them were images she'd posted before. A few videos were mixed in between. I clicked play on one of them.

She was walking with her phone held up in one hand and an iced coffee in the other. She sipped from the coffee, walking and holding the phone up as if this were a natural way of life.

I clicked the arrow to get to the next video.

In this one, she was standing in a dressing room and holding a purple dress in the air by the hanger. "Date night," she said. "What do you guys think? Should I buy this?"

It was a brief video. No longer than seven seconds.

Date night? With whom?

I checked the date. It was recorded in June. I rolled to the next video. Eve was wearing the purple dress she'd just asked for opinions on. The neckline cut very low, revealing lots of cleavage. She was smiling as she sat on the hood of a car. Car horns beeped in the background, whizzing by.

"What?" she called, lowering the phone. "Oh, yeah! I'll take a scoop, babe!" She looked at the camera again. "I'm having so much fun, guys. I never thought I'd fall in love. That sounds so stupid of me." She giggled, and judging by her glassy eyes, I could tell she was drunk.

She hopped off the trunk of the car and puckered her lips as she looked into the camera. Then it cut off. But something before the cutoff caught my eye. I clicked the mouse and dragged the time back a few seconds. The car she was sitting on was red. *Metallic* red, like Lincoln had said. I hit pause on the video and zoomed in. The car's emblem was just to the right of her hip.

"An Aston Martin," I whispered.

My phone buzzed in my pocket. I fished it out to answer

it. "Nico? Got anything for me?" I asked as I clicked the mouse to see the next photo of a cup of vanilla ice cream.

"Not yet. Just calling 'cause I haven't had a chance to look into this Victor person yet. My mom needed a lift to an appointment, then wanted to run errands, so I've been out all day. I should be back in about an hour or so. Just grabbing dinner with her now."

"Okay, yeah. That's fine." It wasn't really. Something told me this Victor guy was the same person driving the Aston Martin and I needed to know who he was, what he looked like, and when he last spoke to Eve.

"I'll text you as soon as I have something."

"Thanks, Nico."

He hung up and I sifted through more videos. None of them showed the Aston Martin again. Neither did any of her photos. Giving up, I moved away from the laptop and searched through the nightstands. Pills. THC carts. Cough drops. Earrings. Sinus relief spray.

I shuffled through the closet but had no luck there. She kept her closet tidy and even color coded her clothes. I lowered to a squat to check her shoe boxes, hoping to find anything that might give me a clue as to where she might be or what she was doing.

Nothing.

With a huff, I made my way back to the laptop, slumping down in the chair and rubbing my forehead. I was getting a headache from all this thinking and wondering. I stared at the screen before sitting up again and clicking through the files. I checked her apps next. There was a black app I hadn't seen before with an icon of a box with three dots above it called ThoughtBox.

I gave it a click and it opened to the main page. The words WHAT'S ON YOUR MIND, EVE? were written across the top of the page. Below that were separated boxes, all with different dates. The latest was from September 2nd.

A sync button was at the top and I gave it a click. More boxes appeared in seconds.

September 3rd.

September 4th.

All dates when Eve was in Sage Hill.

My heart sped up a notch as I gave the most recent date a click and several paragraphs appeared.

"Holy shit," I breathed as I scrolled through one entry after another.

I'd found Eve's digital journal.

Eve Castillo journal entry

It feels like something bad is going to happen. I can't shake it. I can't tell if it'll happen to me or someone else. I can't sleep so I'm currently watching TV with a fire going in the lake house.

My stomach has been hurting all day. I think Alex and Damian were too rough. I should rest but I can't. Like I said, something bad feels like it's going to happen. Could it be guilt? Maybe I should go home. Perhaps I need to reconsider everything and focus on my priorities. So what if Victor doesn't want me? I'll be fine.

I never should've come here.

CHAPTER FORTY-TWO

I didn't think things through when leaving Eve's house. A part of me screamed to calm down, go back home, and process my thoughts before acting, but I couldn't. Instead, I jumped behind the wheel of my car and drove to Sage Hill. *Again.* I was an idiot, I know. But the adrenaline coursing through me was hard to control.

Along the way, I gave Kennedy a call. She didn't answer the first time but did get around to it on my second try.

"Kennedy Windsor," she answered.

"Hi, Kennedy. It's Rose. I—I think I found something, about Eve. I don't think she felt safe in the cottage and there's some guy she talks about a lot named Victor, but I have no idea who he is. I don't think I've met him. There are also other things I saw that might help us figure out what happened to her."

"Okay, okay. Slow down," Kennedy insisted. "What exactly did you find?"

"I found recent journal entries on her laptop, but there's proof in here that she was with Alex and Damian while staying at the cottage. She talks about stuff they did."

"Good Lord." Kennedy sighed. "Alright. Where are you?"

"I'm on the way to Sage Hill. I should be there within the next hour."

"Right. Well, you can't come to the sheriff's office. Reed is here," she said in a lower voice. "I'll send you my address. You can meet me at my place. My shift is almost over."

"Okay."

"You called at a good time," she added. "My friend got back to me, and I also received a call from the DA. I told her about Eve and what we suspect. It has piqued her curiosity and she wants more details. The more proof we have, the better our chances are of bringing them in for questioning."

"Okay, good." Questioning wasn't enough, but it was a start. Perhaps they'd slip or more proof would be revealed. Who knows, maybe there would even be a confession.

"Drive carefully," Kennedy said before ending the call.

Once she'd sent her address, I tapped it, and my phone provided me another route.

Kennedy Windsor lived in an apartment on the second floor in the heart of town. The parking lot was massive but hardly filled with cars. The complex was well kept. I took the stairs up and gave her door a knock.

In a matter of seconds, she answered. It was interesting seeing her out of uniform. She wore jeans and a graphic T-shirt with an ice cube wearing sunglasses. The words TOO COOL were above it. "Come in," she said, stepping back.

I walked past her, and the smell of baked chicken and spices flooded my senses. A candle was lit on the center of her glass dining room table. The rug in her living room was furry and black. Her furniture was suede brown. A corgi mix circled my ankles, sniffing at me.

"That's Pinto," Kennedy said after locking the front door.

"Hi, Pinto." I squatted, giving the dog a rub on the head. He sniffed my hand then chuffed before twisting around and trotting away.

"You really think something bad has happened to her, don't you?"

I faced Kennedy, who had her arms folded and an expectant look on her face.

"I really do," I admitted. "At first, I thought it was just Eve being Eve. She can be flaky and sometimes she just flat out ignores people. But this time it's different. She's *too* quiet about it."

Kennedy dropped her arms and shook her head as she walked past me. "I used to have a friend like Eve. Do you want something to drink?"

"Um, just water is okay." I watched as she opened the fridge. "What do you mean, you had a friend like Eve?"

"The flaky, self-absorbed kind," she said, plucking a water bottle out and carrying it my way. "We're no longer friends."

"Oh." I accepted the water when she offered it to me. It wasn't until I took a few chugs that I realized how thirsty I was. The bottle was nearly empty.

Kennedy laughed as she returned to the kitchen, grabbed another bottle, then handed it to me. "When was your last full night of sleep?" she asked, making her way to the stove to stir something in a pot.

"Not sure, honestly. Two nights ago, maybe." I shrugged, finishing my first water then opening the next. I hadn't slept much with Jayson last night in the hotel either, though he'd slept like a baby. I envied how calm he was, how none of this was truly his concern.

"You should rest. Seriously, you can't get anything done running on empty." Kennedy turned off the stovetop and sat on the sofa. "Come on, sit. Tell me about these journal entries you found."

I sat with her, placing my purse on my lap to dig the laptop out. Once I'd signed in, I started to hand the journal to her.

"Oh—hold on." She shot back up and returned to the kitchen to retrieve a box from one of the cabinets. When she returned, she was sliding her fingers into a pair of latex gloves. "Evidence." She sighed before taking the laptop from me and pressing a finger to the mousepad.

"She wrote in there a lot," I said as she scrolled and clicked. "But there's this one entry about them that sort of surprised me. May I?"

She nodded, turning the laptop my way. I clicked on the entry about Eve spending time with Alex and Damian then turned it back to Kennedy.

Kennedy's brows furrowed deeper with every line. "Wow," she finally said.

"Right?"

"Are you sure this actually happened?" She lifted her gaze to mine. "How do you know this isn't fabricated? That she didn't make it all up as some sort of fantasy in her head?"

"I don't think she would. Eve is very promiscuous and loves sex. I wouldn't count it out."

"So, she had a threesome with the brothers, and they *killed* her because of it?" Kennedy raised a brow. "Sorry, I'm just not making sense of it."

"I can't piece it together either, but if that's all they did, why are they being so secretive about it? And why did they have her purse? Eve makes pretty good money doing what she does. What if those guys did something to her and took her purse so they could try and use her cards or drain her accounts or something?" I was reaching now, but I needed Kennedy to side with me on this and get the same sense of urgency I had. Every passing hour left a colder trail.

"The purse thing is odd, yes, but it's not enough, Rose." She handed the laptop back to me after closing it. "Nothing in this can be used as full-blown proof, at least not enough to spark an investigation. Unless we find Eve or discover a body or blood—*something*—there's nothing I can do."

I swallowed my frustration.

"But like I told you, I spoke to the district attorney. She'll likely give me guidance on the matter. It could take a few days but—"

"Are you kidding me?" I tried my best not to frown. "We don't have a few days, Kennedy. She could be trapped somewhere or even dead!"

"I understand that, believe me," she said, holding up patient hand, "but I can't go hunting the Reeds down based on a purse and a virtual journal."

I slid my eyes to Pinto, who was sitting on the love seat licking the top of his paw with his eyes closed.

"What if I get picture proof that Eve's car is in Sheriff Reed's garage?"

Kennedy frowned. "I hope you aren't telling a cop you plan on breaking and entering into another cop's home."

"Of course not," I lied. "I can sit in my car nearby and wait for him to get home after a shift. I'll snap a pic when he opens the garage again."

Kennedy suppressed a groan. "I think you need to get some rest. Think this through a bit more and let me handle it. I know you want to act now, but you don't want to tip the Reeds off and make them paranoid. If Sheriff Reed catches sight of you lurking around his house, he'll find a way to shut this down. That's the last thing I want happening again."

My brows puckered. "What do you mean *again?*"

Kennedy paused, realizing she'd slipped up. "It's . . . nothing."

I kept quiet, watching as she rubbed one of her nails with the pad of her finger. I'd learned a long time ago that silence made most people want to talk more.

When the silence went on for too long, she cut a glance at me. "He assaulted my dad at a bar." She sighed. "I had just completed my training at the academy and my dad took me and my brother out for drinks to celebrate. Sheriff Reed comes in all loud and boastful. My dad and brother decided to play pool, but when my dad was going for the pool sticks, Reed snatched one of them out of his hands.

"Reed told him he was gonna have to wait his turn and said he was going to play with his boys once they arrived. My dad doesn't take shit from anyone so he just grabbed another stick and told him once Reed's friends arrived, he'd take a break so they could play. Reed got pissy about it and punched my dad in the face. Just like that."

I gasped. "Are you serious?"

"Yes. And the worst part about it is there were people who saw this happen but all of them sided with Reed. But he didn't realize that I'd been recording the whole thing. I had proof that he swung first. We filed a report and were even thinking about suing, but Reed reached out a few days later and offered me a job. He said he'd give it to me, but only if I redacted the report and deleted the video."

"And I assume you did?"

"Wouldn't be wearing the uniform if I hadn't," she grumbled, peeling the gloves off. "Believe me, I didn't want to. I told my dad I wouldn't, but he didn't want my opportunities limited. He wanted me to get the job, to make some money, make a difference in this shit town. Work a few years in Sage Hill so we could move to Raleigh or Charlotte." She shrugged, but I didn't miss the sadness in her eyes. "My dad insisted I take the offer, so I deleted the video, and we pulled the report. There isn't a single day that I don't want to punch James in his face for punching my father in his."

"You hate him," I said.

"I don't hate him. I just don't like that he's running this town or that so many people think he's a good person. He's a snake who loves hiding in the grass."

"Damn," I murmured.

"That's why I believe you about Eve's car. I wouldn't put it beneath James to hide the car to save his ass or even his nephew's. The last thing he wants is his name tarnished. He can't afford to lose votes as the sheriff around here. It's the only thing that gives him purpose and power." Kennedy stood and walked to the trash can to dump the gloves. "But like I said, book a hotel or head back home. Get some rest. I'll take it from here." She stepped toward me when I stood, placing a hand on my shoulder. "I want you to know you can trust me, Rose."

I pressed my lips, wanting to smile, but finding it hard to. "I hope so." It was hard to trust anyone around here, but I had faith in Kennedy.

When I was inside my car again, I debated whether to go back to Charlotte or book a hotel in Green Pines again. Then I thought about Kennedy's story. James assaulting her dad. A white man carrying injustice like a weapon. It wasn't a new circumstance, but it still pissed me off. He was no different than Robert Cowan—men in power who will do anything to keep it that way. It was time for that vicious cycle to end.

I started my car and left the parking lot, but instead of booking a hotel or going home, I took the road that led to James's neighborhood.

CHAPTER FORTY-THREE

The sheriff's truck wasn't in his driveway. I hoped he wasn't home . . . and that he didn't have a partner sleeping inside. Parking at the start of the cul-de-sac, I switched off my headlights and drew in a breath. My phone buzzed in the cupholder, and I grabbed it, seeing a call coming in from Nico.

"Hey, Nico."

"Rose, you all good?"

"Yeah, I'm fine."

"Cool. I'm sending . . . what . . . on Victor McDonnell. Not much . . . him, really but there was . . . I saw that I . . . a coincidence."

"Nico?" I said.

"Rose?" His voice crackled through the receiver.

"I'm still here. Nico?"

"Just . . . for you. I'll . . . an email, okay?"

The phone beeped and I pulled it from my ear, seeing that the call had failed.

"Fuck," I muttered. I had no service in this area. Of course, I wouldn't have any right now, when I was about to do something completely illegal.

Whatever it was, Nico would text or email it to me. I'd head to Flip Stacks and check it out, but first I needed to get into James Reed's house and take pictures of Eve's car. I popped my door open and climbed out, tucking my phone into my pocket, pulling my hood on my head, and taking the sidewalk that led to his driveway.

All the other houses on the lot had their porch lights on. James's didn't. I couldn't help thinking he kept the house in the dark because he was hiding something. A *big* something.

Once I approached the front of his house, I checked his garage for a security camera. There wasn't one there, but that didn't mean his doorbell didn't have one.

Seeing as James was the town's sheriff who likely worked all kinds of hours, I didn't think he'd have time to care for a dog. Not only that, I had searched for his Facebook account and didn't see any pictures of pets. He was also single, so no partner or wife at home.

I walked around the house where a silver wire fence was and gripped the top. The gate creaked as I lifted a leg to balance my foot on it. Once I had a good position, I jumped and landed on the other side. James's backyard was sparse. A dingy hammock was tied to a tree, two chairs and a table were near the back door, and dusty old shoes were piled in the middle of the yard. An umbrella was set up in the center of the table, leaning sadly to the left.

A motion light came on and I rushed to the side of the house. I waited, keeping my body close to the house, hoping not to trigger the light again. I gripped the handle of one of the sliding doors, hoping James was the type to assume his house would never be broken into. It was locked.

I cursed under my breath before looking to the left where I saw a window. I hurried that way just as the motion light flickered on again, highlighting a section of the yard.

Luckily, the window slid wide open. I had anticipated an alarm going off. If it had, my plan was to hurry in and get out in less than two minutes. This was enough time to make a run for it before authorities showed up. To know he had no alarm was interesting. What kind of cop didn't have home security? *An arrogant one who thinks he's invincible, that's who.*

The window was big enough for me to fit through. I went for one of the chairs near the table and carried it to the window before climbing on it. Inside the house, it was dark, minus a hallway light. I looked down and realized this window was right above his kitchen sink. Sticking a foot in, I tapped until I felt a hard surface. Then, I pushed my other leg through and bent backwards in a limbo sort of way to get all the way in. I wound up on the counter, close to the edge of the sink.

After climbing off, my shoes landed on sticky linoleum. The house was quiet. A clock ticked somewhere in the distance. I needed to hurry up and get out of here. I walked toward the lit hallway, checking left then right. There were four doors. His garage was likely close to the kitchen, so I checked the first door. It was a linen closet. The door next to it was a pantry.

I turned and unlocked the door behind me. *Bingo.*

I spotted the pickup truck from the hallway light. After flipping a light switch on, Eve's car appeared on the other side of the garage. Not that I had any doubt about it being hers before, but seeing the bobblehead belly dancer on her dashboard solidified this was indeed her vehicle.

"Okay. Let's see." I snatched my phone out of my back pocket and took a photo from where I was. I took another photo of the front, a picture of the license plate, then recorded a video to show proof that I was inside James Reed's garage. I could probably get charged for this, but he'd never know it was me who'd taken the footage.

It shouldn't have surprised me to see a Confederate flag pinned to the wall where his tool cabinet was. Once I had what I needed, I was ready to hightail it back to the kitchen and put everything back where it belonged. But then I heard a car door close on the other side of the garage gate. I heard heavy footsteps and a deep cough. Heart pounding, I rushed for the garage light and turned it off just as the gate began to open.

CHAPTER FORTY-FOUR

There was only one thing I could do.
Hide.
The only problem? There was nowhere in the garage to hide. If I hid in his truck or Eve's car, he'd probably spot me. So instead, I dashed back into his house, closed the door, and hustled to the pantry.
It wasn't a very large space, but there was just enough room between the shelves and the door for me to fit. I had to suck in to close the door completely. The shelves dug into my back, but I held steady as I heard a door open. I prayed he wasn't the kind to look for a snack as soon as he got home.
Those same heavy footsteps thudded through the house after the door slammed. A deep sigh filled the quiet. I settled my breathing as best I could, then took out my phone to switch it to silent. My hands shook so badly while doing it, I was glad it hadn't slipped out of my hands and dropped on the floor.
The footsteps started up again and were lighter this time. I assumed the person was barefoot now. The fridge opened. I heard a loud pop, like a can opening. Loud gulping. Then silence.
"What the fuck?" a deep voice growled. It was definitely James.

His feet thundered through the house, and it sounded like he'd slid the patio doors open. It was now or never. If I could make a run for it now, I might be able to sneak out through the front door.

I cracked the pantry door open and looked to the left. He wasn't there. Pushing it open wider, I looked toward the kitchen and saw the top of James's head on the other side of the kitchen window.

"You've gotta be fucking kidding me," James hissed.

I stepped out and bolted for the front door. My hands shook violently as I fumbled with the locks.

"Hey!" he shouted.

I swung the door open, ran out as fast as I could, and didn't stop until I made it to my car. I yanked the door open, climbed in, started the ignition, and reversed out of the cul-de-sac just as James came storming out of his house. He glared right at my car, despite my headlights flashing forward. He may not have seen my face, but he knew exactly who I was. I swear the menacing scowl on his face was constructed by the devil himself.

CHAPTER FORTY-FIVE

I had a feeling James was going to reach out to Alex and Damian after seeing me. Call it a hunch, but it would likely be the case. He realized I was on to him. He knew I was searching for answers and only those men had them. Now was the time to send his warnings and get his ducks in a row.

I drove quickly, making sure to get a good distance away from James's neighborhood before stopping in the lot of a closed grocery story and sending the photos I had to Kennedy. Afterward, I typed in the address for Twilight Oaks in Maps. Once I had it, I put the car in gear and drove in that direction. My phone went in and out of service to the point of frustration. There was an email from Nico with an attached document that I couldn't open because the server kept failing. The photos I sent to Kennedy failed.

I should've gone straight to the diner and used the Wi-Fi. Instead, I wanted to get more proof that James and the Reed brothers were hiding something. There was only one person harmless enough to feed me more details. It was now or never. I took the rocky, winding path that led to Twilight Oaks but didn't park at the house. I decided to park along the main path, wedged between a line of trees just out of sight.

It was about a minute walk to reach the Reeds' house from there. I collected my gun and attached the holster to my waistband, my phone, tossed my hood on again, and marched along the gravel. It wasn't until I'd neared the house that I asked myself exactly what the fuck I was doing. Why was I breaking into houses and sneaking onto people's property for a woman who'd *betrayed* me? For a friend who likely wouldn't have been doing the same for me if she suspected my life was in danger.

In all reality, I should've stayed in Charlotte and waited until Kennedy contacted me to say she'd found a body or something. Yes, it'd have been horrible to know there was a body at all, but at least I'd have been safe.

Instead, I was doing this—reckless acts that made no sense. All this for answers. All this so I could prove I wasn't crazy. All this while hoping I would never find a body—that I'd find Eve safe and sound instead, tucked away in some hotel and ruminating over all her stupid life choices.

I walked along the edge of the woods, studying the Reeds' house. I wasn't sure which window belonged to Rory's bedroom. I kept a good distance as I ventured around with quiet steps. A motion light flickered on, but it shone the opposite way, so I took that opportunity to move closer to the house.

The first window I came across revealed their living room. A large body was sprawled out on the couch, one hand on the floor, head thrown back over the arm of it. Damian. I could hear him snoring through the window.

I walked to the right, ducking to keep my head below the windows. The next window revealed a small kitchen with a four-top table. The walls were made of dark paneled wood, the fridge looked a decade old with magnets all over it, and there was an open laptop on top of the table. Familiar stickers decorated the back of the laptop.

I stifled a breath.

Eve's other laptop.

Someone passed by the window, marching so hard their steps sounded like thunder. I ducked. A door creaked open then slammed shut. Footsteps thudded along the pavement on the front side of the house. I kept my back glued to the side, hidden in the shadows. Then I peered over just a bit to see Alex opening the door of his truck and leaning in, searching for something.

While he was occupied, I made a dash for the back of the house. Two windows were here. One window was closed and curtained so I couldn't see a thing, but another window was partly open at the bottom, revealing just a sliver of a bedroom. This room was painted teal, the bedspread gray, white, and pink. A pink rug covered the center of the carpeted floor. And sitting on top of the bed with her legs crossed and a sketchbook on her lap was Rory.

It took everything in me not to bang on her window and call her name. Doing that would've scared the shit out of her. She'd have made too much noise and alarmed her brothers. I couldn't have that. I lowered a bit and took in the size of her bedroom. Her door was on the right, closed and hopefully locked.

Drawing in a breath, I took out my phone and tapped the icon for the flashlight. Then I lifted it, waving the light at the window like a small beacon. I noticed Rory's pencil pause, then she lifted her head with her thin brows drawn together. I gave the window a gentle tap with my finger.

She put down her sketchbook and pencil, uncrossed her legs, and climbed off the bed.

Her eyes expanded when she saw me. She yanked the blinds up by the string before lowering to a squat. "Rose?" she whispered after pushing the window open. She looked at me before her eyes traveled past my shoulder where the lake was in the distance. "What are you doing? You can't be here."

"I know. But this is important, Rory. I *really* need you to tell me everything you know about your brothers and Eve." She blinked at me, panic seizing her features. "I—I can't. I've already told you too much and now Alex is pissed. He said he's glad you checked out 'cause you can leave us alone now."

Yeah, I'm sure he is. "I know about Eve's car. It's in Sheriff Reed's garage. Why is it there, Rory?"

She panicked even more, her eyes growing wet. "I—I don't know. I think they agreed to put it there for now."

"For now?"

"Yeah. Until they can get rid of it and make sure no one finds it."

"But why? Why would they get rid of it? What did they do to her?"

"They didn't do anything to her," she retorted quickly. "Not in the way you're thinking."

"So, tell me what I should be thinking then, because right now, your brothers and the sheriff are the primary suspects in Eve's disappearance."

She made a throaty, nervous noise while glancing over her shoulder.

"I'm not letting this go until I know what happened to her, Rory."

She blinked at me, a tear skating down her cheek.

"Just tell me if you think they're guilty of something. Can you tell me that?" I asked.

"They aren't guilty. They're just . . . confused and didn't know what to do."

"About what?" I asked with a little less patience now.

"About the body," she whispered.

My heartbeat slowed in rhythm. "The *body*?"

"Yes," she said as my chest tightened. "*Eve's* body."

CHAPTER FORTY-SIX

"So, she's..." My words failed me. My tongue felt heavier in my mouth, thick and swollen, like I could choke on it. "She's dead?"

"Yes. But they didn't kill her, Rose. I know they didn't," she pleaded. "My brothers would never do something like that."

"Then why do they have her things? Why did they have her purse? Why is her laptop on your dining table right now?" I demanded, anger lacing my tone.

"I—I don't know. Please," she whimpered, throwing her hands up to calm me. "I really don't know. But I'm telling you, they *didn't* kill her."

Kill. It was such a strong word. Someone *killed* Eve.

"How do you know they didn't kill her?" I asked, eyes misting as I focused on her.

"Because I was up that night when she invited them over for dinner. I... snuck over and saw them through the window. They were all having a good time, and I was a little jealous because I don't get invited to hang out or do anything. They had music playing. She even shared her ice cream with them, but they didn't like it and laughed it off. Then they started doing *stuff*... you know? Stuff that I couldn't really watch for long because it just felt wrong and nasty. But she was clearly liking what they were doing to her."

The threesome. Right. I nodded, waiting for her to continue.

"I sat by the lake for a while with my feet in the water. I was on the dock near Twilight Oaks. It was getting late," she went on, wringing her fingers together. "I heard Alex and Damian going home. I heard them laughing and had even heard Eve yell goodbye to them. It was quiet for a while and I knew they'd look for me soon, but I wasn't ready to go home. I wanted to rinse that scene away, of what they were doing with her. Then I saw someone else pull up to Twilight Oaks. They were driving a red car."

"Did you see what kind of car it was?" I asked.

"No. Just that it was red and looked *really* expensive."

"Did you happen to see the person driving it?"

"Not really. I saw, like, a silhouette when I walked back to the main path. It was definitely a guy. I heard him knocking on the door as he called for her. I think she let him in because it got all quiet." Rory's face became pale, and her eyes bounced around, rehashing the details. "But then I heard screaming. *Eve* was screaming. I went there so I could get a closer look and see what was going on. I saw her run out the back door to the top of the hill. The guy caught her, threw her over his shoulder, and carried her back into the house. She was beating on his back and screaming for him to put her down. I—I couldn't really see his features. But he was, like, average height maybe." Rory's throat bobbed as she shook her head.

"My phone rang, and Damian asked where I was. I went home after that, but I didn't hear screaming anymore. I figured they'd worked out whatever the problem was. But the next day, Alex was supposed to clear up the house after Eve checked out and . . . he found her body right there. Right in the living room. I heard him rush back to the house and tell Damian and they both panicked."

"Shit," I whispered, squeezing my eyes shut. "So—w-what did he do? Where is her body now?"

"She's—"

Rory's bedroom door swung open. Alex appeared behind her just as she sucked in a sharp breath and twisted around.

"Alex," she called.

Alex grimaced as he looked past her and right at me. "What the fuck are you doing here?" he barked.

"No! Alex, wait!" I heard Rory scream, but I was already running away.

I ran into the depths of the woods, trying to find the way back to my car but it was so dark, and it only got darker the deeper I went in.

"Rose! Get back here!" Alex hollered.

I veered to the right, refusing to stop until I made it to the safety of my vehicle. Instead, I was near Twilight Oaks. Way off track. The cottage was pitch black in the night, none of the lights were on inside or out.

"Damn it," I hissed, just as I heard heavy footsteps closing in behind me.

I had two choices. One was to take the main path back and search for my car, but Alex would see me out in the open. He could catch me. I had no doubt he was much faster than me.

The other option was to keep running ahead. Make it to the other side of the lake and ask for help. There was Eddie and the Abbots. They could help me.

I booked it, launching myself forward, past Twilight Oaks. I ran so hard my lungs began to ache. I could hear Alex grunting behind me, shouting for me to stop.

I refused.

For all I knew, Rory had made that story up and her

brothers had killed Eve. She could've lied about seeing Eve and some man afterward. But the red car . . . she'd seen the red car too, just like Lincoln had. That car had likely come by more than once.

Being so lost in thought caused me to trip up. My foot snagged on a root, and I shrieked as I tumbled forward and slammed down on my knees. My palms sank into the damp ground and leaves clung to my hands. I shook them off and stood up, ready to run again. Before I could, something clutched my hood and stopped me.

"Come here!" Alex yanked on my hood and hauled me backwards.

He pulled so hard I collapsed on my ass. Then he stood above me, nostrils flaring. Streaks of moonlight streamed through the towering trees and the shadows made his face look like a demon's. The sharpness of his cheekbones, the dark furrow beneath his blond brows making it hard to see his eyes—it was terrifying.

My heart slammed in my chest as I slid back on one hand. With my other, I snatched my gun out of the holster and pointed it at him. I could see his eyes now, big, blue, and round.

"If you don't get away from me, I'll shoot you!" I yelled.

"You wouldn't shoot," he said. He hadn't backed up, but he hadn't moved forward either.

I pressed down on the safety. "I swear to God I will."

He breathed raggedly through flared nostrils, throwing his hands up. I used that moment to push myself to a stand but kept the gun pointed at him.

"I don't know what you did to Eve, but you're not getting away with it."

"I didn't do shit to her!" he bit back.

"That's a lie. You slept with her!"

Alex blinked. "She wanted that! She told us that was what

she wanted! Are you fucking kidding me? I can't believe this shit is happening again!"

"And then you killed her, right? You took all her things and you've hidden her body." I applied a little pressure to the trigger. "Where the hell is she, Alex?"

"You're so wrong about all of this. So fucking wrong," he grumbled, then he lunged forward and tried to grab my gun.

So, I pulled the trigger.

Eve Castillo journal entry

My therapist explained why I might be allowing the people who've wronged me back into my life so easily. I was groomed to be this way. When Pa abused us, he would also reward us the next day. Whenever he was too harsh on a Saturday, that Sunday he'd be in a much better mood. Smiling. Laughing. Hugging us. Kissing our foreheads. He'd bring home treats—cookies, ice cream, donuts, Popsicles. When he brought them, he'd tell us that he was thinking about us and he loved us so much he wanted to bring us something special. Then two or three days later, he'd be at it again.

Shouting.
Hitting.
Punishing.

It was an ongoing cycle. It's probably bad to admit this, but I was ready for the punishments to happen just so he could love us again the next day. For a while, I assumed he felt guilty for hurting us. I'm not quite sure that was ever the case though.

He would do different things, like take us to amusement parks. Drive us to the mountains for hikes. Take us to the mall and let us shop for whatever we wanted. He'd also take us to the movies and buy us popcorn, slushies, and all the candy we wanted.

It's like he wanted us to think he wasn't that bad of a person. He wanted us to think he was a good man with flaws. Someone we should understand and accept because he was human, and humans made mistakes.

But good people don't accidentally break your arm.
Or accidentally hit you in the face.
Or force you to take freezing-cold showers because

you spent too much time taking a warm one the night before.

Good people don't mock you when you start your period. They don't look at you and say, "Look at that. You're a woman now," just to follow it up with, "Shut the hell up, little girl. You don't know shit," the next hour.

Goodness was never within him. I realize now the rewards were just another form of control. My therapist thinks I accepted Lincoln again because he rewarded me with the funnel cakes and kettle corn. He treated me to a nice night out after hurting me badly. He wasn't doing it for my sake, but for his. He needed that cycle to continue, just to prove to himself that he could be a good person.

It's a shame I've been subconsciously accustomed to it. Now the same is happening with Victor. And I have to admit, out of all the men I've encountered in my life, Victor's anger scares me the most.

CHAPTER FORTY-SEVEN

Alex cried as he buckled, then he fell completely to the ground. I'd shot him in the thigh. It wasn't my intention to kill him. Just hurt him. As he hollered in pain and called me all sorts of derogatory names, I ran around him. He swatted at me, trying to catch me by the ankle but missing.

I could see flashing red and blue lights behind me as I ran to the other side of the lake. That had to be James. I refused to stop, not until I made it to a place with service. Or another phone with service. I checked mine as I made it out of the woods but had no bars.

"Come on," I wheezed, throwing my arm in the air. I twisted around, dying for just a bar. Just one. I tried calling Kennedy just to see if the call would go through. It failed automatically.

"Damn it."

I spotted Eddie's house a short distance away. A swirl of hope washed through me. I ran up the short hill, thighs burning, lungs on fire. Through the wide-open windows, I could see his entire living room. A fire was going, the TV on, deep corduroy sofas. A woman was in the kitchen cutting an apple on a cutting board. She was tall, slim, with shoulder-length sandy-blond curls that reminded me a lot of Emily's. Her skin was several shades lighter than Emily's beige.

Then I saw Eddie appear in the hallway and walk around the corner wearing sweatpants and a long-sleeved shirt. He plucked an apple slice from the cutting board but not before kissing the woman's cheek. The woman grinned.

I knocked on the window and they jumped. "Sorry!" I yelled as the woman pressed a hand against her chest. "I'm so sorry! It's me, Rose!"

Eddie glanced at the woman before hurrying to the patio doors. "Rose? What in the world? What's going on?" He slid the door open and looked me over.

The front of my sweats had a hole on the knee now, along with a dirt stain. I was filthy from the fall, but I was safe. Safe for now.

"What happened? Are you okay?" he asked, eyes widening again.

"I—I'm fine," I told him. "I'm really sorry to bother you, but can I use your phone? I don't have cell service out here."

"Who are you?" The woman appeared at Eddie's side. She folded her arms and looked me over with puckered brows.

"I'm Rose Gibson. I'm truly sorry for interrupting your night but there is a guy out there—well, *three* of them actually. The Reeds, remember?" I asked, eyeing Eddie.

Eddie nodded. "Yeah, the Reeds. What about them? Hold on, are they trying to *hurt* you?"

"I think so. I found out the truth about my friend. She's dead. I think they killed her." I wanted to break down and sob at that very moment, but I held it together with a quivering lip. I could cry later.

"My goodness." The woman cupped her mouth, eyes widening with horror.

"Their sister told me everything and now I have to call someone. I need this person to come here." I held up my phone. "I recorded the whole conversation I had with their sister."

"Damn." Eddie blinked a few times, confounded, before

looking past me and out the patio doors. "Come in. Quick." He ushered me inside and I thanked him as I passed through.

"Can I get you a water? Anything?" the woman asked, suddenly more concerned about my well-being.

"No. I'm okay. I could use a phone call though."

"Well, our cell service sucks here too, even with the Wi-Fi," the woman said. "But we do have a landline. It's in Eddie's office." The woman pursed her lips and dropped her eyes to the gun in my hand. "Honey, I'm so sorry but I'd really prefer not to have any weapons in the house. I know you were protecting yourself, but I have a three-year-old daughter and . . . well, you know?"

"Oh, right." I forced a laugh. "I'm so sorry. I'm not thinking straight."

"I'll keep it outside on the table with the safety on," she said. "You can grab it when you leave. Is that okay?"

"Of course," I said as she reached for it. I handed her the gun, and she accepted it but held it at a distance like she was carrying a fragile bomb. As she went to the patio doors, applying the safety, Eddie faced me.

"That's my wife, Gina." He chuckled. "Don't mind her."

"No, no. I get it. One hundred percent. I wouldn't want a stranger's gun around my kid either."

"I'll show you the way," he said, already walking down the hall.

I glanced over my shoulder before following him. Just to the right, over the top of Gina's head, I could see the police lights still flashing between the trees near the Reeds' house. Sheriff Reed would come this way soon.

I had to make this quick.

CHAPTER FORTY-EIGHT

"It's just in here," Eddie said in a low voice as he pushed a door open. "Sorry for all the whispering and murmuring. Emily's asleep. She passed out right after our boat ride."

"No worries. Again, I'm really sorry for intruding like this, Eddie."

"Oh, please. Don't be," he said. "It's better that you came here. I told you I didn't trust those boys or that damn sheriff. It's a good thing you made it this way. They could've killed you too. My God. I can't imagine how scared you are right now."

"I was scared," I confessed. I swallowed thickly, staring at the tips of my dirty shoes. "I . . . ended up shooting Alex," I said through shaky breaths. "He was chasing me. He tried to take my gun and I . . . I shot him."

"What?" Eddie's jaw nearly dropped. "You serious?"

"Yeah."

"So that's what that noise was," he said, eyes wandering out of the room. "Gina said she heard something, but I thought it might've been people hunting in the mountains."

"No. It was me." I pressed my lips.

"Shit. Well, if the Reeds are involved, that sheriff is gonna cover for them. I'm sure the whole department will cover for them."

"There's a cop in their department. Kennedy Windsor.

She doesn't like Sheriff Reed, so she's agreed to help, but she needs more proof. She's been in touch with the DA, so we're prepared. I just need her to come here, see things for herself and hear Rory's confession on the recording."

"Right. Of course. Well"—he gestured to the landline—"take as much time as you need. I'll keep an eye out for any trouble."

"If they come knocking, please tell them I'm not here," I pleaded.

"Of course, yeah. I won't let them get to you. Not on my watch." Eddie left the room, and I took a moment to breathe in and out and compose myself.

I picked up the phone and dialed Kennedy's number after checking my cell for it.

She answered after the third ring. "This is Kennedy."

"Hey, Kennedy! I need you to come to the Reeds' house. Like, right now. I have more proof. I got a confession out of Rory and a recording of it on my phone. She said her brothers are behind this, and so is James! Can you come this way? I can give you the address."

"Wait . . . what the hell? Why are you at the Reeds' house?"

"I'm not at their house right now. I'm at one of the neighbors'. Alex chased me after I spoke to Rory. He tried to attack me so I, um . . . well, I shot him. He was going to hurt me. I could see it in his eyes."

"You *shot* him?" she screeched.

"It was self-defense. I know it sounds bad now, but I had no choice, Kennedy."

"Good Lord, Rose. I told you to stay put and to let me work on this." Her voice was huffy, like she was moving around, probably collecting her things so she could leave.

"I couldn't stay put. I told you they were behind this. I went to James's house. I got pictures and footage of Eve's car in his garage."

"And how did you manage that?" she snapped. "Did he invite you in?"

I said nothing in response. Instead, my eyes wandered to the right at a trophy case built into the wall. Medals of all kinds were there, gleaming beneath a recessed light.

"You know what? Never mind, just stay put," Kennedy fussed. "Who are the neighbors you're with?"

"Um . . . his name is Eddie. His wife is Gina. At least I think that's his wife. They live in the house across the lake from the ones the Reeds rent out."

"Okay. Stay there until I arrive. And please don't shoot anyone else. Fuck, this will be a mess. I'll have to call the DA now, let her know what's going on." She cursed again.

"I didn't mean for it to escalate," I said, eyes carrying to the left of the trophy case. "But if I hadn't looked, Kennedy, if I'd never come here, I never would've found out what happened to Eve. They're guilty and—"

My mouth parted as my eyes widened. I stared ahead, lowering the phone with trembling hands and stepping around the desk. On the wall was a car emblem. An *Aston Martin* emblem.

"Kennedy," I whispered into the phone as my pulse quickened. "Hurry. *Please.*"

"I'm coming. GPS says sixteen minutes."

I put the phone back on the receiver, then studied the emblem. There were photos beneath it of Eddie with his wife and daughter. Vacation photos. Candids. In many of them, he was wearing a hat with the Aston Martin logo on it.

I left the office and ventured down the hallway. Eddie and Gina were murmuring to each other in the kitchen. I couldn't see them but could definitely hear what they were saying.

"Why did you even let her in?" Gina hissed. "We don't know a thing about that girl."

"She was being chased, Gina. The fuck did you want me to do?"

"She could've shot us too! Did you think about that? She could've been lying!"

"You're being dramatic," Eddie grumbled. "Like always."

"I want her out of here," Gina snapped back.

"Well, we can't rush her out. You saw her. She was scared, G. Someone is trying to hurt her."

As they continued talking, I opened one of the hallway doors quietly. One was a bathroom. The one next to it was a closet full of pool floaties and life vests. Another door led to a guest bedroom. But the door closest to the kitchen, just around the corner from Eddie and Gina, was the garage door.

I pulled it open . . . and my heart dropped to my stomach.

CHAPTER FORTY-NINE

Metallic red Aston Martin.

Just like the photos.

Just like Lincoln and Rory saw.

With shaking hands, I flipped the light switch on to take in the full details of the car. It was spotless as it glistened under cold white light. Beside it, a black BMW was parked.

"What are you doing?" A deep voice rose behind me.

I gasped, pressing a hand to my chest as I twisted around.

Eddie stood there with his brows drawn together. He looked from me to the car.

"I—sorry. I was looking for the bathroom," I told him.

He gave me an odd look. Then he smiled and pointed back with his thumb. "It's just across the hall."

My heart raced faster. "Thanks," I said. He moved back to let me pass.

I stepped by, gripping the doorknob for the bathroom and walking in. I pretended to use the bathroom, flushed, washed my shaking hands, then stared at my reflection for a bit, trying to make sense of the car in Eddie's garage.

Rory said a guy had thrown Eve over his shoulder. That he'd taken her into the house while she was screaming and suddenly the screaming stopped. Mrs. Abbot said she'd heard a scream too. My hands were still shaking as I dried them off.

I pulled out my phone, desperate for some kind of signal. There was finally one bar. I went to my emails with Nico and tried opening the attachment again, the one with Victor McDonnell's name on it. Relief washed over me as the attachment slowly loaded, revealing words first. The blur faded so I could read them clearly. I cupped my mouth.

Victor E. McDonnell. That was the name on the credit card in Eve's wallet. That same name was on this document, except the E wasn't an initial. It was a full name.

Eddie.

Victor *Eddie* McDonnell.

Everything in my stomach turned sour. My hands rattled harder as I read the address Nico had highlighted. An address to a house on the same circle as Twilight Oaks. Right on Aquilla Lake. *This* house. Slowly, an image appeared at the bottom. Grainy at first. Then it cleared. A photo of Eddie himself, smiling and wearing golfing attire.

"Oh my God," I whispered.

My mind went back to Eve's photos on her laptop. The video of her saying yes to ice cream. Of taking pictures on the hood of a red car. The entries in her digital journal. The guy she didn't want to name at first and a person who had clearly broken her heart and used her. A guy she'd met in Miami. A guy who would never choose her . . . because he had a wife, a daughter, and had created a whole life. They clearly made great money. He had everything he needed here.

I was in the belly of the beast. I tucked my phone back in place and drew in a few deep breaths. It was fine. Eddie—or Victor—didn't know what I knew. I could leave now, say I'd figure things out for myself. They wouldn't care. They wanted me gone anyway.

I had no idea what Eddie had to do with Eve. All I knew was that I couldn't figure it out here. Everyone on this lake had something to do with her death and it made me want to throw up.

This was bigger than me. A monster with so many heads that just kept growing more.

I opened the door but was shocked to see Victor still standing in the hallway.

"All good?" he asked, eyes bright.

"Yeah. I'm feeling much better now. Thank you."

He gave me a concerned once-over. "You look a little sick. You sure you're okay?"

"I'm good, Eddie. Really. The friend I called, she actually said she's on the way and I don't want to take up any more of your time, so I can wait outside for her. It's fine." I pointed toward the kitchen, where the patio doors were. Where my *gun* was. "Probably safer to wait out back, right?"

"Uh, sure. Yeah." Victor gestured to the kitchen. I moved ahead.

As I rounded the corner, I spotted Gina standing in front of the island counter. She wasn't alone. Emily was in her arms, her legs wrapped around Gina's waist and her head on her mother's chest.

"She heard some of the noise," Gina said, giving me a cold smile.

I forced a smile and grabbed the door handle, lugging it open. I searched the outdoor table for my gun, the last place I saw Gina put it, but it wasn't there.

"Rose?" Victor called.

I looked over my shoulder at him, heart thudding, pulse swimming loudly in my ears.

"You're probably looking for this." He raised my weapon in the air, smiling again. Only this time, the smile didn't reach his eyes.

When the smile vanished, he pointed the gun at my face.

CHAPTER FIFTY

"Eddie!" Gina screamed as she stepped back. "What the hell are you doing?"

"Get inside," Victor demanded, still glaring at me as I threw my hands in the air.

Call me crazy, but he looked like a completely different person now. That cheeriness he carried was now concealed by a darkness I couldn't comprehend. His hazel eyes were murky, his lips pinched tight, his nostrils flared.

He seemed like such a simple man before. Not overly toned. Not very tall. Your average build. But as he stood there in this moment, I could see that he had strength. With his spine stacked and his chest out, he looked sturdier.

Deadlier.

"Eddie!" Gina yelled again as she clung to her daughter.

"Take Emily back to her room, Gina. *Now.*"

"I don't understand what's going on!" she cried.

"There's nothing to understand!" he barked over his shoulder. "Just fucking take her!"

I stepped away.

He noticed.

He grabbed my forearm and yanked me into the kitchen. I yelped as he wrangled me close.

"Eddie, please," I pleaded.

"You shouldn't be so fucking *nosy*, Rose. But you can't help it, can you?" he growled in my ear. "Fucking reporters. Can never stay out of people's business. Go that way." He released my arm to shove me away, then pointed at a door on the opposite side of the kitchen.

I shuffled forward, biting back tears.

"Open the door," he ordered.

I twisted the doorknob, only to be greeted with darkness. He reached around me and tugged on a string connected to a bulb, revealing a long stretch of descending stairs to a basement.

"Go on." He nudged the center of my back with the gun.

"Eddie, I don't understand," I breathed, taking the stairs down slowly. "Why are you doing this?"

"Because I'm not stupid," he muttered. "I know you know."

"Know *what*?"

"About me and Eve."

I shuddered a breath. "I don't know anything."

Scoffing, he nudged me again. When I made it to the basement floor, he moved around me but kept the gun pointed my way. The basement was mostly empty, minus a kayak and a few folded chairs.

Grabbing one of the chairs, he unfolded it, then pointed at it with the gun. "Sit down."

My legs were like Jell-O, but I did as he instructed.

Someone clambered down the stairs and it didn't take long for Gina to appear. "Eddie! What in the hell are you doing?" she hissed at him. "You're scaring me! You're scaring *Emily*!"

"Gina, grab that rope over there," he called out, ignoring her.

She frowned, looking to where he was pointing with his free hand as he stood behind me. Her mouth trembled as she took all the stairs down and looked from him to me.

"Eddie, I'm not letting you do this." She squared her

shoulders, attempting a defiant stance, but I could see the fear in her eyes. "You're being stupid. Always getting yourself mixed up in these terrible situations! This woman didn't do anything to you!"

"Gina. Get the damn rope," Victor growled through gritted teeth.

Her breaths came out unsteady as she waited him out. Then she caved in and turned for the rope stacked on top of a box in the corner. She handed it to him, but not without giving me an apologetic look first. I looked away, trying to stop my body from shaking.

"Is this about that girl?" Gina asked, stepping back as Victor placed the gun down. I glanced at it as he began to unravel the rope. He'd placed the gun too far away, but if I lunged quickly enough, I could make it.

"The one who called my phone?" Gina proceeded.

"Just go back upstairs," he muttered, shaking the rope out.

I glanced at the gun again. Then at Gina. She was eyeing the gun too. Her eyes connected to mine, and she shook her head, silently pleading with me. I could imagine her thinking *don't do it, don't do it.*

Fuck that. I was doing it.

I shot out of the chair and yelled as I pushed past Victor. He dropped the rope just as I was about to grab the gun and shoved me to the right. Gina shrieked as I fell down on my side. Victor stormed my way and started to reach for my throat but I caught his wrist. I wrapped a leg around his ankle and brought him down to the ground with me. A move I'd mastered in my jiujitsu defense classes.

I was about to climb on top of him and aim for his Adam's apple, but he pushed me off and slammed me onto my back. The back of my head hit the cement floor. I was left with no choice but to freeze as the pain took over.

"Don't be stupid, Rose," Victor snarled. He wrapped a hand around my throat and used his other to grab the gun. I glanced at Gina and groaned. She had backed up with her hands cupping her mouth. Frozen too.

Victor tightened his grip around my throat, and I clawed at his hand. His jaw ticked as he pointed the gun at my head. "You're going to get back in that chair, and you're going to be still. You won't try anything else, or I swear I'll put a bullet through your head right now and end your worthless life."

His eyes flared as I choked. Black seeped around the edges of my vision. My grip slackened as I lost oxygen. Just when I thought I'd lose consciousness, he let go and I inhaled a sharp breath.

Is that what he'd done to Eve?

Choked her to death?

Victor jerked me off the ground and lugged me to the chair again. I slumped in it, rubbing my sore throat, still dragging in deep breaths. This time, he tucked the gun into the waistband of his sweats before snatching up the rope. He gripped my shoulder to pull me back, then wrapped the rope around my chest. As he went lower, I felt it digging into the lower part of my ribs.

I winced. "Eve," I croaked, swinging my eyes to Gina. "Are you talking about Eve? Is she the one who called you?"

"Yes! That's her name!" Gina said, her misty eyes wider. "I was right, then. Wasn't I, Eddie? You were *fucking* her." The anger seemed to throttle her. "You lied to me! You said she was a friend—a colleague. You said nothing happened. I canceled our fucking divorce because you promised it was nothing! You promised you would focus on our family and our future! I should've known you were lying!"

"I think he killed her, Gina," I rasped. Right after, Victor slapped me so hard I saw stars.

"You don't know shit!" he spat in my face.

Blood flooded my mouth as I closed my eyes and groaned.

"I don't know what you did to the other girl, but you need to leave this one alone." Gina stepped forward, tipping her chin. "I should've known not to trust you. I should've listened to my instincts. You let her go now, or I'm calling the police."

Gina clenched a fist as Victor stepped closer to her.

"I'm not letting her go, G. And you aren't calling the cops on me. You're not foolish. You know how bad this will make you and the company look."

Gina's hand shook. "I don't care. You've underestimated me enough." She twisted around and stormed halfway up the stairs.

Before she could make it, Victor raised the gun.

I screamed when the gunshot echoed through the basement.

CHAPTER FIFTY-ONE

Victor cursed as he watched his wife collapse, belly first, on the stairs. Everything fell silent after that, but to my surprise, Gina's head was still moving. That's when I realized he'd shot her in the calf. Blood trickled down her leg as she moaned. She began to cry as she reached for the gunshot wound, but in doing so, she ended up skidding all the way down the wooden steps.

Victor clutched her good leg, flipped her over, and dragged her across the basement on her back. She cried out as he fumed, hiking her up and pressing her back to a wall.

"Eddie, are you kidding me?" she cried. "You fucking shot me!"

I looked down, noticing the bottom of the rope wasn't tied at my waist. He'd knotted the rope around my chest and behind my back, but not at my waist. I shifted my arm, trying to move the rope's end, but that only caused the knots above to squeeze tighter.

"You don't understand, Gina. I did what I had to do for you," Victor said.

"What did you do, you asshole?" she demanded, wincing again.

"She was going to ruin us and everything we've built! She

found us here and she threatened your company—our marriage. She wasn't going to stop until she took everything."

Gina grimaced. "You mean everything *I've* built!"

Victor looked taken aback as his wife glowered at him. "You wouldn't have been able to build any of it if I hadn't been keeping Emily with me every day," he retorted. "This weekend is the first time where you're actually with us, and you aren't even really here, Gina! You're still on your fucking phone. Still emailing. Still on those stupid Zoom calls."

"I can't just stop working because you want to watch a fucking movie, Eddie! God—oh, my God. My leg. It's bleeding badly!"

"Daddy?"

Victor twisted around and most of his anger seemed to rinse away in an instant when he heard the small, innocent voice. Emily stood in the middle of the staircase holding a pink teddy bear and gazing at the puddle of her mother's blood on the step below her.

"Oh, Em, baby." Victor hustled across the basement, hiked up the stairs, and scooped her up. "Come on. Let's get you back to bed, baby. Come."

It was frightening how quickly he could change up. Menacing at one point and sympathetic the next. Victor glared at me over his shoulder, tossing a warning look that said *don't try a fucking thing.*

The door slammed shut, echoing through the basement. I dropped my head and closed my eyes again, thinking of a way to get the hell out of here. Why had Victor killed Eve? Surely whatever she'd done couldn't have been that bad—not to the point where he needed to *murder* her.

"He killed her." I opened my eyes and cut my gaze to Gina. She was already staring at me.

"How can you be sure?" she asked.

"That's what I've been told." My voice cracked. I cleared

my throat. "The Reeds—they live across the lake. The girl, Rory, said they found Eve's body one morning in their rental house. They said she was already dead."

"But how could it have been Eddie? I mean, how did you know for sure?"

"I didn't know for sure . . . not until he pointed the gun at me."

"God." Gina squeezed her eyes shut. "I'm so sorry this is happening," she breathed. "*So, so* sorry."

"It's not your fault."

"It is!" she wailed, throwing her head back. "I—I knew he was seeing someone else. I knew he was having an affair. She wanted to be sure that I knew. She just kept coming back, bragging, telling me to leave him. She told me she'd been sleeping with him for *months*. I asked Eddie about it, and he confessed to it. I wanted a divorce, but he suggested marriage counseling. He wanted to make things work . . . for Emily. I wanted the same thing, so I stayed. I wanted to move on from it and he said he'd take care of the pregnancy and that he would convince her to—"

"Wait, *what*?" My throat thickened with emotion. "Pregnancy? What are you talking about?"

"She was pregnant with his child! She sent me a photo of the pregnancy test. Her blood work. *Everything*. She could've photoshopped it, sure, but something told me she wasn't joking. This felt real, and that was going to be my last straw with Eddie. I wanted to be done."

"When was this?" I asked. "When did she send you the photo?"

"About two or three weeks ago, I think. I was so angry. I told him I'd take everything from him, including Emily, if he didn't fix this. It just doesn't make sense that he'd go and kill her. I thought he'd have her get an abortion or pay her to leave us alone. I'd even suggested that he do that."

"But she didn't," I whispered.

Of course, she fucking didn't. Because that's Eve. She craved the upper hand. She liked being the one in control because, for the longest time, she was powerless. She probably didn't even love Victor. She *used* him. Saw what he had with Gina and wanted it for herself. She blackmailed him, infiltrated his life. Found out where he lived. Now I could piece it together.

She knew Victor and his wife owned a house on Aquilla Lake. He probably dealt with her way beforehand and told her to terminate the pregnancy. She didn't want their affair to end, but I bet Victor stopped responding to her because he wanted to fix his marriage.

She likely got upset and wanted to get back at him, so she thought of ways to bother him. She lucked out with finding the cottage and only booked it to be near him. She wanted to disturb his peace, prove that he couldn't just use and discard her like trash. She was slowly causing him to unravel. Setting off his temper. Pushing him too far. Always pushing people too damn far.

Victor must've appeared at Twilight Oaks twice. The first time, when Lincoln left, was probably to serve her a warning. Mrs. Abbot said she saw Eve walking around their side of the lake. Victor must've noticed her too and that set off his alarm. Things were going good with his wife, but Eve was lurking around, ready to sabotage it.

But the second time Victor visited her was his last straw. She must've done something horrible—something to *really* set him off. So, he killed her. But it didn't make sense that he'd left the body for the Reeds to find. Why hadn't he covered his tracks?

Unless . . .

He saw Eve with Alex and Damian that night. That, or she told him all about it. She probably bragged and shoved it in his face. She probably never got rid of the baby. And if she was carrying Victor's child, how did that make him feel, knowing she was intentionally ruining herself because of the seed he'd planted? How did it make him feel to know she was still carrying the baby at all?

Victor wanted to pin the blame on Alex and Damian. She'd had sex with them at the same time. Their DNA was likely all over her, *inside* her even. Even if the police found out the baby was Victor's, he could've admitted to the affair happening, but said Eve was stalking him and his wife. He could've fabricated a whole story to protect himself and then pinned her death on the Reeds, and he would've gotten away with it . . . if I hadn't intervened.

Knowing this, it was why Alex had taken her things, cleared the house, and got rid of the body. They had no clue who killed her but knew they'd be suspects if her body was taken in for forensics. They likely consulted with Sheriff Reed right away and told him everything, swore their innocence, and that was why he assisted them. That was why he had Eve's car. The broken necklace in the fireplace I couldn't fully understand, but the Reeds could've tried burning that along with her clothes to get rid of evidence.

Thinking about it now, Sheriff Reed knew how this would play out if anyone else other than him discovered Eve's body. He knew a dead girl who'd slept with his nephews would jeopardize his reputation and status, so he helped them cover it up.

The only question remaining was what the hell had they done with her body?

CHAPTER FIFTY-TWO

Victor stormed down the stairs with a roll of duct tape in one hand and the gun in the other. I squirmed in my chair while Gina whimpered, watching as he marched my way while pulling the tape off the roll.

"You killed Eve because she wouldn't get rid of the baby," I said as he stretched the tape.

"Stop talking."

"She came here to get your attention, didn't she?"

He stepped behind me. "She ruins lives."

"So that means *kill* her?" I asked, alarmed.

"I never meant to kill her, damn it!" he snapped. "She was yelling and hitting me. She ran out of the house bragging about how she was going to tell everyone I was the father of her baby. She was reckless and kept saying if she couldn't be happy, neither could I. I tried being reasonable with that bitch. I tried *so hard*. I brought her back to that house to try and talk some sense into her. And she . . ." He paused, drawing in a ragged breath. "She said I was a shitty husband. A shitty dad. She said she was going to tell her followers and the whole world that I raped her and purposely got her pregnant. She was going to rant about our company and reach out to our partners. She said she'd make sure I never saw Emily again by the time she was done. I just wanted her to shut up so we could work out a solution, but she wouldn't, so I grabbed her by the throat and—"

"You choked her to death," I whispered.

He growled and brought the tape to my mouth, wrapping it twice to shut me up.

Then he huffed. "Like I told you, Eve ruins lives. She deserves what happened to her. You should know all about that. All she ever talked about was how she fucked your husband. How she betrayed you." His mouth twitched to fight a smirk. "Makes no sense that you even came looking for her after what she put you through. I bet you're glad she's dead."

My chest tightened at the vulgarity of his accusation. He was wrong. Even though Eve had hurt me, deceived me, made me feel lower than I'd ever felt in my life, I never wished death upon her. Had I wished for some sort of karma? Yes. But more like her falling in love and being betrayed too. Or having her life ruined so she could understand how it felt to hurt and to lose faith and confidence in yourself.

To stare in the mirror and wonder what was so wrong with her. To search for all her flaws while wondering what was so bad that the man of her dreams felt the need to sleep with her *best* fucking friend. I wanted her to know what it felt like to *not* be enough for someone. That's what I wanted to happen to Eve. Not death. But it seems she found that out with Victor. She wasn't enough for him . . . and her anger about it got her killed.

Gina groaned as she clung to her leg. "Eddie, you need to stop this. You have to let us go," she pleaded. "You can't keep us down here forever. People will come looking."

Victor walked around me, side-eyeing Gina. "Think about Emily and what will happen if she loses both of us. Let me go to her, Eddie. Please." Gina tried standing, crying out in pain as she pressed a bloody hand to the wall.

Victor stepped in front of her and pushed her back down. "Emily will be just fine with me." He faced me, pointing the gun my way. "I'll make it look like a suicide with you. You were angry. Hurt about what Eve did. Wanted to find her but couldn't so you killed yourself with your own gun. I'll put your body in the woods, set it up just right."

No one would believe that. I wasn't suicidal. I cared about my life.

"As for you, Gina. You either cooperate, or I'll have to *remove* you too."

Gina squeezed her eyes shut as Victor walked back to me and pointed the gun at my forehead. A strangled noise caught in my throat as he applied slight pressure to the trigger.

This was it.

I was going to die.

I couldn't believe it.

I tried to scream behind the tape and make him stop. I could bargain with Victor, tell him that I'd let this go, that I wouldn't say a damn thing. But someone stormed down the stairs.

James Reed appeared with his gun drawn and aimed it at Victor. He should've shot him. Instead of studying the damn scene, he should've shot Victor first and then inspected. Instead, Victor took the opportunity James hadn't and swung his arm to shoot at him.

CHAPTER FIFTY-THREE

Though Victor had shot at the sheriff, he missed. James dodged the bullet just in time, then charged across the basement to tackle him. Both men slammed to the ground and a brawl ensued.

Another person clambered down the steps—Damian. He stopped at the last step, watching James and Victor scuffle and grunt. Then he looked at me. Then Gina.

"Get them out of here, Damian!" James shouted as he mounted Victor, reeled his arm back, and punched him in the face.

Damian hustled forward, dropping to one knee next to me to untie the rope. He breathed hard, muttering incomprehensibly. Damian was still working out the knots as Victor slammed James into the wall, making him hit the back of his head. James crumpled from the blow and while he was disoriented, Victor whacked him across the face with a solid fist.

Both guns were on the ground and not too far away from where the two men were standing.

I moaned and Damian flicked his gaze up at me. I bobbed my head and darted my eyes to the guns. He peered over his shoulder just as Victor twisted around.

"Shit." Damian sprang across the basement for one of the

guns. He grabbed James's and tried getting mine too, but Victor was faster.

I wriggled out of the remainder of rope just as Victor aimed the gun at Damian. James reached for Victor's ankle and gave it a hard yank, which caused him to buckle and fall to one knee. The gun went off and a bullet pierced the ceiling.

Clearly pissed, Victor threw his foot back and kicked James square in the face, knocking him unconscious. Damian slapped the gun out of Victor's hand and while they scrambled over one another to get it, I finally freed myself and sprang out of the chair.

I pulled the tape off my mouth while running to Gina. "Hey. Gina?" She looked loopy now. She was losing too much blood.

"Gina, can you hear me?"

"Emily," she mumbled. "Please. Get Emily."

"I'll take you to her. Come on. I need you to stick with me." I helped her up and she cried out as more blood dripped down her leg and accumulated on her foot.

Damian and Victor were squaring off now, tackling each other, slamming into the kayak, punching, kicking, grunting. Damian was making sure to kick or shove the guns farther and farther away so neither of them could reach them.

I could have left Gina and saved myself, but it was unlike me. I kept thinking about their daughter, how she'd need at least one of her parents to navigate this world. And it couldn't be Victor. I had no doubt he'd have killed everyone here and run off with Emily.

With all my strength, I lifted Gina up and threw her arm over my shoulder. We went for the stairs, her stumbling, me huffing as I held most of her weight. My face was swollen, and blood was thick around my nose. Gina was a champ. She didn't stop, not even when we made it to the kitchen.

"Mommy!" Emily screamed.

I looked toward the hallway where Emily was standing.

"Oh, Emily! Baby!" Gina hobbled toward her. It seemed she hadn't been shot at all with how quickly she reached her.

"Gina, we need to get out of here right now," I said.

"Yes—uh, my keys. My keys are right there. On the hook on the wall."

I rushed to the hook she was pointing to and followed her to the garage. She slammed a bloody hand into the button to open the gate and hustled to the BMW.

"Alright. Come on, baby. Get in." Gina's voice wavered as she put Emily into her car seat. Her hands shook as she tried strapping her in.

"Here. Let me help." I swapped places with her. "You get in the passenger seat."

Gina swallowed then nodded, moving out of the way.

"Where's Daddy?" Emily asked as I clicked the chest buckle into place.

"He's . . . busy." I forced a smile at her, clicking the bottom buckle in. "You're okay."

Gina was already in the passenger seat. I closed the door and push-started the car, ready to peel out. Before I could, I spotted a figure standing in the driveway behind the car.

Victor.

He stood in the way, holding my gun again. He started to raise it and that's when I slammed my foot down on the gas pedal. Victor dodged to the left as I peeled out. I switched gears, putting the car in drive and drifting off. A gunshot went off. I gasped and ducked. The car made a weird clunking noise and veered to the right. I tried gaining control of the wheel, but the car seemed to have a mind of its own as it spun out of control.

Gina screamed. Then her side of the car slammed into a tree.

Emily began to cry.

He was going to end up killing us.

"Shit." I pressed on the gas, but the car wouldn't budge. "No! Come on!" I pressed again and could hear the car wheels rolling, the engine roaring, but the car didn't budge.

"We're stuck." Gina squeezed her eyes shut. "Damn it, we're stuck."

I looked through the rearview mirror and spotted Victor trudging toward the car.

"Gina, get Emily out of here, find the keys to your husband's car, and leave. Okay? I'll lead him somewhere else, so he doesn't try to hurt you just to get to Emily."

"What?" she squealed.

"I don't think he knows you two are in the car. He wouldn't have shot otherwise. He'd never hurt Emily."

"But he'll kill you." Gina panicked as she reached for me, but I was already climbing out of the car.

Yeah. He probably was going to kill me, but I'd rather it be me than her.

I closed the door before she could say anything else, shooting a quick glance at Emily, whose face was crumpled with worry and her eyes were full of tears. Then I made a run for it. Another gunshot pierced the air, striking a tree trunk.

I could hear Victor's rapid, heavy steps behind me. On one hand, I was glad he was coming after me and not Gina. On the other, I wished that I loved running, like Eve. I wished I'd spent more time on the treadmill because this much exertion was foreign to me. Every limb in my body ached.

Regardless, the need to get away from Victor was what drove me. My adrenaline had spiked, and I refused to slow down. I ran through the dark woods, unsure which direction to go in. If I could make it back to Twilight Oaks, maybe I could find a place to hide long enough until Kennedy arrived.

I stumbled over a tree root but caught myself. Victor's huffy breaths sounded closer, louder.

Owls hooted in the distance. The treetops swayed, rustling the leaves. Branches groaned with and creaked. My lungs felt like they were about to collapse. But I kept running until I spotted a light ahead. Twilight Oaks. I'd never been so happy to see that little cottage.

The front porch light was on. I hustled around the house and dashed through the backyard, but before I could reach it, another gunshot rang. This time, the bullet grazed my upper arm. I cried out and stumbled. Unable to catch myself, I fell. I started to get up again, despite the burning of my arm, but someone clutched a handful of my braids and wrenched me back.

"You should've minded your own fucking business," Victor growled as he pulled back hard enough to slam me on my back.

The breath whooshed out of my lungs. My ears started to ring. I coughed, trying to kick him away, but he stepped back just enough to glare down at me. His head swayed as he scoffed.

"You're pathetic, Rose," he spat out. "I see why Eve didn't respect you. What kind of woman allows the shit you did? What kind of woman knows their friend fucked their husband and *still* looks for her? You're so damn desperate." He leveled the barrel of the gun on me. "Maybe this is what you want. You must have some kind of death wish. I'd hate my life too if I were you."

"Leave her alone!" a high-pitched voice screamed. Rory charged toward Victor with a shovel in hand. She gave it a swing, aiming for his head, but he caught it by the handle with his free hand.

I rolled over as Rory struggled to take the shovel back. He hung on to the handle, grunting as he did. Then, with a smirk, he released the handle and Rory tumbled backwards. I pushed to a stand and started to run off, but Victor caught me, hooking an arm around my midsection and hauling me backward. He slammed me down on the ground again and I yelped from the pain.

"All of you are pissing me off now!" He dragged me by the hood of my jacket, going down the hill that led to the lake. Rory started to chase after us with the shovel again.

"No, Rory! Stop! He'll hurt you too!" I fingered the zipper of my hoodie, ready to pull it down and escape the arms, but Victor stopped and slung me around to grip me by the back of my neck. I could smell lake water now, its fresh scent invading my senses.

My knees slammed into the cool water at the shoreline. Then Victor shoved my face forward and plunged my head under water.

CHAPTER FIFTY-FOUR

I was going to die.

I should've known it from the first night I spent in Twilight Oaks. I sensed something was off. I knew something had happened to Eve. There was a gut feeling and it's never wrong. But, still, I stayed. Like a fool I stayed.

Perhaps Victor was right. Maybe I *did* have some kind of death wish. Perhaps I *did* hate my life. Maybe, subconsciously, this was the result I wanted. I have felt nothing but unfulfilled since I saw Cole and Eve that day.

I've felt empty, like there's a gaping hole in my chest that grows bigger every day. Sure, my family and friends keep me somewhat centered, but some days it doesn't feel like enough. Some days, I just want to quit and run off, start a new life. Forget about the past and all my worries.

Victor's grip tightened on the back of my neck as I thrashed, trying to come up for air. Water filled my nose and mouth. My eyes burned with each panicked blink. No. Dying wasn't what I wanted. Not by a long shot.

I threw back an arm, trying to swing at him, but he held on tighter, shoving me deeper.

I could hear my heartbeat slowing in rhythm. My gasps and moans catching in my chest.

And then I heard a voice.

A familiar whisper.
I'm here, Rose.
Eve.

A muffled pop sounded off. Victor's hand slipped from the back of my neck, and I jerked my head out of the water, gasping for as much breath as possible. I pressed on my hands and knees, sucking in oxygen as I tried to orient myself.

Then, to my left, I saw Victor's body. He was face down, bleeding from the shoulder blade and wincing. His eyes were wide as he stared at me. A short distance away, holding a shotgun aimed in Victor's previous direction, was Griffin Abbot. Behind him was Selma Abbot, whose eyes were wide and panicked. Griffin's nostrils flared as he swung the barrel of the gun to Victor again.

In the distance, Rory stood, and Alex approached with a heavy limp. Rory turned to him, throwing her face into his chest. His thigh was bleeding too, from where I'd shot him. I instantly regretted it.

I fell down beside Victor, shivering.

"Lower the weapon!" Kennedy's voice blared in the distance. I heard something thud on the ground and Griffin's deep voice telling her that he was only helping.

I'm not sure how much time passed before I heard Kennedy read off Victor's Miranda rights while yanking his arms back to cuff him. He was still staring at me, an absent look in his eyes.

"You should be thanking me," Victor rasped, ignoring Kennedy. Water was in my ears, so his voice was muffled, but I understood. "She's dead. She was always your burden and now that burden is gone." He said all this with a sneer.

Kennedy hauled him up just as another deputy appeared. She handed Victor over to him with a firm set of instructions, and when another cop showed up, Kennedy pointed at Alex and said something. The deputy hesitated before walking to Alex and, reluctantly, grabbing his upper arm and leading him away from the scene. I was surprised Alex didn't resist, or protest, at least.

Kennedy started back my way. I turned my head to look up. The sky was velvet blue and splattered with stars. The trees hovered, towering like skyscrapers. It all swirled into one big starlit mosaic.

Then I saw someone standing above me, wearing the same brown hoodie she'd worn in the camera footage from Flip Stack's. She smiled at me before lowering to one knee. Her eyes were rimmed with tears. She touched my face, rubbed my cheek. It was now I noticed the transparency of her skin. The slight glow to it.

She whispered, *I'm so sorry, Rose.*

"Rose?" Kennedy called. Her voice was faint as she pressed a hand to my neck to check my pulse. I glanced at her. She was a blur. "You're okay, Rose. I'm right here."

I looked to my right again. Eve was still there. Her tears had fallen. She grabbed my hand while it rested on my stomach and gave it a squeeze. It was most likely my imagination that Eve was there, giving me what felt like her final goodbye. I wondered if all this time she'd been whispering to me and pointing me in the right direction because she knew I'd never give up.

I'm so sorry, she whispered again.

Believe it or not, despite the mess she'd created and the hurt that still lingered in my chest, I *forgave* her.

"It's okay," I mumbled.

The last thing I remember is smiling before closing my eyes and drifting out of consciousness.

Eve Castillo journal entry

Here's something people are aware of but will never fully accept. Hurt people really do hurt other people. It's the biggest fucking cliché but it's one hundred percent true. We hurt others because the pain inside us runs so deep and throbs so hard that it's impossible to ignore. No amount of therapy, of traveling, of journaling, of reading self-help books, or any of that worldly bullshit will help.

Because once you realize no one will apologize for the way they treated you, you build resentment. Anger. Envy. You want others to feel that too, just so they can understand you a little more. All so you can say, "Do you feel that? The crack forming in your heart? Yeah, well, it's only going to get bigger as the days pass and there isn't shit you can do about it."

I wish I wasn't the kind of person to hurt. I wish I had a good heart like Rose, like Zoey. I wish I was a good person who was okay living life at bare minimum. I can't blame anyone for my actions. I'm responsible for anything that comes my way. Like Pa, I do bad things. I try to reward men with my body, my words, my smile, but eventually it doesn't work anymore, and I'm caught up in a web.

All I know is no matter how hard Karma hits me, I'm ready for her.

Whatever she gives me, I'll probably deserve it.

CHAPTER FIFTY-FIVE

"I believe I can pinpoint why you returned to Sage Hill even though you knew it was dangerous to do so." Cristine studied me from the other side of the room as she sat in her plush, oatmeal-colored chair.

She smiled as I digested her words. It had been four days since the madness in Sage Hill. My upper lip was still a bit swollen, and I swear I could still feel Victor's grip on the back of my neck, squeezing with intense pressure.

"Help me understand it," I said, sighing as I rubbed the top of my spine.

Cristine closed her notebook and placed it on the coffee table. "Your mother went into a burning building to save one of her coworkers and never came back out."

My chest constricted at the mention of my mom. I ignored the knot forming in my throat, nodding as I waited for her to continue.

"Based on what you've told me about your mother, she was a very selfless and loving person. She literally sacrificed her life to try and save another. And I think, whether you realize it or not, you have a deep desire to be just like her. You feel you have something to prove now that she's gone. Or perhaps you think you need to fill her shoes.

"On the surface, you tell yourself you'd never run into a fire or, say, jump into an ocean full of sharks to save someone . . . but that's exactly what happened when it came to Eve. The danger was there. It was imminent and you *knew* this, but you returned to Sage Hill anyway. You were hoping to save someone. But it's impossible to save everyone, Rose."

"I know," I murmured.

"You carry a lot of weight on your shoulders. And you're so hard on yourself. Do you know that?"

I nodded again, a rawness coating my throat.

"You have to realize that every situation you encounter doesn't have to be solved by *you*. Unless it directly impacts your life, sometimes you have to let things run their course."

"But if I hadn't looked for Eve, I might've never found out what happened to her."

"True, but it was still out of your control."

I huffed a humorless laugh. "I feel like I'm being scolded."

"No, no. I promise I'm not scolding you," she replied in a gentle voice. "I just want you to open your mind to the facts. Sometimes we have to face these ugly truths in order to protect ourselves. Just like the situation with Cole and Eve. You never saw it coming. There was absolutely nothing you could've done to prevent it. I know you tell yourself if you'd come home sooner, or if you'd called ahead of time, that it never would've happened. But it would have. Maybe not that day, or the next, but eventually. Why? Because you can't control other people's urges or desires, even if that person promised to commit themselves to you."

Wow. That was a tough pill to swallow.

"So, I want you to work on this," she went on, straightening in her chair. "I want you to start focusing on your well-being and putting yourself first. It's a miracle what happened in Sage Hill. You used your resources and exposed the truth. You saved a mother and a daughter, kept them united. You put a horrible man in custody for murder, they were able to find your friend's body, and you helped a town get rid of a crooked sheriff." Dr. Cristine gave me a proud smile.

"That's true," I murmured.

"Though you did all those things, eventually you'll have to put them behind you. Don't let it linger or weigh you down. Keep going." She studied me for a moment, her eyes softening. "You say you saw Eve the night you found out who murdered her. Do you truly believe she was telling you goodbye?"

I nodded. "I do."

"And do you truly forgive her?"

I gave the question some thought. "I have moments where I get angry. It feels ridiculous sometimes, resenting a dead woman and all," I said, huffing a laugh. "But yes, I truly do forgive her."

"That's good." She gave me a warm smile. "So, start there. Forgive and move on. Forget about Cole. Forget about Sage Hill. Forget about what *was* and focus on what *is*. You have the right to be angry when you need to be, and sad about your friend the next, but what I want you to remember, Rose, is that Eve's choices had absolutely *nothing* to do with you. She was never your burden. She was battling something within herself. And sometimes those battles are the hardest to conquer."

CHAPTER FIFTY-SIX

Sunlight bounced off my white ceramic coffee mug. I sat at my desk, watching how the light reflected off of it, making the papers shine whiter. Ever since I discovered everything about Eve, I found myself appreciating the little things. I realized after all that I had gone through, that I needed to slow down.

Yes, I was at work, but at the moment I had no deadlines or stories to report. I was sure something would come up within the next couple of days, but right now it felt good to sit and work through a few returned edits from Twyla. It seemed like my life had completely changed in a matter of days. After the incident with Victor and Eve, the story was one Twyla wanted front and center on *Premier Daily*.

The hook was: Reporter's Search for Missing Best Friend Becomes a Deadly Encounter.

It's not exactly the headline I would've gone for, but it was already getting a lot of views and traffic. Herbert covered the story and interviewed me, Gina, and Rory. Twyla insisted that I write the piece, but I was glad to offer the opportunity to Herbert. The last thing I wanted was to slip back into that dark place. I'd provided Herbert as many details as I could over several bottles of wine in my apartment. In my opinion, he deserved a promotion and he'd gotten it because I'd moved up to senior reporter.

Sure, it could've been because of Twyla's pity. But still, a win was a win. *Take that, Janna and Bree.* I picked up my coffee and took a deep sip. A knock sounded on the door and Twyla popped her curly head in.

"You have visitors," she informed me. "Should I send them in?"

"Yes, please." I smiled, already knowing who was about to walk through my door.

Twyla opened the door wider, and Kennedy walked in with Rory trotting behind her. Rory carried a container of brownies in her hand, which made me laugh.

"Are you trying to make me fat, Rory?" I asked, giving her a hug.

"No. I was just bored," she said over my shoulder. She didn't seem as hollow as she had been a few weeks ago. It seemed like since her brothers had been taken into custody, she was shining a bit brighter. Sad to say, considering how much she loved them.

"Have a seat. Please." I gestured to the chairs on the other side of my desk.

"We won't be here long," Kennedy assured me, adjusting her hips in the chair. "Just wanted to pop by and let you know James and Alex Reed will be going to trial. According to Damian, Alex and James suggested burying Eve's body in their mother's grave."

"What were they charged with?" I asked.

"Concealment of death. They're facing serious felonies."

"Wow." It still hit me hard that it was Eve's *body* now and not just *Eve*.

"Yep. Took a couple days but we pried the truth out of him. Alex is the one who did the digging. Damian tagged along because James threatened that if he didn't help, he would frame him and put him in jail for Eve's murder."

My throat thickened with emotion. Rory let out a deflated sigh.

"The good news is Rory won't have to face the foster care system again," Kennedy went on, smiling warmly at the teen next to her. "Since Damian was threatened and provided us a full confession, his lawyer worked out a deal with the DA and she pulled some strings. He'll do two years of community service and will be on house arrest for eight months, but at least he'll be home."

"Thank God," Rory said, wiping fake sweat from her forehead.

"Oh, now you want to thank God?" I teased.

"Uh, yeah! He saved my life and yours!" She looked at the ceiling and said, "So sorry for blaspheming you, my heavenly Father. I'll never do it again."

I smirked. "Well, I'm glad you'll still have one of your brothers, at least."

"Yeah, me too." Her smile slipped a bit. "We're thinking about traveling after his two years are up. Getting out of Sage Hill. I'll be ready to graduate by then and we can make plans now. I think it's time we branch out."

"That would be nice. You should definitely do it."

"Right. Well, I really swung by because I've been informed that they'll need Eve's body for just a few more days," Kennedy told me. "Just to be thorough with evidence. Once we have everything we need, we'll have her body delivered so you can give her a proper burial."

"Okay. Thanks, Kennedy. I really appreciate everything you've done for me."

Kennedy's eyes sparkled. "It was my pleasure, Rose."

I forced myself to look away as my tears threatened to take over. As if Kennedy noticed, she reached for Rory's Tupperware and removed the lid. Her nails were pink and red this time.

"Let me try one of these brownies and see what all the fuss

is about." She plucked one out and bit into it. As she chewed, her eyes expanded, and she shifted her gaze to Rory. "Girl! What? These are good!"

"Yeah? I'm thinking about selling them," Rory said, bouncing in her seat as Kennedy devoured the rest of her brownie, then grabbed another.

"You sell these and you'll make enough money to travel and live wherever you want," said Kennedy, her mouth half full. "My goodness, they're so gooey and chocolatey. A glass of milk would hit the spot."

"They *are* really good," I said, taking a brownie for myself.

Rory grinned and grabbed one too. "To a peaceful future," she declared, holding her brownie in the air.

We tapped brownies.

"To a peaceful future."

That I could promise myself.

EPILOGUE

I hadn't read all of Eve's journal entries the day I found them, only the most recent ones about Victor and her trip to Twilight Oaks. After some time, I was able to read a few more and my heart ached for her. There was an entry that nearly broke me down and one I would probably never forgive myself for.

That night when I caught Cole and Eve, I hadn't realized that she'd been triggered. I mean, she'd still gone through with it, but something Cole did had put her in a frozen state. I'd been around Eve long enough to know that when she froze, she didn't care what happened to her. She just went with the flow, let things carry out, gave an empty stare like she wanted to be as far away from her body as possible. She often waited for the worst to pass, then smiled the next day like nothing happened.

That fear I saw in Eve's eyes that night wasn't only because she'd been caught red-handed. It was because she'd lost control of her own mind. I couldn't fully blame her for what happened. I left that night. Blocked Eve's number. Blocked Cole's too, before I had to unblock his to settle a minor dispute with the divorce.

It pains me because I never gave Eve the chance to defend herself. I just flat out ignored her. Neglected her. Wrote her off. She tried coming to my job. To my dad's. She tried calling me from Zoey's phone a few times but when I heard her voice I instantly hung up.

I may not have wanted to forgive her in that moment, but I would have eventually. That didn't mean she'd be my best friend again or that we would be close. No, that never would've happened. But at least I'd have had the peace of mind to understand and let go of my bitterness.

I sat with that guilt as I stood in front of her grave, staring down at her tombstone. It'd taken a full month to get her body. Her funeral was a week ago. Now she'd been put to rest six feet under. This was surreal in the worst way. The friend who'd felt like a sister to me, now dead. Her life cut short at thirty-two years old. When you think about it, that isn't very many years. She still had a chance to grow, to better herself, to take control of her life.

"Rose?"

I lifted my head when Zoey called me. She smiled as she held a bouquet of purple and pink flowers in one hand, Eve's favorite colors. Daddy and Diana were walking in our direction too.

We made a promise to ourselves to visit her and Mom's grave every week and to not take these moments or our lives for granted anymore.

"You okay?" Zoey asked.

I smiled at her.

Zoey would always know Eve was a good person and that she loved her. I made sure to delete all the journal entries and then the app so Zoey would never find it. Of course, all of it was still on the laptop Eve had in Sage Hill, and some bigger truths would leak when it came to the trials for Victor, Alex, and James, but that laptop was still in evidence. And when the trial came, I'd deal with those truths in that moment.

Zoey deserved to remember the best of her sister.

I smiled. "I'm okay, Zo."

She hooked an arm through mine. Tears accumulated in

her eyes, but she blinked them away, allowing a smile to take their place. When Daddy and Diana met beside us, we stared at Eve's tombstone for a while. No one said a word. Honestly, there weren't any words powerful enough to say.

Despite Eve's mistakes and her past, she was family, and we loved her. It would always feel like something was missing now that she was gone, just like it felt with Mom. A gentle breeze caressed my skin, and I closed my eyes, thinking about my friend. Our childhood. Our laughs. Our fights. Our goofy moments. Our sleepovers. Our pinky promises. Our late-night Oreos and milk. Movie nights with wine. Hugs and tears. Whispered secrets and promises.

I was going to miss her. But I was also going to make sure that I lived the rest of my life like she did.

Carefree.

Unapologetically.

Because no matter how wild Eve was, she only wanted to love and be loved. The least I could do was continue carrying her love with me.

ACKNOWLEDGMENTS

This story was trapped in my mind for almost four years, so finally being able to write it was the best feeling ever. The words flowed from my fingers and all I kept wondering was *what happened to Eve?* It wasn't until I started writing that it all came together and wow, was that an adventure.

I want to thank my family for keeping themselves afloat while I was locked into this novel. It's tricky being a mom, wife, and author, but I wouldn't be successful in my career without my family's sacrifices. So, Juan, Julien, Kai, and Micah—thank you, my boys. I love you all so much.

To my wonderful agent, Georgana, you are a light in this world. Even though my thrillers scare the crap out of you, I thank you for supporting them as if they are your own book babies.

Hannah and MJ—you already know the deal. I love you ladies so much! Best alpha readers ever!

To my lovely queens on my ARC team—THANK YOU FOR ALL YOU DO FOR ME! I will never say it enough to you ladies, but thank you. I adore you all so much.

And lastly, I have to give gratitude to my readers. If you're reading this right now, I appreciate you so much. Whether you fell in love with my words or not, just know I'm grateful that you gave my book a chance at all. An author cannot exist without their readers. I will never take mine for granted.

Thank you for being on this ride with me.

Discussion Questions

1. If you'd fallen out with your childhood best friend but they disappeared and you knew in your gut something was wrong, would you look for answers? Or would you let it go?
2. What do you think about Eve overall? Is she a friend you could forgive?
3. What emotions did you feel when meeting Sheriff Reed and the Reed brothers? What about Rory?
4. Rose's therapist mentions that she may have taken the initiative in finding Eve due to the tragic way her mother died. Do you think Rose's mentality is that she *must* help people in need, or else feel like a failure in life?
5. Considering her past, were Eve's actions and behavior understandable?
6. Did you figure out who Eve's murderer was when you met them, or did the reveal surprise you? If so, what was it about that person that surprised you most?
7. Do you believe Rose really saw Eve by the lake after discovering the truth?
8. What do you think would've happened if Deputy Kennedy Windsor had allied with Sheriff Reed instead? What would've been Rose's outcome?
9. Why do you think it was so hard for Rose to let go of the search for Eve despite Eve's betrayal?

Visit our website at
KensingtonBooks.com
to sign up for our newsletters, read more from your favorite authors, see books by series, view reading group guides, and more!

Become a Part of Our
Between the Chapters Book Club
Community and Join the Conversation

Betweenthechapters.net

Submit your book review for a chance to win exclusive Between the Chapters swag you can't get anywhere else!
https://www.kensingtonbooks.com/pages/review/